shattered dreams

BOYS OF BELLEROSE
BOOK 3

JAYMIN EVE

TATE JAMES

Tate James

Jaymin Eve

Shattered Dreams: Boys Of Bellerose #3

Cover design: Emily Wittig
Editing: Jax Garren (line).

For everyone who loves their book boyfriends with baggage...
angst is the spice of romance, after all.

follow us

For book discussions, giveaways, and general shit talking from Tate or Jaymin, please check out their reader groups on Facebook:

Tate James – The Fox Hole
Jaymin Eve – The Nerd Herd

content warning

Boys of Bellerose is a rock star mafia reverse harem story where the female main character finds her happily ever after with more than one lover. It's a four book series, so cliffhangers should be expected throughout, until they find their happy ending.
This series touches on darker themes and includes both graphic sex and graphic violence.
Some characters have traumatic pasts, and there is mention of miscarriage, drug use, addiction, and murder.
Please also note that the mafia world described within Boys of Bellerose is a fictional one and differs somewhat from the real world. Because creative license is more fun!

Should you have concerns, please apply discretion in deciding if this story is right for you.

- Tate & Jaymin

one

BILLIE

EIGHT YEARS AGO...

My little girl kicked me from the inside, and my breath hitched, making me pause on my way up the front steps of my parents' house. It was *such* a weird sensation, having another human growing inside me actually *moving* and making her presence known. *Her*. My daughter.

I'd just come home from my eighteen-week scan, where they'd confirmed I was having a girl. I'd burst out crying, and the poor sonographer had to pat me on the shoulder and offer tissues until I calmed down.

That was my fault for refusing Angel's offer to come with me. But he had enough trouble already, without adding my scan appointments.

She'd started kicking a week ago, and at first I'd thought it was just muscle spasms. Or gas. But the lovely sonographer today confirmed that it was indeed my baby girl stretching her legs.

Eighteen weeks. That meant it'd been a whole twelve weeks since I'd lost Jace. Since I'd lied to him and said I was in love with Angel. Actually, that wasn't even the lie, I *did* love Angel... but I'd told Jace that I *didn't* love *him* anymore. That Angel and I wanted to be together *without Jace*. That we'd been sneaking around behind Jace's back and didn't want to keep lying to him about *our love*.

I had nearly choked on my lies so many times, but I'd clung tight to the knowledge that he'd thank me one day. Maybe ten years from now, when he was an international superstar with platinum records on his wall and a stack of Grammys, he'd look back on our breakup and realize that I'd done it *for him*.

"Calm down, baby girl," I whispered to my belly. "I know, I'm hungry too."

I hunted through my oversize tote bag for my house keys, then unlocked the door before registering that my mom's car was in the driveway. She was usually at work for a few more hours at least, so it was odd. Not *that* odd, though; maybe she'd just gotten the afternoon off.

For some reason, I didn't call out as I stepped through the front door. Raised voices echoed through the house as I closed the door quietly behind me and placed my bag on the floor.

Frowning, I moved further down the hallway toward my parent's bedroom. That seemed to be where the shouting was coming from, and my curiosity demanded I listen in—mainly because my own heavy guilt made me assume they were arguing about me and the baby... and Angelo.

We'd announced last week that we were going to get married after the baby was born, and *neither* of our families had taken it well—his worse than mine, but mine were far from encouraging of the idea.

"...you insane? If..." my dad was saying, his tone agitated and angry, "...going to kill us all. Not just you, Tina, *all of us!*"

Whoa. What?

I stopped dead in the middle of the hallway, my hand pressed to my belly like I could somehow protect her from the words my father was saying. *Kill* us? Who? Why? Surely, he was just being dramatic and not literal with that statement.

"...being dramatic, Christian..." My mother echoed my thought, her voice quieter and some words too muffled for me to make out. "...never find out. I know what I'm doing, besides the fact... only... for *you*! You and Billie, and that cursed baby. Otherwise..."

Dammit, the missed words were driving me insane. I needed to hear more. If they were talking about me and my little girl, I needed to know what was going on. On silent feet, barely daring to breathe, I crept closer to my parent's bedroom, where the door stood open a few inches.

"This is insane," my dad exclaimed with a slightly hysterical laugh. "Tina, these aren't just white-collar criminals. This is the goddamn *mafia*. If they find out what you've been doing—"

"They *won't*," my mom insisted, sounding frustrated. "You are the *only* person who knows, so unless you've told someone..." She trailed off, leaving the implication hanging in the air between them.

A tense silence fell then, broken abruptly when my dad jerked the bedroom door open and found me standing there. Listening.

His eyes went wide and round, his breath sucking in sharply. "Billie. How much of that did you hear?"

I shook my head slowly, my brow furrowed with

confusion. "Not enough... Are you guys going to tell me what's going on?"

Dad glanced over his shoulder at Mom, who was staring at me with an ashen complexion, her fingers pressed to her mouth.

"No, honey," Dad said quickly, flashing me a fake smile, "Mom and I were just discussing her work. It's nothing to worry about, okay? Come on, you look hungry; I'll whip us up some banana pancakes for dinner."

"Christian, that's not a healthy dinner," Mom called after us, but Dad already had his arm wrapped around my shoulders, guiding me toward the kitchen. He knew I loved breakfast for dinner more than any other incredible meal he could have made.

I glanced up at his brittle smile as we started pulling out ingredients for pancakes, and cautiously poked him for information. "That sounded like a serious disagreement with Mom," I commented, keeping it vague. "Anything I need to be worried about?"

A stricken look passed over his older but still handsome face, then he shook his head. "Nothing at all. Just a stressful time of year for Mom's work. Tell me about your scan today! Did you find out the sex?"

Excitement bubbled through me, and I brushed my

worries aside. Instead, I focused on telling my dad the good news about my baby girl. My healthy, happy, baby girl, who would be entering the world in just four and a half months.

All worrying thoughts evaporated from my mind as Dad pulled out his paint swatches after we finished the pancakes. He'd been working on decorating a nursery upstairs, and now that we knew I was having a girl, he wanted to revisit our color scheme.

As with every day lately, my energy bottomed out way earlier than I'd normally go to bed. Yawning, I hugged my dad goodnight, then went to tell Mom the same. She was in the study, where she and Dad both had computers set up.

"Good night, Mom," I said from the doorway. "I love you."

She glanced up from her computer and smiled gently. "I love you too, Billie Baggins. Sweet dreams."

Upstairs in my bedroom, the same one I'd had since I was born, I fell asleep easily—the pregnancy exhaustion was insane—but sadly, I didn't *stay* asleep. Sometime before midnight I woke up desperate to pee and groaned as I dragged myself out from under the blankets.

Something itched my nose, and I sneezed on my way

to the bathroom. I tried to stay as asleep as possible, hoping not to fully wake up, so I left the lights off and my eyes mostly closed. I sneezed again while peeing and wrinkled my nose. I'd been so fucking sensitive to smells lately, and right now I could smell someone's chimney smoke almost as though it was right here in the house.

A scream rang out from downstairs, and I nearly fell down the toilet as I jumped in fright.

What the fuck?

Something shattered, and another scream reached my ears. Mom.

"Mom?" I called out like an idiot. I'd seen enough horror movies to know that was a bad, *bad* idea, yet in the heat of the moment, I couldn't stop myself. I needed to see if she was okay, so I hurried for the stairs to check on her. Maybe she'd fallen?

The smoke was inside the house, though. It was *inside* and way too thick for chimney smoke. Besides, it wasn't winter. Why would the fireplace be going when it was eighty degrees?

"Mom?" I called out again, coughing through the smoke as I hurried downstairs. Something was on fire. We needed to put it out, but how? I knew Dad had an extinguisher somewhere. Kitchen? No... garage maybe.

I hurried for the garage door, only to find it locked.

What the hell? That door was never locked. Not in my whole damn life had that door been locked.

Confused, scared, and sick with worry, I grabbed a tea towel off the kitchen bench and ran it under the tap before covering my mouth and nose. Inhaling smoke couldn't be good for my baby girl, but I needed to make sure my parents were safe...

Breathing through the wet cloth was marginally easier as I hurried along to my parents' bedroom. It was empty, but the smoke was thicker. Where was Dad? Maybe they were in the study?

A noise in the hallway made me jump with fright, and I darted back out of the bedroom to see a shadowy figure disappear down the hallway toward the front door. It was a man, based on size, but he was way too broad and tall to be my dad. He disappeared into the night before I could even get a word out, slamming the door behind himself.

Panic nearly paralyzed me, but I forced myself to move in the direction of the study. That was where the smoke was coming from.

Not trusting metal door handles, I pushed the door with my foot and nearly collapsed from the heat. The air down low was easier to breathe, so I stayed on hands and knees as I crawled into the burning office, my face already streaming with tears. They were in here. Both of them.

"Mom?" I croaked from behind my wet cloth—which was now almost dry. "Dad?"

It was nearly impossible to see, but my hand fumbled across something. A shoe. A *foot*. I chased it up my mom's unmoving body until I touched blood. So much blood.

Sobbing and coughing, I frantically searched for a pulse. Nothing. She was dead.

"Dad?" I wailed, searching on hands and knees until I found him too. Then I nearly vomited.

I needed to get out. *Now*. Before I died too. Not to mention my baby...

Gritting my teeth against the screams of anguish welling up inside me, I crawled on all fours out of the burning office. It would only be a matter of minutes before the whole house caught alight. I couldn't still be here when that happened.

Staying low, I scrambled along the hallway to the front door. The door I'd *just* seen my parents' murderer leave through. And it was locked.

"What?" I exclaimed, tears choking me. "No!" Disbelief made me stupid, and I stood there for precious seconds, yanking on the handle like it was some kind of mistake.

A wave of dizziness washed through me, making me nauseous, and I dropped back to the ground. Fuck. I needed to get out. Now.

"Help!" My cry was a pathetic croak as I pressed my face to the floor. The fire was spreading fast; if I didn't get out now...

Key. I needed a *key!* Dad had just changed the locks last week—now I knew why—and the front door automatically locked on exit. Where were my keys?

Staying low to the floor, I hunted for where I'd dropped my handbag earlier when I came home. I'd put my keys back in my bag, hadn't I? Or... shit, maybe tossed them on the table? *Fuck!* Why couldn't I remember?

Dizziness tilted the room sharply, and I crashed to the side, pain shooting through my belly. Had I just hit something? I couldn't see, everything was so dark now. My lungs were tight. So damn tight.

Hacking coughs shook my body as I searched the ground for where I'd dropped my cloth. Finding nothing, I tried to pull my pajama shirt up over my nose and mouth, but it was like trying to smother a forest fire with a drink bottle. Utterly pointless.

My lungs burned, tightening more with every gasping breath I drew, and my vision went hazy. I couldn't give up, though. I couldn't just quit. Not when my little girl was depending on me... I needed to survive for *her*. My baby and Jace's.

Drawing together all my strength, I crawled through the living room, determined to get to the window. If I could open it, I could get out. If I could get out, I could breathe. My baby could live.

Coughing, choking, dizzy as hell, I dragged myself up and yanked on the window sash.

It didn't budge. Not even an inch.

Desperation made me scream, then I coughed so hard I blacked out, falling awkwardly to the floor. I refused to give up, though, and fought my way back into vague consciousness as I got back onto my hands and knees to find another exit. Any exit.

My belly radiated with pain, but I had to grit my teeth and continue on.

Sometimes, though, determination simply wasn't enough. As I crawled out of the living room, heading for the stairs, a blast of intense heat exploded somewhere nearby, and my strength failed.

I failed.

two

JACE

PRESENT DAY

Fucking chaos reigned around us, and my ears rang to the point that I couldn't hear anything. But I could feel the aftereffects. The heat and the scent of what I could only liken to sulfur and concrete dust surrounded me, as the building continued to tumble and burn behind us.

Billie hung loosely in my arms, her head flopping around despite my attempt to keep her safe. The fucking panic at not knowing if she was badly hurt or just knocked out rode me as hard as it had the night in the field. Everyone needed to stop trying to kill us, because it was eating away at the last threads of my sanity.

When I was a few feet from the entrance, I paused and turned back to the building, needing assurance everyone else had gotten out safely. Billie remained limp in my arms, so I shook her gently.

"Wake the fuck up. Please, Rose."

I couldn't even hear my own words through the ringing in my head, so chances were she wouldn't either, but I had to try. I was just about to place her on the ground to check her for injuries when Angelo and Vee appeared through the doorway. *Thank fuck.* He was helping her to get free, but before they could get out, more of the building started to collapse around them. "Move it," I shouted, hoping they were less hearing damaged.

Grayson, who was in the doorway helping Rhett, left him outside and headed back in. He'd clearly seen exactly what I had. This fucking glass monstrosity was coming down like a flimsy house of cards. A cold, lifeless building, decorated with the worst art, including that giant sculpture of what I had to assume was an oversized dick, since it had a shaft and balls...

As my eyes lifted toward the piece, just visible through the glass entrance, the fucking cable snapped. Just snapped, sending the giant piece crashing toward the ground. At the same time, Grayson was hauling Vee out, but Angelo was still inside.

My shout was lost in the collapse of half the building, the sculpture landing right where Angelo had been. Sprinting back to the doorway, I was thankful that Grayson was always aware of his surroundings. He managed to get Vee to the ground in time to catch Billie as I tossed her into his arms on my way past.

He bellowed some shit at me as I continued into the building, and my hearing had come back online enough that I definitely heard *"Stupid fucking irresponsible..."* He wasn't wrong, but I also didn't give a fuck. Not that he could even talk; he'd be right there with me if he wasn't taking care of two injured women and Rhett.

In the background sirens blared, but they'd be too late to save Angelo.

Maybe I was already too late, but there were only a handful of people in the world I'd run into a burning building for. Angelo was one of them. Billie and Angelo were my oldest friends, my fucking family, and sure, we'd fought for near half our friendship, but that didn't mean the love had ever died.

It just got compressed under hate.

If they were dead, I wouldn't be able to hate them anymore. I had to ensure they stayed alive and well so I could resume my normal toxic relationship of simultaneously loathing and missing them.

Once inside the building, the heat and smoke were already thicker than a few seconds ago when I'd seen the sculpture fall and land on Angelo. Glass crunched under my boots as I ducked down low, hauling up the collar of my dress shirt to cover my mouth.

"Angel," I called, coughing through my words. The ringing in my ears had moved deeper in my head, to the point my brain felt like it was shaking. I'd suffered a head injury from the force of the explosion, but I couldn't succumb to it yet. Not until they were all safe.

More smoke billowed in from farther back in the building, but Angelo had only been a few steps inside the main foyer. He couldn't be far from me.

Practically crawling, I managed to bump into his legs, which were only visible when I was right at his side. The black-clad pants led up to a shard of glass lodged firmly below his left knee. His right leg looked burned as well, but there were no flames, as if he'd managed to get them out. Somehow.

Whatever the case, Angelo was injured and needed medical attention now.

I was about to grab his left leg to drag him out of

the room, when my rattled brain kicked in and reminded me that half of him could be trapped under the fucking sculpture. I'd probably pull his head off by doing that.

"Angel!" I rasped. "Don't you be fucking dead, you hear me. I still need to beat your ass a dozen or more times, and if you're dead... it means my fun is over."

And part of my soul would die because he was one of my brothers. There were Rhett and Grayson too, but Angelo was the first, and I couldn't imagine a life without him in it.

Moving up his body, the fucking relief I felt to see him free of the sculpture, with just a nasty cut on his forehead, almost knocked me to the ground. The dick sculpture had clearly clipped him as it fell, but he'd managed to move enough that it hadn't crushed his skull in.

At least I hoped it hadn't. The wound was bleeding, but more of a slow seep, rather than the gush of a deeper, more serious injury. Not that any head injury couldn't be serious.

But at least he had a chance.

Coughing and trying to breath shallowly, I wedged my arms under Angelo, cursing him for being such a giant fucker. Luckily, I wasn't small by any means, because hauling his bulk out of here was going to take all of my strength.

Trying not to jostle his head any more than necessary, I lifted him into a fireman's hold and took one step after another, heading in the direction of the door. I got a little turned around at some point, but the firefighters entered the foyer before I managed to wander into a damn wall and escorted me out into the fresh air.

My lungs were screaming at that point, the smoke filling every crevice of my body, and when they shoved oxygen on my face–while also taking Angelo from me and hauling him off into an ambulance–I spent a good ten minutes hacking my guts up.

"You're a fucking idiot." Grayson took it upon himself to yell at me. "You ran in there injured and without a plan. Next time, fucking wait for me to help you. "

"Angelo didn't have any extra time," I rasped, pulling the mask briefly down. An EMT started pushing me toward one of the ambulances then, forcing my mask back on my face. Grayson shook his head, looking stern, but he didn't stop them from doing their job. I pulled my mask back down again. "How're Billie and Rhett?"

His dark gaze drilled into me as he huffed. "Injured, but they should recover. Billie had some sort of seizure, though, while I was holding her, so they'll most certainly take her in for tests."

"You're all coming in," a short, blonde woman said. She was dressed in an EMT uniform and looked about twenty years older than us. She had a serious, no-nonsense face. "You were in an explosion. Every single one of you needs to be checked out."

"Where's Billie?" I shot back, before she firmly shoved me onto a stretcher and got the mask back on.

"She's in another ambulance," she said quickly. "They're taking her straight to the hospital since Mr. Taylor is correct about her possible seizure. Mr. Silver is with them as well since he has a head injury."

What the fuck? Why was Billie seizing? She had been unconscious, but I hadn't seen any visible injuries to account for that reaction. Maybe it was just the whole ordeal affecting her. I mean, the area was like a war zone right now, with medical service, police, helicopters, and more all around us. It would be a lot for anyone to handle, let alone someone who had gone through the death of her family before.

The EMT forced me to lie back so they could wheel me to the closest ambulance, and I saw her try the same with Grayson, before he eyeballed her hard enough that she backed off. "We suggest getting checked out," she said, but the rest was cut off as two men loaded my stretcher into the vehicle and the doors were closed.

One had gotten in with me, but he was still chatting with the other guy as he got a drip set up. "Can't believe we're treating fucking Bellerose," he said, shaking his head, acting like I was either unconscious or hard of hearing. "Someone tried to blow up Bellerose."

Considering the mild ringing in my ears, I genuinely worried that I had damaged something permanently in my hearing, and how the hell would I make music the same after that? The fine tuning of my hearing was how I found the best sound. "They didn't succeed," I managed to get out before he lifted my mask once more, looking a little embarrassed.

"We'll have you at the hospital in a minute, Mr. Adams. Please, just try and lie as still as possible. I'm getting some oxygen and fluids into you, and the rest will be assessed in triage."

I nodded, letting myself relax back into the pillow. What a fuck of a day. Flo's funeral, then Tom the Fucker's request, and then someone tried to kill us. Again. My damaged hearing had nothing on the fact that all of us could have died today. Today, when we were mourning our friend who was killed in the last attempt. I'd already lost Flo, and I could not handle losing any others.

Angelo and Billie could have died today.

Rhett and Grayson.

My family.

My new aim in life was to figure out who was behind the farmhouse and then this bombing and tear them into tiny fucking pieces. Then I'd burn those pieces and scatter their ash into the closest pig shit I could find.

It was the only fitting ending.

I'd spent the past few days feeling sorry for myself, hating Billie harder than ever because she'd kept the truth of my child from me. A child who had died in a fucking fir—

I sat bolt upright, scaring the poor guy who'd just finished fixing my drip in place. But I'd finally figured out the real reason Billie was having a seizure. *It had to be the reason.* She'd been unconscious, maybe stuck in some sort of triggering flashback. I'd seen her face when Angelo had landed in a campfire, and here we were, in another fire. Another fire where people she loved were hurt. Like her parents. Like her... *our* baby girl.

"Sir, you need to relax." The guy attempted to push me back, but he had no hope of moving me. I might party like a rock star, but I worked out like a bodybuilder. It was the only way to exorcise my demons.

Ripping the mask free, I nailed him with a glare. "I need updates on my friends. Are we all heading for the same hospital?"

He blinked, and I could tell he had no fucking clue. To his credit, though, he did ask the driver, who called back, "Yep, they have enough room at Naples General to take everyone. No need to split the group."

That was a relief. "I need to see Billie," I said shortly. "The blonde who was taken first. She's been in a fire before, and her seizure could be a reaction to past trauma. I mean, check injuries first, but I need to let the doctors know her history."

He nodded, understanding that until they took me seriously, I wasn't going to stop. "Mr. Adams, I assure you that you and your friends will have the best care available. I'll personally make sure that you get to speak with Billie's doctor and the other band members." He paused, eyes shifting between me and the driver briefly before he leaned in and lowered his voice. "Any chance for an autograph? I'm a huge fan."

I wanted to tell him to fuck off, but an ally when we got there could come in handy.

Relaxing back into the bed once more, I nodded. "You ensure I get to see Billie and Rhett when we arrive at the hospital. And immediate updates on Angelo.

Then I will get you all the signed band merch you can handle."

The smile on his face was goddamn beaming, and I tried to remember that we needed fans to keep making music. Today, though, when someone had tried to fucking murder me and everyone I loved, it was a hard reminder.

Bellerose had saved me once, but it felt like my downfall now.

three

BILLIE

Why did people always seem to think that running water was soothing? It wasn't. At all. It just made me need to pee, and then I'd always end up anxious because it's never a time or place where restrooms are convenient. So there was little wonder why I was shifting uncomfortably in the overstuffed armchair, trying desperately not to look at the stupid decorative fountain in the corner.

"How are you feeling today, Billie?" the smartly dressed woman opposite me asked, her head tilted to the side with curiosity.

I didn't answer. What the fuck did she want me to

say? It'd been a week since the explosion—the *fire*—that nearly killed us all, and I'd met with Dr. Candace every day since the hospital discharged me for my *physical* injuries. My mental ones were another matter. They were the reason I was sitting here, talking about my *feelings*. Again.

My therapist gave a tiny sigh, one I wasn't meant to hear, then tried again. "Do you have plans for Christmas?"

I laughed bitterly. "With who? All my family? In my home? Oh wait, I don't have either of those things." Okay, sure, maybe the reasons I was in therapy were more than just the bomb at Big Noise. Maybe, just maybe, I needed the help to work through some of my past trauma.

It still didn't mean I had to like it.

"Billie, we both know that's not true," she said with a small shake of her head. "Just because they're not related to you doesn't mean that Rhett, Grayson, and J—"

"Don't. Do *not* tell me that Jace *holier-than-thou* Adams is my fucking family." I all but spat those words, the instant anger ripping through me so fast my hands shook. "Rhett and Grayson are..." Fuck. What were they to me now? We *had* been lovers, I guess. But now? Now, everything felt so different. Broken.

I swallowed my emotions back, my knee bouncing as I tried to hold my need to pee.

"Okay, so let's talk about where you're staying when you leave here today," Dr. Candace suggested with a small grimace of disappointment. "I understand you've already been discharged. Tell me about what your plans are."

Discharged. Yep, I sure was. Although the hospital had cleared me of my injuries the day after the explosion, I'd been kept under psychiatric hold thanks to my *episode* during the fire. Jace had lobbied for it harder than anyone else, claiming I was "a danger to myself and others" like some kind of fucking—

"Billie?"

"Sorry," I murmured, wrapping my arms around myself. "Um, I'm going to stay with Gray again, I guess. I don't really have any other options..." Poor Billie Bellerose. No home, no family, no hope...

"That's not what I heard," Dr Candace disagreed with a gentle smile. "You could have gone to Rhett's home; I know he offered." I was fairly sure Dr. Candace was a Rhett Silver fan. "Or the Riccis'—"

"No," I snapped, cutting her off. "I won't go there. If I do, then..." Then Giovanni would be insufferable. Creepy. Dangerous. I wouldn't put it past him to try and force his own baby into me just to ensure the family line continued. Gross. The idea sent a deep shiver through me.

Dr. Candace just pursed her lips thoughtfully. "Will you tell Grayson about your past? I know you said Rhett and Jace both know about the fire, but you've kept Grayson in the dark. Is there a reason for that?"

She'd asked this once before, six days ago when we'd met for the first time and I had to spill my guts over why my mind had snapped during the fire. How I'd become locked in the memory of my parents' death. How I'd remembered *more* than ever before... and that new information had terrified me.

I shook my head. "Maybe one day," I croaked. "Not yet. I can't... I don't want to revisit it all. Not after Angel..."

"What if Rhett or Jace tell him your story? About your parents' death and Penelope?" Her question was entirely valid, but that didn't mean I had to like it.

I shrugged. "Then I guess it saves me from telling him. Besides, he knows some..." I couldn't totally remember what, though. A little about Penelope, because he'd rescued us from the woods right after that emotional confession to Jace. But not the fire or my parents, and no one beside Dr. Candace knew about my recent memories. About how I'd heard my mom and dad fighting over something the day they'd died or how they'd been killed not by the fire, but by someone slitting their throats..

"So you have no problem with Grayson knowing but just don't want to tell him yourself," my therapist clarified. I squinted at her in frustration.

"Yes, isn't that what I said?"

She gave a slight shake of her head, then flashed a quick, reassuring smile. "I'm just making sure you understand what you're telling me, Billie. And that in turn helps me understand where your reservations lie. Do you think Rhett or Jace *would* tell anyone your story? It's very personal."

The waterfall continued to trickle, and I glared daggers at it. *Goddamn, I needed to pee.*

"Billie?"

I sighed. "No, they probably wouldn't. Rhett has too much respect for my privacy."

Her brow arched. "And Jace?"

Was an arrogant son of a bitch. "Would never want anyone to see *me* as the victim. He already got a verbal spanking from Gray when Gray didn't even know the whole story. No way would he risk falling from his own pedestal by garnering sympathy for *me*. His fucking Lilith."

"Is that how you see yourself?" she mused, watching me carefully.

I had no issue with therapists. None. I would have voluntarily come to her if I'd had the money and means. Jace hadn't needed to try and commit me. But the fact that he had, the fact that I *wasn't* here of my own volition, it made me want to resist at every damn turn. Even to the detriment of my own health.

"Let's talk about music," she suggested, changing the subject.

"What about music?" I replied, confused and suspicious.

"You collaborated a lot with Jace before Bellerose was signed, didn't you? I understand you have songwriting credit on most songs from the debut album." She smiled like this was a good thing. "That must be something you enjoy doing with him?"

I scowled. "How do you—" Songwriting credit? Since when? "It's something that I *used* to enjoy with him, yes. And with Angelo. And then, more often than not, we'd all end up naked, which is how I ended up pregnant at sixteen. My parents were very proud." Okay... that was a little more caustic than she deserved, given how nonjudgmental she'd been with me.

My little snaps of anger never seemed to phase her, though. She just nodded like she was making mental notes—never physical ones, she never scribbled away on a clipboard like a stereotype—then continued with her line of conversation.

"What instrument do you play?"

"None of them," I muttered. "At least, not well. Not like..." Not like Jace or Angelo. Or Rhett and Gray. Or Flo... "I play guitar and piano a little, just enough to get the tune out of my head and give it to more talented musicians."

"I see," Dr Candace murmured. "Have you worked on anything recently?"

I nearly said no, then remembered the song I'd come up with while we were in the woods. The same one I'd told Jace he couldn't have, only to hear him putting the most heartbreakingly perfect lyrics with my melody when he thought I was asleep. Then we fucked the next morning.

"Yes," I admitted, "but only because I was bored."

"How did you feel while you were creating music, Billie?"

Alive. "Um, okay I guess?"

She nodded, her expression giving none of her thoughts away, as usual. "Is *okay* the level you judge much of your existence on? Just *being okay* is what you aim for?"

Damn. That one stung. But she wasn't wrong. "Yeah, I guess life hasn't really been one to give me tequila to go with the limes. There's no turning most of my shitty life around, and... yeah, being *okay* means I'm not dying in an alley somewhere."

Another nod. Another warm expression and no judgment. "Do you ever have goals or dreams? Do you make plans to turn *okay* into more? To raise that level and keep it raised?"

A sad, hard bark of laughter escaped me. "Goals and dreams are for a different life. A different fucking person. I exist. There's nothing else, and I won't waste my time and energy hoping for more."

Her kind smile dimmed just a fraction, the first negative reaction she'd shot my way in many minutes. "I don't think that's true, Billie. From what you've told me, and the background I know, you have a lot of reasons to be hopeful. I know it's scary to dream for a better future, but it's also healthy. It forces you to change circumstances, to refuse to accept bad treatment, and to create a life that's more than just *okay*."

Scary? Was she fucking kidding? It was absolutely terrifying, and it felt like one more shattered dream and I'd be broken beyond repair. Jace fucking Adams seemed to think I already was.

"Thanks, doc," I drawled, forcing the mood to shift with my attitude. "I'll take that into account when I'm being almost murdered for the twentieth time in a year. Merry fucking Christmas to me."

"I'm glad you brought up the attempted murders," she said in one of her rapid shifts. "As we've discussed, life-or-death situations are very triggering when you've suffered a previous loss. It brings up the old trauma. With that in mind, I believe it's time for us to discuss some techniques that might help you deal with flashbacks."

Dr. Candace had already attempted to impart these techniques during our first couple of sessions, but I'd been less than receptive, especially on the eve of the last fight I'd had with Jace. But the truth was that "seizure" on the day of the attack wasn't my only flash-back. There had been moments since the explosion during the day and night when I found myself in this space between the past and the present, unable to truly differentiate which I was in. It was affecting me too greatly to keep turning down the help. Even if that help was being somewhat forced on me.

"Okay," I said with a nod. "I need to let the past go because it's breaking me."

She leaned forward, her expression so open and kind that I alternated between wanting to cry and punch her in the face. This shit hurt, and while it wasn't her fault, she was here now, picking at the wounds. Or was she suturing them? Both hurt, but one would eventually allow me to heal.

Either way, I was here now, and I'd listen.

"You are stronger than you think, Billie," she told me, and fuck if there wasn't a tiny ring of truth in her tone. As if she truly believed what she was saying. "Look back at what you've overcome. Look at where you've been and where you are now. Being here in therapy, for starters, is a great show of strength. It might have been forced on you, but you still participate with me. I've had a lot of therapy sessions with people who were mandated to be here, and let me tell you, it's generally screaming, trashing my office, or silence that cannot be broken. You. Are. Strong."

And fuck. There she went, making me want to cry again.

"And you *will* let the past go, as soon as you deal with the trauma."

She was saying exactly what we both knew. I'd suppressed the pain and loss for so many years, that it had built up too big to be contained any longer. My brain wouldn't allow it.

Dr Candace's next smile was broad, as she kept her focus firmly on me. "Therapy is going to help you let go of your past and move forward to a stronger, more fulfilled future, but in the meantime, here are my suggestions for dealing with the current flashbacks and trauma episodes."

I found myself leaning forward, desperate to hear her next words.

"Start with learning to recognize the prequel to an attack so you know when it's about to happen. When you feel it coming on, I want you to take five deep breaths and count backwards with each one. Slow, sure —keep yourself focused on counting and breathing."

She continued on, listing out multiple steps that had me grounding myself in the present by finding familiar objects and focusing on them, repeating out loud that *this is not real, this is not my life now*, seeking out a stable person that I trusted to help me through, and a few others.

"It sounds simple, but it's more difficult to implement when you are lost in the trauma," she warned me.

What else was new? Nothing in my life was ever simple, and I had the sense that this might be harder than even my normal.

Luckily, I was well used to dealing with difficult shit. It was the story of my life, after all.

four

BILLIE

Whenever I left a therapy session, I felt wrung out, like I'd just run a marathon or puked my guts up for six hours. Usually, I was ferried back to the hospital, where I'd sleep in my less-than-comfortable bed, but today was different. Sort of.

I'd been discharged, finally free and ready to mentally take on the world... according to the overwhelmed hospital, who really needed my bed. I had no idea what to expect when I left the therapist's office. No idea if anyone would be waiting for me.

Not like Bellerose could just hang out in the street,

ready to greet me when I emerged. And aside from them, I had no one.

When I pushed the glass doors open, stepping out into the icy air that was whipping around, I let out a small gasp. Despite my previous thoughts, two members of Bellerose were standing on the sidewalk, baseball caps pulled low, huge glasses on. But there was no way Grayson could ever hide his bulk. And Rhett's tatts were always distinctive, especially when he was the crazy person not wearing a jacket in this weather.

The pair stood there, no security, no fanfare, smiling their perfect fucking smiles at me.

The tears I'd been suppressing in the therapist's office refused to remain at bay any longer as my feet moved faster, and I sprinted the last ten feet to throw myself at both of them. They caught me with ease, arms wrapping around me.

"Aw, Billie, you missed us," Rhett said in his joking tone. "My little Thorn."

It wasn't as if I hadn't seen them over the past week. Once I'd established that everyone was alive and on the mend, there'd been time to visit, but it had not been exactly comfortable in the hospital with no privacy, the sterile surroundings keeping us uneasy.

It hadn't been the same, but this... this felt right.

"How are you?" I asked Rhett as we pulled apart and I could see his face. He'd been knocked out in the attack and had a few cuts and bruises, most of which were fading now, turning a lovely yellow-and-green color, from what I could see around the edges of his band shirt and jeans anyway.

"Totally fine. I've had worse injuries in bar fights," he snorted.

I wasn't at all surprised.

Tilting my head back, I met the unwavering stare of dark brown eyes. "And you?" I asked softly.

Grayson's serious expression didn't shift. "You know I wasn't injured, Prickles. I'm more than okay, especially since you're coming home today."

Okay. There went that fucking word again—and the reminder that I had to start striving for more than *just fucking okay.* Maybe the word I should be focusing on was *home.* A word that had my heart aching for all the right reasons. Feeling myself soften, I stepped closer to Gray and placed my hand on his hard chest, relishing the connection.

I did the same to Rhett, and for the first time, I was starting to understand the *grounding* the therapist had talked about. Two things that made me feel present stood right before me.

Just had to keep these boys with me at all times.

"How was therapy today?" Rhett asked, his expression growing serious enough to match Grayson's. In the reflection of his glasses, I saw my own expression fall. I hated the reminder. I hated the weakness in myself for not being able to deal with this. No matter how many times Dr. Candace called me strong, she had no idea how weak I truly felt.

"She said it's going to take time to unravel all my trauma, and I have to come back for two sessions a week. In the meantime, she gave me some techniques to try," I said with a shrug. "To deal with the flashbacks and PTSD. I might need your help with that, if I'm asleep or if I don't catch it in time."

"You have our help, support... whatever you need," Rhett replied instantly. He leaned down and kissed me gently, and it felt like I was grounded again. *More.* For the first time since the explosion, I felt like myself.

This is what I'd needed all along—to be away from the hospital. Away from loneliness... back with my rock stars.

"She's not a terrible therapist," I admitted, when I caught my breath again after his kiss. "She's kind and understanding. I'm less than pleasant most of the time, but she hasn't shown any frustration." It was on the tip of my tongue to suggest that maybe Rhett should go and see her too. But I also didn't want to be Jace, forcing therapy on someone. That fucker.

"So, we're heading home," I changed the subject. "Which home?"

"Ours," Grayson rumbled without hesitation. "Yours and mine." Rhett elbowed him quickly, and he finally smiled. "Yours, mine, and Rhett's."

"I moved in!" Rhett sounded so fucking pleased with himself that I had to smile, then stronger emotions took over. Just the thought of being with Rhett and Grayson together, in a safe place, had me all fucked up.

"Your house is the safest," I choked out. "Makes sense." The tears were burning again at their casual reference to *our home.*

Rhett just laughed and hugged me again, harder this time, so my feet left the ground briefly.

It was at this point I noticed that we were finally starting to draw attention. The boys had been incognito, but I wasn't in any sort of disguise, and unfortunately these days, thanks to that fucking blog, my own infamy was growing.

Gray, too, noticed the people stopping and staring. The whispers growing stronger around us. Wrapping an arm around my shoulders, he quickly ushered us into his blacked-out SUV, which was parked nearby. He deposited me into the front passenger seat, while Rhett climbed into the middle seat behind us. Gray screeched out of there just as the paps showed up.

They'd been tipped off, but it was too late.

When we'd been driving for a few minutes, weaving through the midmorning traffic in downtown Naples, I had to ask them the question burning through my brain. "Where is Jace? Did he move in too?"

The silence was strong for seconds, as if no one really wanted to talk about Bellerose's lead singer.

"We're having a little break from Jace this week," Rhett said. I turned to find his expression neutral. "He's mostly been in the hospital with Angelo anyway."

Angelo. I'd been doing my best not to think about my former best friend turned lover, turned enemy, then fake baby daddy. He'd been hurt the worst in the attack, and the one time I'd managed to drag myself to the ICU to visit him, I'd broken down in gut-wrenching sobs and moans.

Not that it had mattered. Angelo was in a coma and had no idea I was even there. I'd sat at his bedside for an hour until his "bestie" showed up. That had been Jace and my first fight post attack, done in whispered, hate-filled accusations. Everything had gone downhill after that, and I'd found myself involuntarily admitted to the psych ward.

Fuck Jace.

"No news about Angelo still?" I asked, wondering if they'd heard anything. My last update had been three days ago from one of the nurses who was a Bellerose fan and had tried to stay on my good side by slipping me extra treats with my meals and keeping me updated about Angelo and the others.

"Jace isn't exactly talking to us," Grayson said shortly. "That bastard needs therapy too, if you ask me."

"All of us need therapy," Rhett said with a sigh. "What do you really think of this chick, Billie? Can we trust her not to sell our story to the press?"

That was an excellent question. I liked her for sure, but money turned even the nicest people. "I honestly don't know. Maybe we should wait and see if any of my sob story makes it into Dirty Truths."

The loss of Penelope when I was sixteen wasn't common knowledge yet, but it also wouldn't be that hard for people to dig up that information. My name was known. I'd gone to the hospital after the fire and miscarriage. The information was there for them to find with enough determination and dodgy bribes. Maybe I needed to tell the therapist something that wasn't known by anyone else and see what made it into the news.

"If I get a chance, I'll test her professionalism," I told the guys. "Then we can decide if she's a good fit for the rest of the band."

"I don't love you being the sacrificial lamb for this," Rhett muttered, his brow drawn in a sullen frown in the mirror. "Just go about your normal sessions. You'll figure out her true intentions soon enough. It always becomes obvious over time."

If anyone would know, it was these famous guys.

Rhett continued, "The ship has sailed on trusting anyone, but I reckon we're about due one loyal person coming out to bat for our team."

Gray and I exchanged a look, then my lips twitched with a smile as I turned to look at Rhett in the backseat. "How many metaphors did you just mix, Zep? I thought you were supposed to be a songwriter."

His own mouth curved in an answering smile, the mood instantly lightening. "Mixed metaphors are the spice of life, Thorn, and should be used liberally. Like butter. Or lube." He shot me a wink, and my body flushed with heat. Oh yeah, I'd definitely missed him.

"Well, I'm glad that she's helping you, little hedgehog," Gray said, reaching out to place a hand on my leg. I loved when he gave me those little affectionate touches, so at odds with his whole tough-man image. I covered his hand with my own, keeping it.

The three of us slipped back into oddly comfortable silence for the rest of the drive to Grayson's house, and on arrival I quietly noted some new security upgrades. Not the least of which was a perimeter fence with electronic gates where you used to be able to walk right up to the front porch.

"How'd you get this done the week before Christmas?" I asked, blinking at the fresh work.

Gray shot me a quick smirk. "I know people."

Rhett scoffed. "He means that he paid people. Anyone will work over the holidays so long as they're well compensated for it."

My brows lifted, but Gray just shrugged as he parked the SUV in his garage. "We have a little surprise for you, Prickles."

Butterflies fluttered through my chest. A surprise? Were they going to cover themselves in chocolate sauce and let me lick it off? Wow. One week without sex and I was turning into a man, constantly thinking about it.

Eager to see what they were talking about, I clambered out of the car and followed Gray into the house with Rhett behind me. Whether they'd done that deliberately or not, I wasn't sure. But it gave me a calm sense of security to be surrounded by my guys.

"Billie!" A high-pitched scream echoed through Gray's house, and I sucked in a sharp breath of fright. It eased a second later when Vee shoved Grayson aside and threw herself at me like an amorous octopus. "Oh my god, you're here! And you look amazing! How do you feel? I can't believe they kept you so long!"

"Fucking hell, Valentina, let the girl breathe," Rhett growled, gently peeling my new growth off and giving me a scrap of space. "At least let her sit down before you grill her."

Vee flushed and offered me a sheepish smile. "Sorry. I missed you."

It was sweet but... weird. She was Angelo's wife, and we hadn't ever spent a whole lot of time together. But she had saved us. All of us. And nearly gotten killed in the process.

"It's okay," I replied with a reassuring smile. "I just need a coffee, I think." I looked past Vee to Grayson with a hopeful look. He nodded back, his gaze soft and affectionate, and that fizzy warmth of happiness filled my chest once more.

We moved into Grayson's living room, and I glanced around curiously. Christmas was tomorrow, but he didn't have a single decoration up. No tree, no lights, not even a cute Santa stashed somewhere. It made me curious about Gray's stance on Christmas, since it used to be one of my favorite holidays. Before my parents had died, anyway.

"How are *you* feeling?" I asked Vee, refocusing on the gorgeous redhead perched beside me on the leather couch. "You look... better." Her face was also a rainbow of bruising, and there was a thick line of stitches cutting from her eyebrow up into her hair where part of her scalp was shaved. She wore a long sleeve top and sweatpants, but I'd bet the rest of her looked equally painful.

She grimaced. "I look awful, I know. But I *feel* better. They discharged me after only a day, but I can't exactly go back to my family, so..."

I gave an understanding nod. "Gray brought you back here. Makes sense. I'm glad you're safe, Vee. You risked so much for us."

She gave an uncomfortable shrug. "You'd do the same, Billie. I know you would."

A few months ago, I wouldn't have been so sure that I would. It'd been me against the world, and I wouldn't have put anyone else higher than my own survival. Now, though? Yeah, she was right. There was nothing I wouldn't do for my found family. The boys of Bellerose.

five

GRAYSON

The sound of Billie crying woke me, and I leapt out of bed like my ass was on fire. Before I had even fully woken up, I was in her room—a guest room that Rhett and I agreed was the nicest for our girl—and sliding under her covers.

"Shhhh, Prickles," I breathed, wrapping her trembling form in my arms and holding her close. "It's just a dream, beautiful girl; you're safe. I'm here. You're safe." I whispered the reassurances against her hair, relief washing through me as her sobbing eased.

It took a few minutes, but eventually her trembles subsided and her breathing calmed.

"Gray?" she mumbled in a voice husky with

emotion and sleep. "What...?"

"You were having a bad dream," I told her quietly, not releasing my hold on her tiny form. I wasn't ready to let her go... and I never would be. Rhett could just suck it up and learn to share. So could Jace, for that matter.

Billie's breathing hitched, but her arms looped around my body to hug me back. "Fuck, I'm sorry. Did I wake you up with my screaming?"

It tore me apart that she couldn't even rest in her own head. "No, you were just crying. I'm a light sleeper and was listening for you anyway."

"Where's Rhett?" she asked, pulling back from my chest to blink around with confusion. She and Rhett were sharing a room because we didn't want her to be alone—nor did she—and Rhett seemed to only sleep well when he was holding her. I got it, but I was jealous as fuck.

I listened to the sounds of the house for a moment, searching for an answer. Then I gave a small nod when I worked it out. "He couldn't sleep, I think. It sounds like he's downstairs talking to Vee. She's also having a hard time with nightmares. We're all a bit... tense."

Billie's laugh was bitter, but she relaxed back into my embrace. "Tense is one word for it. Does her family still want her dead?"

I sighed. "We think so. Angelo would be our best source for info, but seeing as he's currently out of action, we are just playing it safe and keeping her hidden here."

"Mm," she murmured, her cheek against my chest. "Good idea."

We lay there like that for a while, just... cuddling. I couldn't remember ever cuddling with a woman before; it just wasn't my style. I fucked around, sure. But I didn't sleep over, and I sure as shit didn't cuddle. Billie was different, though. Cuddling her was fast becoming one of my favorite things in the whole damn world— after the taste of her sweet cunt on my tongue, of course.

"Do you want to tell me about your nightmare?" I asked eventually, knowing she wasn't asleep by the pace of her breathing.

Breathing that picked up slightly, as if she was already reliving it. "How much of my past do you know about?" she whispered, but it sounded louder in the still night air.

Surprisingly, not much. "Only the basics. Billie Bellerose, twenty-four years old and an only child who grew up in Siena. You lived next door to Jace. Your parents are deceased, and you also lost... a child, which I know from that argument you had with Jace. When he

47

lost his shit. But I didn't ask him for further information, so that's it."

She tilted her head back, and in the limited light, I could make out the widening of her eyes. "You never investigated more? You, with all your research equipment, never looked into the homeless chick that fell into your band?"

My low chuckle filled the room. "I'm not sure what you did to me, but I just kept waiting to hear your story from you. I didn't want to see facts and figures on a page, all black and white and cold. That's not you, little hedgehog. You're warmth and light and so much more than I could ever learn from research."

A small sob escaped her, and I wanted to punch myself in the face for making her cry. But then she wrapped her arms tighter around me, pulling into my body as if she couldn't be close enough. My dick responded, as was to be expected, but so did my fucking heart. It squeezed in my chest, and I had a feeling that I was done for.

This was it for me.

There was never another who could wind themselves around me like this and make me never want to let go.

"The day I was almost shot by Ricci thugs," Billie murmured against my chest, "was the actual best day of my life. Who knew something so terrible could lead to something so wonderful."

That wasn't my experience in life, but now was not the time for my fucked up story. I wanted hers.

"I dream about the fire that killed my parents and almost me," she said suddenly. The relaxed calm of her body vanished as the tension of the past held her tight. "I was sixteen, and I'd just had my eighteen-week ultrasound to confirm I was carrying a little girl. I didn't remember this until these flashbacks started, but that day, when I walked into the house, my parents were fighting. It's weird that I didn't remember, but somehow the trauma of that day was blocked out. At least it had been until now."

Her voice wavered as she spoke, and I just held her as tightly as I could without crushing her. My strength was an asset, but I had to be aware of it in circumstances like this.

She tried to start again, but her voice broke harder, and she was crying once more. "Th-that ni—" Sobs shook her entire body, and I was desperate to kill whatever was hurting her. Only I couldn't.

"Shhhh, baby." I rocked her back and forth. "You don't need to tell me now. I've waited this long for your story, and I will continue to wait until you're ready. With the nightmare fresh in your mind, it's just too raw. We have the rest of our lives to learn about each other."

Her sobs slowed, and she lifted her head once more. Before I could figure out her next move, she pushed herself forward, her lips landing on mine. A low groan filled my throat, and I tried to let her control the momentum of the kiss, but just tasting her had my control shot to shit.

Fuck.

I'd never expected this. I'd never expected that any woman would hold me so enthralled, to the point that the thought of touching another chick had my dick wanting to shrivel up and fall off.

"Gray," she moaned against my mouth, and that was when my thinly held control snapped. I demanded entrance, my tongue sliding against hers, and she opened for me without hesitation. She was so responsive, taking everything, even when I was rougher than I'd like to be.

She rocked against me, lifting one leg so it was resting over my hips, and I was starting to see that my little Prickles was into my dominance. Fucking hell.

Cupping her face, I devoured every part of her mouth, exploring it like I owned her.

Maybe I did, because she sure as fuck owned me.

"Gray, please," she said again, breathy and clearly

on the edge of moaning once more. If that happened, I'd take that offer and fuck her worries away. But that wasn't how we needed to deal with her nightmares and PTSD. I'd been there, and it would just be hiding from it again.

With that in mind, I pulled back from her, hating every fucking second our mouths weren't touching. Every second I wasn't tasting her.

"As much as I want to strip you bare and spend the next few hours making you scream my name," I said, still wanting to punch myself in the face. "You're in the midst of trauma. You're exhausted, healing, and I think what you need now is comfort and sleep."

A strangled laugh spilled from her perfect lips. "An orgasm would really help with that."

I joined her laughter. "I know, baby. And I can give you that, but when we fuck... make love... whatever you want to call it, I want every part of your brain. Every part of you. I'm happy to be your distraction when needed, but for our first time, I need all of you."

I was a demanding, selfish bastard like that.

"You have all of me," she whispered, resting her head against my chest. She yawned a second later, and I knew my instincts about how exhausted she was were right. "Or as much as I can share when Rhett has some of me too."

That part was different. It wasn't like I was happy about sharing her with Rhett, but if there was anyone in the world I would share Billie with, it was my band-mate and brother. "Still fairly confident that you're going to pick me," I teased.

She didn't laugh with me, and I wondered if that was a genuine worry of hers: that I was going to make her pick. Dropping my head to the pillow, I wrapped her up tighter, and she shifted to lie across my chest. "I was just teasing," I told her, loving the feel of her against me. "You don't have to choose. We're figuring out this sharing thing okay for the moment, and there's no reason to end whatever is happening between all of us. It might not be conventional, but it's working, and that's all that fucking matters to me."

"Me too," she said with another yawn, snuggling further into me. "It's working so well. Just need to figure out these nightmares."

Her last words were near incoherent, and when her breathing evened out a few seconds later, I closed my eyes and enjoyed the moment. Sure, I had a rock-hard dick that was complaining loudly at me, especially since Billie was still draped across half my body, but the rest of me was content to be with her like this.

I had no idea what the fuck had happened to me, but I was going with it.

six

BILLIE

I'd fallen asleep in Grayson's warm embrace but woke up to Rhett feathering kisses over the bend of my neck. His light caresses sent shivers of pure ecstasy through my body, and I gave a low moan of appreciation.

"G'morning, Zep," I mumbled, rolling over as I blinked my crusty eyes. "Where's Gray?"

Rhett's smile was pure mischief. "Kicked him out. Fucker was snoring when I came back to bed, and neither of us needed that noise."

A lighthearted chuckle filled my chest. He wasn't wrong about Gray's snoring; the big guy was like a hibernating bear. "What time is it?"

"Time to get up, Sleeping Beauty," he replied, kissing my throat teasingly. "I wanna know if you've been naughty or nice this year."

I must have been half asleep because I didn't understand that comment at all. "Huh? Naughty, obviously." That was what he meant, right? He wanted to fuck?

Rhett's answering chuckle clued me in to the fact that I'd missed the point entirely. "Naughty Billie is my favorite, but in this case I meant... it's Christmas. Merry Christmas, beautiful Thorn."

Shock froze me, and Rhett swooped in with a kiss on my mouth. I *knew* it was Christmas, but I'd just figured we were ignoring the holiday entirely. After everything we'd all been through, it seemed wrong to celebrate. Especially with Angelo still in the hospital.

"Come on," Rhett urged, oblivious to the guilt swirling through my guts. "Grayson is making breakfast." He tugged on my hand to get me out of bed, but I pulled back.

"Um, I just need to take a shower and wake up," I told him with a cringe. "And brush my teeth. I don't want to kiss you with fuzzy teeth and morning breath."

He gave me a long look as I stood up wearing just his t-shirt and a pair of panties. "Thorn, I'd *never* complain about your fuzzy teeth." He tipped his head to the side, his gaze turning predatory. "Maybe I can help you shower?"

Tempting. Oh my god, *tempting*. "Cute. If you do that, then breakfast will go in the trash." Besides, I needed a hot second to get my head straight. To swallow my crushing guilt over Angelo's situation and my part in his injuries. What if he didn't make it?

What if he never woke up?

"You've got a good point," Rhett agreed. "But be quick. I really want to show you... uh... something." His shifty eyes clued me in to some kind of surprise waiting downstairs, and it eased a bit of the sourness in my chest.

Assuring him I'd be fast, I hurried across the hallway to the main bathroom to shower. After my nightmares, I was rocking a stale-sweat smell that had to be as far from sexy as possible, and good god, my breath could knock over a cow.

I took my time working through my brain while I showered, placing all my icky, negative emotions and thoughts into their boxes where they belonged. A little logical reasoning went such a long way, and this was something Dr. Candace had already commended me for being able to do.

Logically, I acknowledged the fact that today was

Christmas and no amount of feeling guilty about Angelo's situation would change that. Nor would he get magically better because I was beating myself up over him being so hurt. Besides, it wasn't like we were heading out to some ritzy party to drink and dance the night away. Rhett just wanted to have breakfast with Gray—and Vee, too—and we all needed to eat. So what difference did it make?

With that logic in mind, I got dressed and made my way downstairs.

"What the—" I gasped as I stepped into what could only be described as the inside of a snow globe. The entire living area of Grayson's house had somehow magically transformed into a Christmas wonderland, just like my dad used to do when I was a kid.

"Merry Christmas, Billie Bellerose!" Vee sang out, appearing from the kitchen wearing an apron that looked like an elf costume. She crossed over to where I stood frozen on the stairs and hugged me warmly.

My responding hug was weak as I tried to take in the transformation. Then I looked to Rhett and Grayson, who both stood near the kitchen in matching Santa pants and hats. That was it. Pants and hats and nothing in between besides rippling muscles and glorious ink that begged to be licked...

"Oh geez, didn't I tell you two to put shirts on?" Vee scolded, then shot me a wink. "I'm going to get you coffee, Billie. You look like you need it."

She disappeared again, and I took a few steps closer to my smirking sexy Santas. "Okay, someone explain," I ordered. "What, when, how, who, why?" I gestured around us at the myriad of decorations filling Grayson's usually impersonal home, right down to an eight-foot Christmas tree decked out in greens and reds with twinkling lights to top it all off.

"Christmas," Gray replied with a one-shouldered shrug. "Last night, with lots of hard work, Rhett and Vee, and because you deserve it."

Well. Ask a silly question, get a silly answer. Not that his answer was *silly*, but it was definitely lacking in meat.

Rhett elbowed Grayson, then turned back to me. "Babe, we know that Christmas used to be a big thing in your family. We just wanted your first Christmas in *our* family to be something really special."

Oh fuck, he was going to make me cry.

I wrinkled my nose and swallowed, trying to hold back the tears. It was incredibly sweet of them, but... "My dad was the one who decorated for Christmas," I told them in a hoarse voice. "He loved the magic so much, and it was easily my favorite time of year. Every-thing glittered, everyone smiled. My parents always seemed like they were extra in love at Christmas... but since they died, I haven't—"

Wait.

"How did you know that it was my favorite—"

My question got answered before I even finished saying it out loud because the front door opened and in walked the boy from next door. My first love, my oldest friend, and now my arch-nemesis. Jace.

Sucking in a sharp breath, I glared daggers. "You."

He lifted his chin, his eyes meeting my gaze unapologetically. "Me. Merry Christmas, Bellerose."

Anger bubbled beneath my skin, and my fingers curled at my sides. The urge to punch him right in the smug face was so intense I was nearly choking on it. But before I could act on that desire, I realized he hadn't arrived alone.

Jace stepped further into the house, closer to me, and revealed his companion limping inside behind him, leaning heavily on a walking stick.

"Angel?" I squeaked in utter disbelief.

His sexy, lopsided smirk was perfection as he met my gaze. "Merry Christmas, Bella."

With a cry I crossed the space between us and

wrapped my arms around him as carefully as I could. He was in bad shape, covered in bruises and sporting a bandage on his head, so I didn't want to hurt him more.

"Hey, Bella, don't cry," he whispered, wrapping one arm around my waist to hold me tight. "Precious girl, please don't cry. I'm okay, I promise."

I was sobbing against his chest, the uncontrollable kind of sobbing that came right from my soul and poured out like floodwater. Angelo just held me and whispered reassurances against my hair, and I forgot where we even were, until Vee gasped out Angelo's name, and I jerked away like he'd electrocuted me.

"Holy shit, A!" Vee exclaimed, rushing over to him as I backed up quickly.

Angelo barely even glanced at his wife, though, his gaze locked on mine as embarrassment and guilt heated my cheeks and caused sweat to roll down my spine. What the fuck was that? I'd just thrown myself at him like we were lovers, and the way he'd held me back was more than *old friends*. Wasn't it?

"Um, I'll get coffee," I mumbled, beating a quick retreat into the kitchen. Vee had already started making the coffee, leaving little left to do, but I needed a hot second to catch my breath.

"Hey, are you okay?" Rhett asked gently, having

followed me. His hand stroked down my spine, and I leaned into the touch, soaking up his strength. "I mean, obviously you're not, but is it something I can fix? Did this all miss the mark? Jace told us—"

My bitter laugh cut him off, and I spun to face Rhett. My protector. "Of course Jace told you about how we used to have magical Christmases together, because he was never around for the ones *after*. He didn't see the Christmas I spent curled up on the floor of a church because my apartment had no heating and the taps had literally frozen solid. He didn't see the way I mourned, thinking how it should have been our baby girl's first Christmas. Typical fucking Jace never looks at the bigger picture."

Pain and regret creased Rhett's face, and I instantly felt like an asshole. It wasn't on him or Gray to know those things. They'd wanted to do something sweet, to make our first Christmas together special. And here I was, wallowing in the past.

"Fuck, I'm sorry," I whispered on a long exhale. "I'm being a bitch, and you went to *so* much effort. I just—"

"Stop it," he cut me off. "You have nothing to apologize for. Nothing. We should have asked, instead of assuming."

I scrubbed a hand over my face and groaned. "Can

we start over? This is all... it's a lot. Can I rewind and pretend I just came down those stairs again?"

Rhett smiled. "Of course you can. Merry Christmas, Tho—"

This time I cut him off by launching myself into his arms and crushing my lips to his. He barely even missed a beat, wrapping his hands around my ass to boost me higher and kissing me back with a low groan of appreciation.

My butt met the counter, and I spread my knees wide, pulling Rhett close as we kissed. His tongue twisted with mine, teasing and licking as his hands smoothed up my thighs. I was wearing a pair of loose boxer shorts, so there was almost no obstruction as his fingers found the edge of my panties.

"Fuck, I want nothing more than to rip these aside and fill you with my dick right now," he whispered in a husky, sex-filled voice. "But I suspect we would have an audience."

"Good guess," Grayson agreed from somewhere behind Rhett. I peeled myself away just far enough to see him pulling a tray of pastries out of the oven. So domestic. "Rhett, put your dick away, and take the coffee through to the living room."

Rhett grumbled but did as he was told after adjusting his raging hard-on in his Santa pants. God *damn,* that was hot. I licked my lips, and he shot me a wink loaded with promise.

Grayson cleared his throat, and I ripped my hungry gaze away from Rhett's retreating form.

"What?" I asked with an innocent blink. "Someone left me all worked up last night, and now all I can think about is sex."

His grin was pure evil as he abandoned the tray of freshly baked treats and prowled closer. "What *idiot* did that?" he mused, trailing a finger along the line of my jaw as he took the space between my legs that Rhett had just vacated.

Tipping my head back, I waited patiently for his kiss, and he didn't disappoint. I sighed into his caress, his huge hand cupping the back of my head with an element of control that turned me on even more.

"Gray..." I whispered against his lips as his festive flag pole thickened against my core. "I want you to fuck me *so* badly."

His lips curved into a smile against my kiss. "Good. The feeling is mutual."

"Oh shit, sorry!" Vee squeaked, clearly having just walked in on our holiday hookup. "God, I have some wicked timing today. Just pretend I wasn't here. Um, continue." She hurried out again, but the moment had passed. Grayson was already putting physical distance between us, even as he slipped a hand into his pants to rearrange. Thoroughly.

"Tease," I accused with a scowl, slipping off the bench.

His laugh followed me out of the kitchen, and I couldn't help smiling to myself. Maybe this Christmas could bring the magic back after all.

seven

BILLIE

Rhett and Grayson had done an excellent job of getting me out of my head, but within minutes of returning to the living room, I was ready to commit murder again.

"Wait, you came out of your coma three days ago, and no one thought to let us know?" I blurted out while Angelo told us about his recovery. My accusing glare snapped straight to Jace, and he just leveled a calm, zero-fucks-given stare back. That stupid nurse in the hospital hadn't even mentioned a thing to me either. Couldn't trust anyone these days.

Angelo looked between the two of us and sighed. "I asked Jace not to say anything until my doctors gave full clearance. When I first woke up, things were... confusing."

The hesitation before he said *confusing* made me suspicious as hell, and I wasn't the only one.

"What does that mean?" Vee asked. "Confusing how? You didn't remember the bomb blast?"

Angelo wet his lips, his gaze darting back at me ever so quickly before he focused on Vee. "No. I didn't remember lots of things. It was scary as fuck, to be honest. I thought..." Another glance my way, then he pasted on a brittle smile, covering for the pain in his eyes. "But apparently that's a normal thing, and it didn't take too long to get caught up. I just wanted to be sure I was recovering before Jace said anything. I'm sorry you were worried, Vee."

I swallowed hard. Of course Vee had been worried; they were married and clearly loved each other, even if their relationship wasn't sexual.

"I'm surprised Jace let you leave the hospital," I muttered, unable to keep a lid on my bitterness. "He's all about control these days, aren't you Adams?"

The infuriating *fuckhead* just cocked a brow at me. "If we have something to discuss, Billie, I'm sure it can wait until tomorrow. Today is meant to be—"

"If?" I spluttered, outrage choking me. "If? *If we have something to discuss?*" Yes, I was sounding like a parrot, but was this asshole fucking serious right now? "You know perfectly fucking well, Jace Adams; don't even try to gaslight me right now. Don't you *fucking* dare."

I was so mad I was shaking. Physically shaking. Grayson shifted to sit beside me, his fingers lacing together with mine and grounding me, but Jace and I were locked in a venom-filled staredown.

"Billie..." he started with a resigned sigh.

I could practically smell the bullshit he was about to spew, so I shook my head. "Save it," I hissed. "You're not fooling anyone." With monumental effort, I shifted my eyes back to Angelo. "Have you heard from Giovanni at all?"

He winced. "Yes. He had someone at that hospital well paid off; they informed him as soon as I woke up. He was right there an hour later, grilling me for info."

Vee paled at that, and sympathy stabbed through me for her. "What about Vee? Is her family looking for her now? Did you tell Giovanni that it was the Altissimos who tried to kill us?"

Angelo gave a small headshake, but Jace interrupted. "Billie, can I have a word in private?"

"No. Get fucked."

Jace rolled his eyes, and it made me want to junk-punch him. Hard enough to neuter him. "Real mature,

Billie." He stood up from his seat and gestured out of the room. "Please. See? I asked nicely."

Sarcastic fuck. "Will you force me if I refuse? That seems to be your MO these days when you don't get your way."

Anger flashed over his face before he got it under control, and I got a spike of satisfaction knowing I'd gotten under his skin. "Billie. Don't be a fucking brat. I'm asking for two minutes of your time in private."

"Jace, just leave her be," Rhett groaned, sticking up for me.

Grayson's fingers squeezed my hand like he was silently asking whether I wanted him to intervene. Somehow, though, their support gave me the push to hear Jace out. It reassured me that whatever he wanted to discuss wasn't something they'd all been privy to. Which meant I was now curious.

"Two minutes," I relented, releasing Gray's hand and standing up. "After that I can't be held responsible for stabbing you with a fork."

Jace didn't see the humor, just gave me a withering glare and pointed toward the corridor leading to Gray's home gym and office. I rolled my eyes but stalked down there anyway, let myself into the gym, and flicked on the lights.

"Well?" I demanded, whirling around to face my

nemesis when he entered the room after me. "What is so important you needed to demand a private audience?"

The door slammed shut behind him, but he didn't stop where he was. Instead, he stalked closer, giving me zero time to react before he grabbed me by the neck and crushed his lips to mine.

Time stood still, my breath catching hard in my throat as he kissed me. Then I foolishly melted and kissed him back for just the briefest moment. In that instant, I forgot how mad I was, how much he'd hurt me, how cruel we'd been to one another, and just remembered the boy I'd once loved with my whole fucking heart.

Then I came to my senses and bit his lip so hard I tasted blood.

He hissed, staying in my space even as he dabbed his lip. "Fair. I shouldn't have done that, and it wasn't why I called you away. I just... acted on impulse."

"Well *don't*," I snapped. "There is fucking *nothing* left between us, Jace, you made sure of that with your epic power play at the hospital."

"This!" Jace roared as I shoved him away forcefully enough to make him stumble. "*This* is what I needed to talk to you about, Billie. This stubborn-as-fuck grudge you're clinging onto. Your fucking victim attitude. Your holier-than-thou disdain and refusal to see the bigger picture. It's *infuriating*."

My jaw dropped at hearing him accuse me of the exact shit he himself was guilty of.

"Excuse me?" I scoffed. "You must be kidding me right now."

Jace took a few steps away, running his hands over his face with frustration while I just watched in shock. Had I stepped into an alternate universe?

"Look. We have our issues, we both know that. But my best friends, my *brothers,* have moved heaven and earth to make this Christmas fucking *magical* for you, Billie. If you're too much of a fucking bitch to respect that and put aside our shit for one damn day, then you're not the woman I thought you were."

Shock and disbelief stilled my tongue, but only for a moment.

"Are you actually serious right now? You think you can come in here and act like you *didn't* have me involuntarily committed to a mental hospital simply because I wasn't dropping to my knees and sucking the great Jace Adams dick? That shit doesn't just blow over with some tinsel and fairy lights!"

He closed the gap between us and grabbed my shirt. In a swift movement he'd spun us and shoved my back against the door, but this time he didn't try to kiss me.

Instead, he just pinned me there, holding eye contact so intense it made my knees weak.

"If that is seriously what you think happened, then we have much bigger shit to deal with. But it can fucking well *wait* a day. Can't it? Use whatever tattered shred of human decency you have left inside that black heart, Billie, and think about Rhett and Gray. Think about Angel. We can go back to war tomorrow, but today I am asking you—*begging* you—for a ceasefire."

Guilt and regret drowned me, and I bit the inside of my cheek to hold back the hot tears pricking the backs of my eyeballs. "You want a truce?" I croaked, making sure I was understanding him.

"Yes," he breathed, looking utterly exhausted. Blood dripped down his lush mouth, and it shouldn't have been as sexy as it was. "Please, Billie. They have been through it all, right alongside us. Today is about more than just *you*. It's about them. Us. All of us. They—we—desperately need to feel like a family again. Even if it's just for one day. Can't you see that?"

His thumb stroked over my cheekbone, and it sent a scalding tremble through me. When had he touched my face?

"Billie... Rose... just one day of peace. For them. It's all I'm asking."

He was playing dirty, calling me Rose like he was

appealing to the old me. The one who'd loved him unconditionally. The one who'd have forgiven him *anything*. She was long gone now.

"I don't think I can," I admitted in a choked whisper. "I'm not that good at faking it, and right now I'd rather swim with piranhas than play happy family with you, Jace."

The agony that creased his face nearly made me gasp aloud, but he chased it away by punching the wall and spinning away from me. Swallowing again, I sought the strength to walk away and came up empty handed. I couldn't leave. He might not be touching me, but he held me captive with his presence nonetheless.

"Fine," he spat. "Then don't. Be as cold and nasty as you fucking want to me, but swap out your language, your tone, for the opposite of what you mean. That way you can get your shit off your chest and *I'll understand*, but everyone else can pretend we're playing nice. Can you do *that*?"

My brow furrowed. "You mean like if I want to say: Jace, dickhead, shut the fuck up—"

"You'd say, *Jace, sweetheart, I love when you talk.*" He affected a sugary-sweet girl voice to demonstrate.

My lips twitched with amusement, but I bit my cheek to hold the smile back. Could I do that? I couldn't agree to a truce from our fighting; the wounds were too fucking fresh. But could I bicker with him in codewords?

"Fine," I agreed. "In that case, Jace, sweetheart, that shirt looks great on you." I fluttered my lashes and smiled as I said it, then spun around and yanked the door open without waiting for a reply.

"Hey!" he barked after me. "There's nothing wrong with my clothes!"

I chuckled silently to myself as I made my way back to the living room. Maybe his idea could have merit. It might be fun to rip shreds off of him while no one else knew what I was saying. And he *did* have a valid point about respecting the work Rhett and Grayson had put in. And Vee, too.

That explained where Rhett had been when I'd woken up in the night, but I was still confused how Vee and I had become such good friends. Maybe she was just bored and starved for female conversation. Not that it was a problem for me; I *liked* her. But I also had a level of guilt when I remembered who she was married to. And everything that had gone down with Angelo and me, no matter how long ago... those feelings had been real back then, and I was starting to think I'd never entirely let him go.

"Is everything okay?" Rhett asked cautiously as I

rejoined them in the living room. "Gray is fetching the first aid kit."

I smiled, sinking into the sofa beside him. "Not necessary. We just had to have a conversation. Right, Jace?" I glanced up at my closet enemy, and he gave a tight smile back. Blood still tinted his lips, but he didn't seem to care.

"Absolutely right," he agreed. "You're such a great communicator, Billie. I really love how you use your words."

Oh. I see how this is gonna go.

Narrowing my eyes, I held his smug gaze as he sat back down. *Game on.*

eight

ANGELO

Billie and Jace trading insults was so familiar that it brought forth more of the jumbled memories that had been assaulting me since I woke in the hospital. Even if they were disguising those insults as compliments. I knew those two as well as I knew myself, and the absolute fury in their eyes couldn't be as easily disguised as the venom on their tongues.

"Jace is such an exceptional song writer that I'm sure he'll have the next few songs whipped up on his own in no time. No worries," Billie chirped, sounding like she was a Jace groupie when we all knew the truth.

The rest of the band had been discussing the

contractual obligations they still had to fulfill, and I'd been resting on the couch watching them do it, all the while wondering how different my fucking life would have been if I'd chosen the rock star path versus the mafia one.

Not that I'd ever had a choice, but waking up in that hospital bed, my head somewhere between eight years ago and today, I'd realized that I'd never really dealt with the pain of losing Billie and the baby all those years ago. I'd woken up thinking she was still pregnant, that we were shopping for baby shit, and that we were going to make this work even without the third to our trio.

Jace had set me straight right fucking quick, and I'd had to grieve that shit all over again.

The glass shard they'd removed from my knee had hurt me less than waking up to that.

"Angel," Vee said, dropping down gently beside me. Seeing her alive and healthy, albeit covered in healing bruises, had my spirits lifting slightly. "I can't believe you're here. It truly is the best Christmas gift I could have received."

My eyes found Billie, who had thrown her head back and was laughing at something Rhett said. Real laughter. The sort that consumed her entire face, trans- forming it from beautiful into something so real it hurt to stare upon her. I'd seen the most famous works of art around the world, and not a single piece compared to Billie when she was like this.

My Christmas gift.

"I've been worried about you," I said to Vee, tearing my gaze from Billie. It was really fucking inconvenient that the past and present continued mingling in my head, making it difficult for me to remember that I'd moved on from Billie. I'd let her go.

I'd had to let her go to save her life. Despite our fake relationship, that still hadn't changed. Without the Ricci heir on board, she was no longer safe from my family. And she certainly wasn't safe from Vee's.

"She's been worried about you," Vee said softly. "You two need to sort yourselves out because life is too short to be without the one you love." Her eyes fell, and I knew she was thinking about Giana, her long-time secret girlfriend who was now in hiding somewhere in Europe. Another person sacrificed to this life we lived.

"You know how I feel about love," I snapped, anger bursting to life. Love, a four-letter word that I fucking detested. A weapon wielded by my father. The guilt he used to get his own way. And the excuse he gave me for the choices he'd made in my life. All for the *love* of his son and family. Yet I couldn't deny what Vee had said. I did love Billie, and sometimes it scared the life out of me that one day I'd turned into Giovanni and use that love to control her.

"You love better than any man I know," Vee said, letting out a breathless sigh. "If my sexuality was a choice, I would have chosen you a million times over. Don't think you're like him. You are nothing like any of the men in our families. You have honor. Billie knows that."

She was stabbing at wounds, and I needed her to stop. "Billie is not our concern right now," I said shortly, straightening out my leg when it began to ache from remaining in the same position for too long. "Our concern is this brewing mafia war and how the fuck we deal with it without becoming collateral damage."

Vee placed her hand on my right bicep and squeezed tightly. She kept her hand on me as she said, "It's Christmas. The family can wait for tomorrow; God knows it's not going anywhere."

That was the problem. The families we were born into was a life. It was a forever life, and there was no fucking *out*. "You're right. Tell me what's happened since we ended up in the hospital."

Vee quickly launched into the timeline of events, from her release and Grayson offering his place as a safehouse—I owed him for that, among other things—to Billie being kept involuntarily in the hospital to deal with her flashbacks. "She got out last night after her therapy session," she continued, "and it is so nice to have everyone here, together and alive."

Nice was debatable. I could do with less Bellerose and more Billie, but that was probably still the fucked-up brain injury talking, as it gave me a front row seat to my teenage trauma. Jace hadn't mentioned that he'd had Billie semi-committed, and I wondered if that was because he felt guilt over it or because he didn't want us to fight again so quickly. Either way, that was a conversation we'd need to have one day soon.

"You and Jace seem good now," Vee said suddenly, her voice low enough that no one else heard. "Did something happen?"

Not something. Everything. "He risked his life to save mine," I said. "When I woke in the hospital and he was at my bedside, I was so goddamn confused. My mind was back when we were eighteen and I was with Billie and Jace was gone, so to see him sitting there..."

I hadn't really known what to think, and it had only added to my confusion.

"But then he set me straight, and we talked about all the shit that went wrong between us eight— well, shit, nearly nine years ago now, and I think maybe we're ready to let the past go."

At least most of it, since there was no way either of

us could truly let Billie go. Not even if we wanted to. We'd both tried and failed, and it was time to learn from that. She was a part of us, and not even nine years apart had changed that.

"We should write a song now," Rhett declared loudly, holding his bottle of whiskey in the air like a salute. "Come on, it's Christmas day, and we already have multiple miracles. Jace and Billie haven't killed each other, Angelo woke from his coma, and none of us have had an attempt on our lives today. Let's celebrate. It's the perfect time to write our next hit."

Grayson, Jace, and Billie yelled their agreement, and it was clear that they were all much further along in their festive drinking than Vee and me. Maybe some alcohol would help with the mental anguish that was apparently wrapped around me, refusing to let go. Fuck the rules around alcohol and painkillers.

Reaching for the cane, I started to get to my feet, but before I could, Billie had jumped up from her spot on the couch and was rushing in to slip under my right side. "Get his left, Vee," she said sweetly. "Let's get him more comfortable."

More comfortable. That brought up some thoughts that were better left for another time. Comfortable with Billie used to be naked afternoons in bed eating, fuck- ing, and watching movies. These suppressed memories had chosen the worst moment to burst into my head and refuse to leave.

Fuck. I'd locked them down once, and I could do it again.

"I've got this," I said shortly when I was up, shaking off the two women. "Just wanted a drink."

"All you had to do was ask," Jace said, appearing before me, a glass of whiskey in his hand. I knew before I even took it that it'd be Yamazaki 21, my favorite whiskey. Drinking on medication was definitely against my doctor's orders, but since when did I follow the rules?

"Thanks," I said softly. "It's the day for a drink."

"Or five," Grayson agreed, moving closer as well.

Rhett let out another cheer. "We do need to celebrate. I know that Flo isn't with us now, and we haven't mourned her yet. But Christmas is for celebration, and I'm going to count all of my blessings today."

There was this brief moment of silence, and fuck if we didn't all bond like teenage girls at a damn sleepover. Upending the glass, I swallowed the shot straight down, and already Jace had the bottle ready for number two.

"Keep them coming," I told him before I dropped back into the couch I'd been trying to get up from. Billie didn't attempt to touch me again, but I felt her eyes burning into the side of my face. The need to look her way was so strong that I almost caved into her pull.

I managed to ice her out until she said, "Will you play bass for them while they're putting music together?" Her voice was tentative. Hopeful. "It might help... seeing as Flo is gone."

Fuck my life and the goddamn mafia crown it rode in on. Tilting my gaze toward her, I knew this wasn't a battle I could win. Not when those hazel eyes were pleading with me to keep playing nice. To make the music today that everyone clearly needed to make.

"Sure," I said casually, even though it was any-fucking-thing but casual.

Billie's face lit up once more, and those painful ghosts that lingered in her eyes faded. Briefly. If music was the key to soothing her soul, then I'd play all goddamn day.

Someone produced a bass guitar from somewhere—thin air was my best guess since it was in my lap faster than seemed possible. Grayson had his sticks out, ready to use them on a small side table, Rhett had retrieved his guitar from a bedroom, and Jace was using a small but expensive-looking portable keyboard. He was a master of multiple instruments—whereas I only played lead and bass guitars—but I hadn't heard of him using the keyboard on his last few albums.

Yeah, I'd kept up with Bellerose. Not that I'd ever admit it to anyone other than Brenda, my source of information.

"Keyboard," Rhett said, nodding his head like he was into it. "I love it. Going old school."

Jace shrugged, dropping his head as he adjusted the sound to his liking. "Figured it was time to go back to the start, to where we made music for the love of it, not because a fucking record label was tapping their fingers demanding a generic *Bellerose hit*."

Billie snorted, and when Jace lifted his head to nail her with his famous stare, she forced a smile across her face. "Old school is a fantastic idea. It makes sense to go back to when you made good music."

She was sweetness and smiles, but this time she couldn't really hide the dig. Jace's lips twitched. The bastard was amused, but he didn't give her anything other than a shrug. "I've always been good, sweetheart. This is just a different sort of good."

"Right," Billie chirped. "Couldn't agree more, *babe*."

She crossed the room to drop down between Rhett and Grayson, and I fought the urge to follow her and yank her out from between them and back to my side. *Not. Fucking. Theirs.*

Only she was.

That would never change.

"Okay, let's start with an old number to get warmed up," Jace said quickly, pressing the keys to the beat of "Existential Crisis," one of their earlier numbers. I knew it well enough to find my place a second later, and once again, it was as if I'd never stopped playing.

Bass wasn't my normal; I'd been lead guitar when I'd played with Jace, but it was easy enough to figure out. Grayson picked up the drums a second later, and Rhett's guitar was there as well. He was a talented musician, there was no denying that, and not a bad guy. If anyone had to take my place in Bellerose, I was glad it was someone like him.

Even if I did want to kill him at the same time.

Billie closed her eyes as the song moved toward the opening chorus, Jace's vocals filling the room with no need for a microphone. I had a feeling he'd chosen this song because it was one of the few that didn't rip Billie to shreds.

Quite the gesture for someone who claimed to hate her and everything she stood for.

When we were done with that, Rhett let out another whoop, and I finished off the last of my drink, enjoying the warmth dripping through me.

I'd almost died a week ago. All of this was bonus content in the life I'd thought was over.

"Okay, let's try something else," Grayson said, his

drumming picking up tempo as he pushed for a faster beat. "Rock out a little more."

Rhett drained his glass dry and grabbed his guitar again. "This is the fucking best. Angel should be our new bassist. Wouldn't that just be perfect? We could be the *boys of Bellerose.*"

Billie's eyes shot open, and she met my gaze.

The past and present flashed before my eyes once more. The past where I'd been part of a different sort of family. One filled with music and love.

Until I'd learned to hate both.

Fuck.

Dropping the bass to the side, I pushed myself up once more and grabbed my cane.

"I'm going to rest," I said shortly, stalking off as best I could in my injured state.

If I was going to let the past go, I needed to do that today—today, while it was still possible— because if Billie held me in her gaze once more, I'd be fucking lost.

nine

BILLIE

The swirl of my stomach woke me the next day, and I groaned as I opened my eyes to find the harsh fucking light of day was trying to drill into my brain. Closing them again, I pushed through the pounding in my head and attempted to remember what had happened yesterday.

Christmas.

Maybe one of the most perfect Christmas days I'd ever had, but I had definitely overindulged in the spirited beverages. A choice that I was paying for this morning.

But I'd wanted to celebrate; Angelo had come home, and there was something different between us. A pull that we'd both attempted to destroy years ago, and yet, it was back.

He'd made music with Jace, which felt like a fist plunging into my chest and tearing my heart free. Angel must have felt the same, seeing as he'd stalked off for a "rest." When he'd returned a few hours later, he'd appeared to have let go of whatever bad mood had taken hold, and then joined the boys and got down to the serious business of getting hammered and writing music with the band.

In my hungover state today, I had no idea if the three "hits" I'd help them write were really as good as I remembered, but it was a day I'd never forget.

A moment of peace in a lifetime of pain.

"You okay, Thorn?" Rhett mumbled, rolling over to drape his arm across my body. "Did the nightmares wake you?"

For once, they hadn't.

He wrapped me up tighter, and I let out another groan. "Nope, not the nightmares. This morning it's the hangover."

Rhett's soft laughter was somewhat soothing, and I appreciated him for being my calm in the chaos. "Shower, painkillers, and water," he told me. "I left the last two on the side table."

Prying my eyes open, dealing with the light, I saw

the tall glass of water and two white tablets exactly as he'd said. "I fucking love you," I declared, reaching over and fumbling to grab them. "I don't know what I did right in my life, but I'm so damn thankful for you."

Rhett's laughter this time was a little louder. "I can't tell if you're talking to me or the pills."

Swallowing them down in one go, I took a soothing drink of water before turning back to the gorgeous man in my bed. "You," I told him, my chest squeezing as painfully as my stomach was roiling. "Definitely you."

He stilled, that laughter dying off, and as he pushed himself up, the sheets falling away from his naked body, I choked back a gasp. His mouth landed on mine hard, and I was reminded that when we fell into bed last night, I'd sort of fell onto his dick as he fucked me until I was sobbing his name.

My core clenched, and I was ready for round two. One that was far less fuzzy.

"I love you too, Thorn. Have since the first moment you stumbled into my alley."

Rhett, my knight in shining armor. He'd never let me down, not even one time, and he was so much more than I deserved.

Nothing more was said as our mouths met again. Rhett's hands cupped my face as he deepened the kiss, and I moaned softly, the fuzzy-headedness fading slightly under his touch. The roiling of my stomach remained strong, but I refused to let that win when I was about to lose myself in some Rhett orgasms.

"Fuck, Thorn. You were sent here to save my sanity, I swear to the rock gods."

"You saved me too," I whispered back breathless. "In every fucking way."

Rhett's eyes darkened until they were near emerald as he slid his hands under my ass and jerked me up and into his body, before he dropped us both back to the bed, his weight crushing me but in the most delicious way.

Opening my legs to allow him closer, I rocked against his hard cock, and he was just positioning himself to slide inside me, when there was a heavy bang against the door. Followed by another. The sound hurt my brain, and if I'd had magic powers, I would have turned whoever was at the door into fucking dust.

"Fuck off," Rhett growled as the thick, pierced head of his cock pushed at my entrance; his mouth dropped to my tits as he sucked roughly on both nipples, one after the other, drawing them between his teeth and tongue until both peaks were hard and throbbing.

The banging came again, more consistently this time. "Get the fuck up," Jace shouted through the door.

"We have music to finish and shit to talk about, and it can't wait for your five minutes of glory, Rhett."

"That motherfucker," Rhett snarled against my chest before he lifted his head once more. "If I come out there, Jace, I'm going to beat your fucking ass. Then I'm going to let Billie have her turn."

Jace's laughter was dark. "I've had more than my share of turns with Bellerose. It always starts well, but in the end, you get fucked in ways you never signed up for." He banged against the door once more. "Now get the fuck out here."

Footsteps trailed away, and Rhett dropped his head down to rest next to mine on the pillow. "I'm going to murder him," he growled, in a very un-Rhett like way. "Strangle him with a mic cord and call it a workplace accident."

A small laugh escaped my lips, even as I pressed them tighter together. Rhett lifted his head and met my gaze, and the next second we were both laughing. "Guess the mood is a little ruined," I said when I calmed. "But I'm taking a rain check on this."

His kiss was swift and full of heat and dominance. "It's a deal, baby. Come on, let's get up."

He was up in a flash, and I tried not to envy that sort of athletic prowess after drinking, when I felt about as nimble as an elephant. Rhett helped me up as well, before depositing me in the bathroom. "You shower first and take your time," he told me, hands wrapping possessively around my hips as he pulled me in for one last kiss. My legs were a little weak when he pulled away, and judging by his smug grin, he was well aware of the effect he had on me. "I'm going out to beat Jace's ass and find out what the urgency is."

With a shake of his head, he turned toward the door, and I lost sight of that hard cock that had almost been all mine this morning. "Don't forget pants," I called after him, and when he turned, I saw a glint of his lip ring around his gorgeous smirk.

"Jace can deal with it, Thorn. After all, it's his fucking fault that I'm as hard as a damn baseball bat."

He was gone before I could comment, and I thanked the stars that Vee wasn't into guys, because I was under no illusion that I was okay with sharing them. Unfair when I expected them to share me, but hey, such was life. I was greedy that way, and as long as we were all happy with the arrangement, then I wasn't going to complain.

Closing the bathroom door, I moved toward the shower, turning it on as hot as I could handle, hoping that would ease the pounding of my headache. The painkillers should kick in soon, but until they did, the throb grew steadily worse.

Sinking to the floor, I drew my knees up toward my chest, wrapped my arms around them, and let the water pour over me as I thought about yesterday. Such a perfect day, but Jace's actions this morning proved that our truce was already over. He wasn't playing nice, and I would do the same because he was an asshole who needed a constant reminder that he wasn't truly a god.

When I had hogged enough of the hot water, I switched it to a little cooler and quickly washed my hair and shaved all the parts of my body that needed shaving before I got out. After wrapping a towel around myself, I brushed my teeth at the sink and dried my hair quickly with the hairdryer in the vanity. Everything I needed was always around when I was with the boys, and it wasn't as if I'd forgotten the life where I barely scraped by and could only wash my hair weekly to try and conserve products, but the memory was dulling.

Now I just needed these nightmares to fuck off and the therapy sessions to end, and life would be amazing. Okay, sure, there were probably multiple mafia families still trying to murder me, but for some reason it didn't feel like that was my greatest concern at the moment.

Here, I was safe, and I would enjoy it for as long as possible.

Dressed in jeans and a sweater, minimal makeup on

and my hair hanging loose down my back, I left the room and found that the boys were back to their song composing from last night. Midnight blue eyes met mine when I stepped into the room, and Jace shot a scowl my way. "We're on a deadline, Bellerose. Maybe you can hurry the fuck up with whatever you're doing in the shower next time."

My return smile was so sweet his teeth should be hurting. "Oh, Jace, sweetheart, it takes a really long time for me to orgasm when you're in the house. Something about your presence just kills it for me. Hence the long shower."

The blue in his eyes faded further, and I barely kept my laughter from spilling free, especially when Rhett barked out a laugh. Before Jace could snap back, I spun and headed for the kitchen. If I was going to deal with his toxic ass, I needed coffee by the boatload. Thankfully, the headache had subsided at this point, but it'd be back soon enough if I didn't hydrate and caffeinate.

Some wonderful person had left the pot half full, so I filled my cup, adding in some creamer and sugar for the extra hit of energy, and sank back against the bench to enjoy it in private. The Christmas decorations were still scattered around; no one had cleaned away the festivity yet. And since they were still working on the song, I wondered if today would end up being as nice as yesterday.

Vague hope, of course, as I spun to add more coffee to my mug, only to find strong arms banding in on either side of me, trapping me against the kitchen bench. Without turning, I knew it was Jace. Fuck, I knew every muscled curve of his bronze skin, even if his body was bigger and harder these days.

"What the fuck do you want?" I grumbled, still facing the bench as I sucked down another gulp of coffee. "Can't you just go back to making bad music and leave me alone."

He remained infuriatingly silent, while still not releasing me from his hold. When I couldn't take the tension any longer, I turned in the very small circle he'd left me and immediately wished I hadn't. His face was too beautiful, and he used it as a weapon far too often. Those eyes, once again a deep, rich blue, bored into me. He leaned in closer, until our faces were scant inches apart. "Did you really make yourself come?" he murmured, the husky tones of his voice stronger since he'd been singing. "In the shower. Thinking of me."

Swallowing roughly, I almost dropped the coffee but somehow managed to catch the handle again. "I—" I cleared my throat. "I think you misinterpreted what I was saying out there."

I sounded breathless, but I got the whole sentence out, which would have to do.

White teeth flashed as his lips tilted up—it wasn't a comforting smile. It was a predator scenting his prey while realizing he was close enough to kill. "We both know the truth, Rose. There's never been another who could get you off like me."

In some ways that was true, but in others, his bandmates were proving it wrong every damn day. "Angelo could," I reminded him.

Jace didn't bite like he might normally. Those two fuckers being best bros again was going to be a real issue for me. "Not like me. Or at least not like me and him together."

Fuck. I couldn't argue there. I was apparently built to enjoy multiple men in the bedroom.

"What do you want, Jace?" I snapped, needing to change the subject. "What the fuck is the point of this?"

Something flickered across his expression, like a brief moment of unease or uncertainty, before it vanished under his cocky smirk. "Just to remind you that no matter how much you try to run from the past, it's still here and it's not going anywhere."

Throwing the mug onto the bench made the last of my precious coffee swish over the side, but that was a small price to pay for being able to slam my hands against his chest and push him away.

Or attempt to push him away.

All that actually happened was I got closer, and Jace leaned into me more, until we were pressed together from the chest down. Chests that heaved as we fought for breath, the proximity enough to have me shaking.

"Jace—" I choked out, and he snarled before he moved his arms further apart on the bench, pushing me back with his body until I was completely trapped between a rock star and a hard bench. His head dropped lower, lips parting, and I could smell that spicy aftershave he had worn since he was a teenager.

It brought back all the memories, and I wanted to cry, even as I was trying to push myself up to bring my face closer to his. Just when his lips were about to land on mine, he paused and said, "Don't ever forget who owns you, Rose. No matter who else has touched you, you are fucking mine."

With a rumble, he pushed away from the bench, and I all but collapsed to the ground, only managing to hold onto the side of the table. Every part of me was on fire, and I desperately wished my lie before about getting off in the shower had been the truth.

I couldn't keep dealing with this sort of stimulation and not have follow through.

My fucking pussy was going to rip itself free in protest and run away from the abuse.

Before I could sob out my frustration, a tall, dark, and deadly shadow appeared in the doorway. Grayson took one look at me and, without asking a single question, appeared to know that I was on the edge of my sanity.

"Come on, Prickles," he said, lifting two coats from a hook near the hallway. "We're heading out for a few hours."

Thank fuck for Grayson. Getting me out of this house and away from the tension was just what the therapist ordered.

ten

BILLIE

The instant Gray drove us away from his house, avoiding the security teams around his house since *today was just about us*, the tight band around my chest eased and suddenly I could breathe again. I hadn't even fully realized how on edge I'd been surrounded by all the guys—and all our secrets —until stepping away from it.

"Thank you," I said softly, turning my face to smile at Grayson.

He quirked a brow. "I got the feeling you needed a change of scenery."

"So much. Shouldn't you be working on music with the guys, though? Now that you're all, you know, jelling

97

and shit?" There was no denying how good they'd sounded last night, and I was ninety percent sure that hadn't been the alcohol influencing my thoughts.

Gray shrugged. "Jace and Rhett needed to bicker over the third verse chord changes, and it seemed like Angelo had some strong opinions to offer. Me? I don't care either way; they both sound good."

"So you're leaving them to fight it out without you?" I gave a small laugh. "Brave. We might need a cleanup crew when we get back. Speaking of, where are you taking me?"

His answering smile was sly. "You'll see, little hedgehog. It'll take us about half an hour to get there, though, so get comfy and take a nap. You look like hell."

I scoffed in outrage. "Rude. I look..." I flipped open the sun visor mirror and winced at my reflection. "Okay, you have a point. Rhett's fault, though."

Grayson groaned. "I'm well aware. You're a screamer, Prickles. I've never been so turned on and frustrated in my own bed before."

My face flamed, as did other parts of my body, and words completely flew out of my brain. It was entirely safe to say that I had *not* considered who might hear us last night, and now I was fucking mortified.

Also kind of smug, realizing that was why Jace was so worked up this morning. Take that, asshole.

Rather than dig myself into a deeper hole of embarrassment with Gray, I took his advice and curled up in my seat for a little power nap. Sleep was incredibly easy to find, too, and I didn't wake again until Gray opened my door to tell me we'd arrived.

"Huh?" I mumbled, blinking sleepy eyes and snuggling deeper into the leather jacket I was wearing as a blanket. "Where are we?"

Gray flashed a smile and smoothed my hair back from my face. "If you get out of the car, I'll show you."

Curiosity won, and I scrambled to unbuckle my seat belt and climb out. We were... in the middle of nowhere?

"Uh... Gray? Did we get lost? And should we be out here without security?" Because it sure seemed like he'd just parked us on the side of the road in a forest dusted with snow and no cars or houses anywhere in sight.

He gave me a side-eye, no doubt reminding me that he was all the security we'd need, then wrapped me up in one of the warm coats he'd grabbed on the way out of the house. Then he added a soft cashmere scarf from the backseat of his car. It smelled just like him, and my mouth watered as I inhaled.

"Warm?" He tilted his head, checking on me. I nodded my agreement, and he turned back to the trunk of his SUV. There, he lifted the floor panel and pulled out a black rigid case.

"Whoa," I blurted as he opened the case, pulled out a handgun, and tucked it into the back of his pants. "Um..."

"Yes?" he asked, shooting me a fake-innocent smirk. He closed the car up and clicked the fob to lock it.

I frowned at our remote surroundings, then narrowed my eyes at Gray. "Are you planning to shoot me and leave my body in the woods? Because if so, I have one dying request."

Grayson reached out and took my hand in his, tucking them both into one of his pockets as we started walking together. "Oh yeah? What is it? Maybe I can accommodate."

It was on the tip of my tongue to tell him, but I still really wanted to know where he was taking me that required a gun. So I just grinned up at him flirtatiously. "I'll tell you when I see where you're taking me. Maybe."

Gray just gave a small laugh. "Well, it's not far. I think it might really help you with all that tension you're carrying around."

My brows shot up, and my lips formed an *O*. Was he taking me to a secluded fuck shack to rock my world without fear of interruption? Because if so, I was one hundred percent in. How the gun played into that scenario, I wasn't totally sure. But Gray was kinda kinky, wasn't he? Maybe it was a fake gun that he was going to use to fu—

"Just up here," he said, interrupting my rapidly smuttifying thoughts.

He pulled me to a stop at the edge of a vast clearing surrounded by towering trees and... not a whole lot else. Where was the sexy fuck shack?

"Ummmm..." I squinted around, then looked up at Gray. "I'm confused."

Always one to show rather than tell, Gray released my hand, then reached into the back of his pants for the gun. Most of me was confident that my joke about him shooting me was just that, a joke, but a quick flash of fear zapped through my chest nonetheless... right up until he aimed and fired *down* the clearing—and away from me—and a puff of colored powder exploded from whatever he'd hit.

Understanding dawned, and I started laughing a tiny bit hysterically. "You have a shooting range out here? That's... you brought me to *shoot targets*. To burn off steam. Shooting shit. Of course."

Gray quirked an eyebrow, guiding me further into the clearing. "Yes. What did you think I meant?"

My cheeks burned as he placed the heavy gun in my hand, wrapping my fingers around the grip securely as his body bracketed me. "Um... not that." Keeping it vague seemed like a good idea.

Gray gave a rumble at my back, his breath warming my cheek as he gently moved my position like I was a life-size doll. I thought for sure he was going to leave it at that and not push me to say it out loud, but then his huge hand gripped my hip and pulled me flush against his body. Against his hard dick pressing into my back.

"Did you think I was bringing you out here to fuck, where no one could hear you screaming and Rhett couldn't suck away your focus?" His voice was a low growl in my ear, and I couldn't prevent the needy whimper that slipped from my throat. Fuck, I was turned on, even while my hands gripped Gray's gun like it was the crown jewels.

Swallowing hard, I tried to find my voice. "Maybe." It was a squeak of a word, and Grayson's answering chuckle nearly made me come.

"Maybe?" he replied, teasing the skin above my pants where his fingers had slipped beneath my shirt. "Hmm, well it definitely wasn't my intention, but I'd hate to leave you wanting, Prickles."

Oh, I liked where this was going.

"Tell you what. Hit three targets, and I'll eat your

pussy before we go back to the house." He punctuated his offer with a nip of teeth on my neck, and my finger slipped.

The shot rang out across the clearing, and I yelped in fright. Needless to say, it did *not* hit a target.

"Careful, baby girl," Grayson warned with an edge of amusement. "Neither one of us needs a trip back to the emergency room today."

I groaned, my hands now shaking. "Can you give me an easier offer? One target?"

He kissed my neck again, softer this time, then brought his hands up to cup mine on the gun. "Don't underestimate my skills as a teacher, little hedgehog. Or my motivation to help you win this." Another butt with his hard dick made me groan. "Now, focus on the targets. I'll guide you through, and we can do it together."

Together. I liked that. I never felt alone when I was with Grayson; he permanently had my back no matter what—something he demonstrated as he calmly spent the next hour teaching me how to shoot accurately. Or *more* accurately than I could when we'd started. Sharp-shooter I was not. But he seemed determined to ensure I was comfortable handling his weapon. His gun, that is. His *other* weapon didn't wilt at all across that hour, and I was utterly astounded at his control and willpower for not acting on what we *both* wanted to do.

"Well, look at that. Three in a row," Grayson commented as the puffs of paint powder exploded at the far end of the clearing. My ears were ringing despite the squishy earplugs Gray had given me, but I was elated at my success.

Quick as I could, while remaining safe, I handed the gun over and spun to face him with a wide grin on my face. "So... pay up."

His answering look was pure filth as he unloaded the gun and tucked it away in what I now realized was a holster at the small of his back. *Phew.* He'd already educated me about how hot guns could get, so I didn't need him burning his ass just to look badass.

"You're so cold your adorable nose is about to fall off," he informed me with a chuckle. "But you did good. Come on."

He started leading the way out of the clearing— back towards the car—and I gave a petulant noise of complaint. Hell, I even stomped my cold foot a little. "Gray, you made me a deal!"

His bark of laughter echoed through the trees. "And I intend to follow through. Keep up, Prickles. I've nearly made a mess of my pants at least six times in the last hour; if I don't get your legs wrapped around my head in the next five minutes, I'll explode."

Well. When he put it like that... I just about sprinted back to the SUV while Grayson's rich laughter followed me along the path. Instead of opening the front passenger door for me, he popped the trunk and pressed a button to flatten the backseats down.

"Uh, what...?" I watched, confused and horny as Grayson pulled a rolled-up blanket from *somewhere* and within a minute had created a perfect, cozy double bed in the back of his vehicle.

"Hop in," he told me with a wink. I did as I was told, and he climbed in as well before closing the trunk hatch. "Now lie down and look up," he whispered.

Again, I did as I was told, then gasped. The panoramic moonroof gave us a perfect view of the moody clouds above the car threatening to drop snow at any moment.

"Gray..." I breathed, admiring the turbulent beauty of those freezing clouds swirling across the sky. "This is perfect."

He reclined on his side, propped up on one elbow as he studied my face. "I had this planned for a nighttime trip so we could look at the stars."

I shook my head. "No, this is better." Reaching up, I

threaded my fingers through his hair and pulled him close to kiss. "Thank you. You're too good to me."

He kissed me back, humming thoughtfully. "About that deal we made..."

I yelped in surprise with how quick he moved, rearranging our position and stripping my jeans off entirely. "Gray!" I gasped as his fingers hooked through the elastic of my panties.

"Too fast?" he asked, pausing to look up at me with a hungry expression on his face.

I shook my head. "God, no. I was just going to say you can't rip those off like in the movies. Real panties don't just—"

He gave a forceful tug, and the fabric bit viciously into my flesh for a split second before tearing away entirely.

"You sure?" He grinned, holding up my shredded garment. "Sure seems like they do."

I moaned, but it was tinged with laughter. "Ow."

He winced, then bent to kiss the sore points where my flesh had taken the force of the tearing underwear the hardest. "Sorry, beautiful, I've been wanting to do that for so fucking long. Let me make it up to you."

His kisses drifted lower, and I gasped when his mouth found my clit. "O-okay," I agreed in a shaking voice. "You can try."

His response was to suck my clit while pushing two fingers straight into my already pulsing cunt. Holy *crap*, that nearly made me come. I had to bite the inside of my cheek hard enough to draw blood just to keep it at bay.

"You're soaking, Prickles," he rumbled, the reverberation of his low voice doing filthy things to my insides. My response was just a breathy moan as I threaded my fingers into his hair and pulled him harder against me.

He gave *incredible* head, there was no question about it. But he'd been teasing me with that massive erection pushed against my back while we shot targets, and now his fingers and mouth weren't enough. I needed *more*.

"Gray," I gasped, writhing under his touch. "I need..." Christ, he'd already turned me down for sex once; what if he did it again? I doubted my ego could bounce back so easily a second time.

"What?" he prompted. "What do you need, beautiful?"

I licked my lips, searching for my voice.

Grayson sat back, patient as a fucking monk, and just watched me while I worked up the courage to ask for what I *really* wanted.

Gritting my teeth, I reached out and gripped his belt

to pull him closer. "This," I said, palming his hard length through his pants. "I want *this*. All of it. In me. Right fucking now."

Surprise and amusement flitted across Grayson's face, but they quickly melted into pure, toe-curling lust. "Demanding, aren't we? I thought our deal was for me to eat your pussy until you screamed the birds out of their trees."

"Gray..." I whined, tugging his belt open and fumbling with his tight pants button. The straining fabric, thanks to his massive erection, wasn't making things easy. "Don't make me beg."

His lips curled in a wicked grin. "I don't know. Maybe I want to hear you beg."

Dammit, Billie. Why did you say that?

Then again, I was so revved up there wasn't much I wouldn't do. "Please, Gray," I moaned, finally getting that pesky button undone and freeing his cock from the denim prison. "Please fuck me properly. I can't stop thinking about how good you'll feel pushing this monster cock into my tight cunt and making me scream with pleasure. I want you to fill me up, then flip me over and smack my ass like a drum while you pound my pussy from behind."

For the first time since we'd met, Grayson seemed genuinely speechless—not just that he was *choosing* to remain silent like he so often did. No, this time he was *stunned.*

Then I repeated what I'd just said inside my head, and belated embarrassment nearly killed me right then and there.

"Holy fucking shit," Gray breathed. "Billie Bellerose dirty talking is officially my favorite thing in the whole world. Do it again."

My hands clapped over my face, and I gave a pathetic whimper of anguish. "No! I don't even know where that came from!"

Gray chuckled, a deeply sexy sound, as he kissed my belly and pushed my shirt up to reveal my tits in the thin lace bra I'd worn. "I do. And I like it."

"You do?" I squeaked, parting my fingers to peek out at him. I was convinced he must be making fun of me, but the look on his face as he unclipped my front-clasp bra was nothing but enthusiastically aroused.

"I really, *really* like it," he confirmed, then sucked one of my nipples into his mouth so hard my back arched and my breathing hitched. "Look at me, Billie. I want you to *see me.*"

This time, I didn't immediately do as I was told. He wasn't telling me twice, either. A moment later he had both my wrists gripped in just one of his huge hands and pinned to the carpet above my head.

"Prickles," he murmured, "I gave an order. You do as you're told and say *yes, sir*." He winked to show me he was joking, but my body jerked with a mind-blowingly physical response, nonetheless. Apparently, I liked being bossed around in bed. At least by Grayson, anyway. If Jace tried it, he'd be choking on his own balls.

Maybe.

I think he would, anyway.

"Yes, sir," I gasped, obedient with Gray like I'd never been in my whole damn life.

His eyes flashed with heat, and his free hand pushed my legs apart. "Good girl," he rumbled, nearly making me combust. His long fingers stroked through my soaking folds, and he groaned when I bucked against his hand. "Easy, baby girl, take it slow."

Without releasing my wrists, he shifted his position until his broad tip lined up with my core. Then he pushed forward, and I gasped so sharply I nearly choked. I knew he was big, I'd just had him in my hand, but sweet baby jesus, he was thick enough to split me in half. Wasn't he?

"Billie," he groaned, his jaw so tight it was obvious he was holding back. "You feel so fucking good." Another push, another gasping exclamation from me. I couldn't help it. "Shit," he cursed. "I don't want to hurt—"

"Please," I quickly breathed before he could get the wrong idea. "Please, Gray, stop teasing. Fuck me hard; I won't break." I was more than wet enough to take him, despite how tight the squeeze was.

He gave a pained groan and shook his head slightly. "Billie, don't tempt me. I'm trying to—"

"Trying to make me claw your eyes out with frustration? You're succeeding. If you don't stop fucking teasing me with this half-penetration shit in the next three seconds, I'll have to—"

"What?" he taunted, his lips curling in a smirk. The bastard had the audacity to actually pull *out* slightly! "What will you do, dirty girl?"

Throwing all my inhibitions to the wind, I placed my lips against his ear and whispered the filthiest, darkest shit I could think of that he might, maybe, be into. Would I go through with *any* of it? Probably not. Okay, maybe I could be convinced. But the dirty talk really seemed to work for him, because he gave the sexiest moan I'd ever heard from Grayson Taylor and then he thrust so hard into my pussy that I really did scream.

"Keep going," I moaned before he could panic. "Please, Gray, *please* don't stop. Fuck... yes!"

"Holy shit." Grunting, he shifted his grip on my wrists, then started giving me exactly what I'd been begging for. He didn't *make love* to me like he'd suggested a few nights ago. Nope, he *fucked hard,* and it was utter perfection. My legs wrapped up around his waist as he pounded my cunt, letting him in deeper and making me shriek. Normally, I'd have swallowed that noise back, but we were literally in the middle of a forest. No one was around to hear my noises except Gray, and he was *definitely* proving that the audio turned him on.

"Gray," I gasped out at some point, "I'm close. So fucking close. Don't stop... *please*, Gray. Please, let me come..." Like I could have stopped it even if I'd wanted to. What a good joke.

I detonated, my pussy locking up in spasms of muscle tension, and my senses all hit the reset button. My vision went dark, and my hearing went mute, tingles erupting over every surface of my skin. Then it all returned in tiny, slow increments as my body quaked with aftershocks.

Gray remained buried deep within me as I rode out the shakes with my legs still tight around his body. Based on his harsh breathing in my ear, he was having a hard time maintaining his composure, and now it was my mission to make him crack.

"So fucking good," I moaned, licking his neck where I could reach him. My wrists were *still* pinned, and I was all kinds of okay with it. Maybe Gray wasn't the only kinky one in this car.

He lifted his head just enough to meet my gaze, his hair falling around us like a curtain. "What was it you asked for earlier?"

My eyes widened, my own plea still crystal clear in my head. "Um... I don't remember?"

His smirk was pure evil. "Good thing I do, then."

Lightning fast he pulled out and flipped me onto my belly. I only got a split second to squeak a breathy *"Oh shit"* before he lifted my hips and thrust back in from behind. The new angle saw his massive cock stretch me in a whole different way, and I spiraled into an instant mini-orgasm that shocked the hell out of me.

"That was unexpected," Gray commented when I finished, "and I'm not even a little bit mad about it. But you *did* request something else."

Yup. I sure had. Crap... would I like this? Probably. It was Gray. I doubted I would dislike *anything* he did to me in the bedroom. Or the car, as it may be.

He lifted my hips again, trying to position me on my knees, but that then didn't give him enough room for his head. It was funny, in a frustratingly sexy kind of way, until he muttered a curse and reached over my head to press the moonroof button. A moment later, the glass retracted and let in a frosty gust of air.

"That's better," Gray rumbled, his head sticking out of the roof while he got me positioned right how he wanted me: ass up, face down, pussy full of his cock. I kind of wanted to see it from his point of view but made a mental note for another day. "Gonna come for me again, Prickles?"

His huge hand caressed my ass cheek. Priming it.

"N-no?" I whimpered, full of shit. Absolutely I was.

Smack. My body tensed at the sharp sting of pain, and Gray hissed a breath through his teeth. "Yeah, you are."

Smack. The other cheek this time. The instant warmth of blood rushing to the skin combated the freezing air swirling into the sweaty car, and my strung out body quaked.

Yeah. I was.

He quickly found a rhythm, fucking me with deep, rough thrusts and just tossing in an occasional smack on my tender ass cheeks, but it quickly pushed me over the edge again. Then again. Then...

"Gray," I whimpered, "I can't—"

"Yes, you can. You come apart so fucking beautifully, Billie. Like a damn goddess. One more time for me, baby girl. One more time and I'll join you this time. Can I come inside you?"

Oh geez, he wasn't the only one getting off with dirty talk. Just him asking that knocked me over the edge for the fifth time... or fourth? Sixth? Fuck, I had no clue.

"Yes!" I cried out as my pussy spasmed around him. "Yes, fuck, Gray, do it!"

He thrust again, still fucking teasing. "Do *what*, Billie? Spell it out."

I whimpered, my whole body shaking. "Come inside my pussy, Gray. Fill me up with your cum. I wanna feel you explode."

That sent him flying, and with his next brutal thrust, he grunted and cursed the sexiest sounds as he climaxed into me from behind. Then he collapsed just barely to the side of me, to avoid crushing me entirely, but didn't even bother pulling his dick out. It was... hot. I liked that he was still inside me as he gradually softened, and without really intending to, I tightened my inner walls.

"Prickles..." he growled with warning. "Don't start something you can't finish."

"Who says I can't?" I replied, full of sass despite how much my body resembled an overcooked noodle. Gray just cracked one eye, giving me a hard look, and I grinned. "Okay, fine. Good point. But in that case, you should really put that weapon away. You're too tempting, Grayson Taylor."

"The feeling is mutual, Billie Bellerose." With a groan of effort, he separated from me and tugged his pants on. The roof was still open, and without his body heat, I started shivering. Clothes. I needed clothes. When had he taken my top off? I didn't even remember that part.

Scrambling around, I dressed as best I could without panties, then Grayson wrapped his leather jacket around me once more.

"You look so fucking good in this," he murmured, tilting my chin up to claim my lips in a kiss.

It was the kind of kiss I'd file in my core memory databank. Utterly perfect, totally sweet, and with the soft flakes of snow falling on our faces as our kiss deepened.

"We should go before I get more filthy ideas," Gray rumbled with reluctance. "Rhett will be ripping his hair out by now. Billie withdrawals."

I smiled, but he was probably not far off the mark. He held my door open and helped me into the passenger seat, then gave a husky chuckle when I winced. Yeah, my ass cheeks were *burning*, and he was way too smug.

"You're sleeping in my bed tonight," he announced as he turned the car on and closed the moonroof. "Fuck Rhett's nightmares, he can stay up with Jace and take a dose of his own medicine."

That shouldn't have turned me on as much as it did, and yet...

Best Christmas ever. Hands down. I was falling head over heels for the boys of Bellerose and never wanted it to stop.

eleven

BILLIE

We returned to a silent house. The first person we saw as we entered the living room was Jace. He'd crashed on the couch, guitar on his lap, and even without us making a noise, his eyes flew open.

He nailed me with his signature glare. "Where have you two been? Security lost their fucking minds when they realized you'd snuck out without telling anyone."

I couldn't help the smug smile that spread across my face; sort of looked like Jace had been worried too. "Gray took me... shooting. It was fucking amazing."

His gaze darted between the two of us, and it was clear he knew that a little more than "shooting" had been going on. I moved further into the room, ready to collapse on the couch too. The couch on the opposite side of the room to Jace. "You're limping," he said suddenly. "Did you get injured?"

A choked laugh escaped me. "Just a hard whack on the ass. Nothing serious. Don't worry."

"Serious enough," Gray said, crossing his arms and nudging one shoulder into the doorframe between the kitchen and living area. "You never told me Billie enjoyed outdoor activities so much."

Heat filled my body, starting with my cheeks and dripping into what should be a satisfied pussy. But she was a greedy girl, apparently. "I didn't know myself."

Jace threw the guitar to the side and got to his feet, stalking off like his ass was on fire. A feeling I knew quite well after one afternoon with Gray. "I do love it when he leaves a room," I said, letting out a long sigh as I sank into the plush couch.

I'd spoken too soon, though, since he was back in moments. He was also shirtless now, wearing only loose shorts, and I couldn't figure out what the fuck was happening. "I'm going to work out," he said shortly.

That he was frustrated made me happier than I'd ever admit.

"Why exactly are you still here?" I asked him, sitting up straighter. "Surely you have your own fancy gym in your own fancy condo."

He didn't reply, choosing instead to shoot me a dark glare before he stalked off, heading for Grayson's state-of-the-art gym.

"I think we all know why he's still here," the big guy said, dropping down next to me on the couch. "Jace is a man filled with demons, those of the past and present, and he has no fucking idea how to deal with them."

"Jace is a piece of shit," I said shortly.

"I fucking heard that," he shouted from down the hall.

Getting to my feet, I shouted back. "Good, I don't care. You tried to have me committed, and I won't ever forget it."

The sound of a door slamming echoed through the building, and then there was silence once more. Silence and Gray, who was waiting for me to rejoin him.

He didn't say anything for a few minutes, just draped his arm around me and tugged me closer to his body. I sank, exhausted, against him, enjoying these last few moments of peace and comfort.

"He didn't try and have you committed," Grayson said softly.

A stab of betrayal hit me at his defense of Jace, and my instinct was to shout and storm off. But part of me couldn't walk away from Gray like that.

"What would you call it then?" I said shortly.

"Jace doesn't always go about it the best way, but his aim was to help you deal with the past. He feels immense guilt that he wasn't there to help you deal at the time of your loss. Steamrolling you into getting help wasn't his finest hour, but the intention was pure."

Bitterness rose in my throat, and I had to swallow multiple times before I could talk again. "Once again Jace tried to pass off the *issue* in his life to someone else. He should have just talked to me. End of story."

"True," Grayson nodded, his arm still holding me tight, as if he knew I was seconds from getting out of here. "But he also isn't a psychiatrist. He doesn't have the skills to help you work through past trauma, and he wasn't sure you'd agree to go without a little push. The doctors were already considering an extended stay in another facility to help you deal. Jace was the one who got them to agree to outpatient therapy with one of the best in the city. He pulled a lot of strings to make that happen. *For* you, not *to* you."

A huff escaped me, and as much as I wanted to keep

holding onto my anger toward Jace over that, it really wasn't necessary. We had so much other baggage that it was probably fine to let the therapy one go. For now. "She really is excellent," I grudgingly admitted. "I'm not upset to be going back to see her tomorrow."

"That's good, Prickles," Gray said, leaning down and dropping a kiss on my forehead. "There's nothing I want more in this world than to slay your demons for you, but some of them are beyond my reach. I'm always here for you, though, whenever you need a little extra strength."

I didn't deserve him. Or Rhett. Or any of them. But I sure as fuck was going to figure out how to be a better person for them all. As Dr. Candace said, "One day at a time when it comes to recovery."

Angelo entered the room then, cane in one hand and Vee holding the other one. Did it bother me that my fake ex-lover was holding hands with his very real wife?

Nope. Not at all.

Not even a tiny bit.

Fuck my life.

"You're back," Vee said in an excited voice. "I've been waiting for you to return."

Why? "You have?" My verbal response was politer than my mental one.

She followed Angelo to the couch near ours, both of

them sinking down, and once again I was fighting the monster inside that said he was mine.

Not mine. Not even a fucking little.

"Now that we're all here, healing, and about to emerge into the world once more," Vee started, "I need to tell you all what I learned that almost got us killed."

The atmosphere of the room grew tenser, and somehow Rhett appeared in the next second, as if he'd been close enough to hear. He sat on the other side of me, the three of us squished together. "Someone should call Jace up," Grayson said. "He's in the gym."

I wanted to protest, but unfortunately, this was important enough that he had to be here. Rhett reached over and picked up a phone resting on the side table. It apparently worked as an intercom, because he was able to connect to the gym room, and a few minutes later Jace bounced up with a towel draped over his shoulders and a lot of bare chest on display. Those fucking shorts were hanging low on his hips, so I could see the defined line of every ab, and the trail that led—

Shaking my head, I forced myself to focus on his face, lest I give him an indication of how much he physically affected me.

Not that he wasn't pretty much well aware at this point.

"What's up?" he said, seemingly calmer than he'd

been when he stormed off. "Rhett said it was an emergency."

Vee straightened on the couch, smoothing her pants down with her hands in a nervous gesture. "I thought it was time to give you all the details about what happened with my family and why we all almost got blown up."

Angelo reached over and grasped her hand once more, squeezing it briefly, and she appeared to relax. "I want to start by saying sorry. I was born into the mafia. It's the only life I've ever known, and I love many aspects of it, but lately the push and pull between families trying to rise to the top has left a bad taste in my mouth."

She met Angelo's gaze briefly, before letting out a deep breath. "I guess it really started when I was forced to marry A. Thank God he's nothing like the rest of the family and accepted that this could only ever be a marriage in name. Never for real. The problem is, though, that females have one role to play in this world: Produce an heir. Male first and then whatever after that. No one really cares."

"The more males, the better," Angelo confirmed.

Vee nodded. "Correct. Now, it's kind of hard to produce an heir when you don't have hetero sex. So Angelo and I lied, saying I'm infertile, which resulted in my father trying to force me to see every specialist in the world. The pressure grew more intense as time went on, and we even discussed possibly just getting me pregnant once and hoping for a boy, but A..."

Angelo shook his head. "I wasn't quite ready to make that choice."

His gaze met mine, and fuck if fire didn't burn in those dark depths. I'd have paid very good money to know what he was thinking in that second, but another part of me wasn't sure I could handle it.

"Then Billie happened," Vee said, and there was no anger in her voice. "Angelo supposedly got her pregnant and I thought that finally I'd be off the hook. As long as an heir was produced for Giovanni, then we should be in the clear, but apparently my father had other plans. He wants an Altissimo to carry the bloodline or some bullshit like that."

She swallowed roughly, her eyes shiny. "I overheard a conversation where he admitted to joining forces with the Wilsons to take out the Riccis. He wants Altissimo to take over the syndicate Giovanni currently rules, and he won't stand for anyone less than an Altissimo to take it. Even if it's my husband's child, that didn't matter. It needed to be *mine*. He told his acquaintance that he'd heard from a doctor that I was perfectly fertile, so he planned to have me raped and a child forced on me by one of the men under his control. He then mentioned the bombs, the setup, and his obsessive need to wipe out the Ricci bloodline. The moment I heard that, I sent Angelo a message telling him I needed to escape and asking him to come get me from my parents house. I didn't stop to grab anything, just headed for the gates, but I had no idea that my father had already informed the guards there that I was to be detained... by whatever means and force necessary."

As her lips trembled, a sob rocked her forward. She got it together just as fast, while the rest of us remained in silence. The level of evil her father displayed toward his own child was not something I could understand, but I had a feeling that the others in the room weren't quite as naive as me. Their silence wasn't of the stunned variety. They just wanted all the information.

"The guards took me by surprise, beating me worse than I'd ever been hurt before. It was just pure luck that as they were dragging me back to the house, I managed to taser one and then mace the other with my self-defense keychain. Angelo arrived a second later and killed both guards, before I passed out from my injuries. He saved my damn life."

She'd saved herself, but he'd definitely helped; she'd been half dead when Angelo arrived at Grayson's, and quick medical attention had kept her breathing.

Vee turned to me then. "The bombs were part two of their plan," she elaborated on her information from before. "The Wilsons organized a location for Angelo and Billie to be at. If the bombs had worked, there would be no more Ricci heirs and the path would've been free for Altissimo to assassinate Giovanni and take the crown. The Wilsons were going to be the fall guys, lest any of the other mafia families grow concerned about an internal takeover."

Gray leaned forward, legs pushing into me as he spread them slightly. "My family has ties to the Wilsons also," he rumbled. "The web they're weaving is getting rather complicated."

"Your family?" Vee said, raising one of her perfectly plucked eyebrows.

Grayson nodded. "I've been out for eight years, but my mother's family is part of the Kahulu cartel."

The stunned look on Vee's face would have made me laugh if this weren't so fucking serious. I wasn't surprised about Grayson; he clearly was more than just a drummer in Bellerose.

"How did you get out?" Angelo asked him.

Gray let out a sad laugh. "With a lot of sacrifice and bloodshed. But you're never truly out, just sidelined. My fame makes it difficult for them to bring me back in, but I've never made the mistake of believing I was totally free."

That statement hurt my heart. Gray was too good for that world. Angel too.

I had literally no skills that could help either of them, but I had to hope that we could eventually come up with a plan that would give those born into these lives a chance for true freedom.

"What about Tom?" Rhett asked thoughtfully. "How does he play into all of this? And why bomb a Big Noise office with all of us there? There's got to be more to this than just trying to kill Angelo and Billie."

Angelo nodded like he was thinking the same thing.

"I have no clue," Vee admitted with a helpless shrug. "I didn't even know Tom's name until Grayson told me what'd happened with the meeting and Florence's estate."

"Shit, that's something else we need to deal with," Jace muttered, running a hand over his hair. "Seems insignificant in the face of bombs and assassins, but for Flo..."

"I'll look into it," Gray rumbled. "For Flo. And because nothing would make me happier than wringing Tom Tucker's slimy, little neck."

That was a statement we could all get on board with. But Rhett's question had struck an uneasy nerve inside me, too. He was right... there had to be more going on. I didn't for a second believe it was just the easiest place to target Angelo and me. No, for some reason the Altissimos or the Wilsons wanted *Bellerose* dead.

But why?

twelve

RHETT

After Vee gave us her version of events, clueing us into this bloody mafia war brewing behind closed doors, the mood was sedated. Everyone needed to process and think it all over, and I was one hundred percent confident I could do my best thinking with Billie in my bed.

Frustratingly, Gray had apparently gone all in on my girl and called dibs on her for the night. Like he was a child. Who the fuck called dibs on another human? She wasn't the last donut, for fuck's sake, she was a *person*.

Okay fine, I was pissy because he'd gotten to her

before me and my complaints about not being able to sleep without her fell on deaf ears.

Gray just flipped me off and locked his door. Then proceeded to give me a heavy dose of my own medicine.

"Remind me again why we need a drummer in Bellerose anyway?" I grumbled to Jace over coffee *way* earlier than either of us liked to be awake. The sleeping arrangements with six of us in a four-bedroom house weren't ideal either, and Jace had been crashing on the sofa the past few nights.

Jace yawned, rubbing his eyes. "Do we? I reckon we'd be fine without. How do you wanna do it? Smother him with a pillow or...?"

"Good morning!" Billie sang, breezing into the kitchen with a flushed face and freshly fucked hair. "Oh yum, that smells good." The groan she gave as she sniffed the recently brewed coffee was pure sex, and Jace choked on the sip he'd just taken.

I smirked, knowing all too well why he was shifting in his seat and avoiding eye contact. Jace, for all his bullshit protests, wanted Billie *bad*. Their little spat of hate-fucking had only made it worse for him, too.

Served him right for being a self-centered prick.

"Here," I offered Billie, "take mine; I just made it." Her grateful smile was enough to light up the darkest corner of hell, and I leaned in to accept her sweet kiss.

"Thanks, Zep, you're my hero."

Jace snorted, and I ignored him. "Anytime, Thorn." Then I slipped my fingers into her messy hair and pulled her back down for a much spicier kiss, knowing it would tear Jace up inside. Sucker.

She gave another one of those sexy moans that got my dick instantly hard, then reluctantly peeled away. "Don't tempt me," she complained with a pout. "I need to shower and change, or I'll be late for my session with Dr. Candace. You're still okay to drive me, right?"

That's right. Her psychiatrist appointment. I flicked a quick glance at Jace and was satisfied to see guilt written all over his face, then nodded to Billie. "Absolutely. I'll join you in the shower to save time, if you want."

Her answering laugh was pure, undiluted crack to me. "Nice try, Zep. We both know that'd make me late for my session. I'll be ready in twenty minutes, okay?"

"Make that thirty," Grayson countered, stalking into the kitchen and swooping Billie up. Her coffee went flying, the mug smashing on the floor, and Gray didn't even bat an eyelid, just tossed my girl over his shoulder and disappeared back upstairs. Fucker.

I glared at the mess he'd left behind and sighed. "No, you're fine!" I yelled after them. "I'll clean this up, shall I?" The only response I got was the slamming of his bedroom door and a squeal from Billie. Lucky bastard.

"I'm just saying," Jace drawled, sipping his still intact coffee mug, "A little murder between friends isn't the worst. I'll hold him down if you want to slit his throat."

Tempting. Really fucking tempting. Except Jace and I both knew neither one of us could successfully hold Grayson down, even while properly motivated. Damn muscle-bound asshole.

"Whose throat are we slitting?" Angelo asked with a yawn, sliding into one of the seats at the table beside Jace. He'd ditched his cane, choosing to hobble around instead. "If it's Grayson's, count me in. What happened there?" He nodded to the mess on the floor, and I groaned. It wasn't going to clean itself up.

A full forty minutes later, the kitchen was sparkling clean and Billie was late for her appointment.

"Sorry, sorry, sorry," she gushed, flying down the stairs at a million miles an hour while still buttoning her shirt up. "I'm here! Let's go!"

I spared a moment to aim both middle fingers up the stairs at a supremely smug and satisfied Grayson, then followed Billie to the garage where I already had Gray's SUV ready to go. Two members of our security team were in another car nearby, waiting to follow us.

"I called ahead for you," I told her as we exited Grayson's newly secured gates. "They know you'll be a little late and said it's fine."

Her sigh of relief sagged her whole body. "Thank you, Rhett, you're a lifesaver. Honestly, I don't know where time went; I was on track and then..." She blushed.

I rolled my eyes. "Then Grayson derailed your train. I get it. I almost kicked the door down to strangle him, but I also can't be *that* mad when I've done the same thing with you... how many times? I suppose it's understandable." Not that I liked it, but it also wasn't fair for me to sulk.

She bit her lip, her whole vibe radiating uncertainty. "Is this weird?" she asked in a small voice. "It is, isn't it? I shouldn't be—"

"You shouldn't be second-guessing your feelings, Thorn. We're all big boys; we can deal with our jealousy. The one thing we all agree on is that you're *worth* sharing. None of us would be happy to walk away at this point." I reached over and interlinked my fingers with hers, giving a little squeeze of reassurance. "Trust me, babe, this is gonna work. Eventually. When Gray stops being selfish."

Her smile was mischievous. "Did we keep you up last night?"

I gave a pained laugh. "You know full well that you did. In more than one sense of the word. At one point I even heard you say, 'Stop making me come; we'll wake Rhett up,' and Gray responded with, 'Good, serves him right'."

Her face flamed red. "Wow. Thin walls, huh?"

"Like tissue paper."

She held onto my hand as we drove, though, and I made a mental plan to remind her how *Rhett Silver* could make her come before we returned home to Gray. Just as we turned into the parking lot for Dr. Candace's office, Billie sucked in a confused breath and turned to me with a little frown on her face.

"What did you mean when you said *we all* agree? You meant you and Grayson, right?"

She was so fucking cute. "Yeah, babe. That's what I meant." If that's what made her comfortable. "Come on, let's head in."

We hopped out of the car in the secured parking lot, security a few steps ahead of us. I pulled a cap over my bright hair before escorting Billie inside. When we got her checked in with reception, the woman told us that Dr. Candace was waiting, so I took Billie back to her office straight away.

I'd told Billie already that I would hang out in the waiting room for her since neither of us wanted her returning to the car alone. Not now, given what Vee had revealed about the Altissimos working with the Wilsons. Although Billie was no longer "pregnant," she would still be a threat to them. Or a loose end.

The security remained vigilant near the front door, and I did my best to ignore their presence completely.

The receptionist returned a moment later and offered me a coffee, which I gratefully accepted. Billie was turning me into a sober, daylight-dwelling human, and it was weird.

Settling into one of the comfy sofas in Dr. Candace's foyer, I pulled out my phone. Billie's sessions ran for an hour, so I could work on the songs we'd uploaded into our shared cloud folder while I waited. It wasn't as easy as having a guitar in hand, but I could hear the music in my head well enough.

About half an hour later, my phone dinged with a message from Jace. Quickly followed by Grayson, then Brenda and Brenda again.

"What fresh hell is going on now?" I muttered, opening Jace's message.

Jace: Bro, check Dirty Truths. Wtf?!

A pained groan rolled out of me, and I ignored the other messages while I pulled up the shit-stirring blog site. I expected to see a blast about Billie being in therapy or maybe a paparazzi shot of me walking into the building and a wild story about how I'm in treatment after my drug bender a month ago.

That would have been better.

"Bellerose Back on Tour**,"** the headline of the most recent article read.

"Fucking what?" I spat, then scanned the contents of the post.

Despite recent speculations surrounding the infamous rock band Bellerose, their label Big Noise Records has announced the band is restarting their broken tour with all new dates and cities to be listed on TicketWizard later today. Our source tells us that the band is excited to complete their tour in honor of recently deceased Florence Foster, with all remaining royalties of the reinstated tour being donated to Ms. Foster's estate.

Bile rose in my throat, and I quickly flicked back to Jace's message and hit the call symbol.

"What the fuck?" I hissed when he answered. "Tell me this is bullshit."

"I wish I could," my best friend replied with fury shaking his voice. "Brenda is in panic mode, but she's not denying *shit*. So—"

"*Fuck!*" I shouted, then instantly winced and mouthed an apology to the receptionist. Luckily, no one other than my security—who were well used to my language—was in the waiting room to witness my meltdown. "Jace we're *not* going back on tour right now."

"I couldn't agree more," he snapped back. "We don't even have a complete band anymore, and I for one refuse to let Big Noise assign a random bassist to take Flo's place."

Ugh, just the suggestion of that made my blood boil.

"Why would they do this?" I asked in a harsh whisper, ducking my head low when the receptionist eyed me curiously. "This makes no sense. After the bomb?"

"I don't know, bro. I don't fucking know. Brenda is on her way over here now; I seriously hope she has answers because I'm at a loss." He sighed in exhaustion, whispering curses on his exhale.

I glanced at my watch. Billie still had half an hour left in her session, but I could interrupt. "We'll be right back."

"No," Jace snapped. "Let Billie finish her session. She needs it. This can wait. Just... take care of her first, and this will all sort itself out later."

I wet my lips, tempted to comment further on that sentiment, but decided against it. "Okay," I agreed instead. "Then we'll be back in an hour. Get some answers out of Brenda in the meantime. And for the record? I'm *not* going on tour."

"We're on the same page, bro. Gray and I will handle it." He ended the call, and I read the stupid fucking gossip post again. And again. Who *was* this asshole, and where were they getting this information?

I just had to hope this one—unlike the rest—was pure fiction. My gut told me it wasn't.

thirteen

BILLIE

Therapy went so much better when I wasn't being a snarky, oppositional bitch. Who would have thought it? "I'm so proud of how far you've come in a week, Billie," Dr. Candace said as she walked me to the door. "Your willingness to open up to me will make all the difference. I'll see you next week."

"See you next week," I agreed, already somewhat looking forward to it.

When I emerged into the waiting area, Rhett was standing near the door as if he was ready to get out of here. Did this place make him nervous? I hoped not because I was still figuring out how to subtly suggest he give therapy a go. Even if it wasn't with Dr. Candace.

"Ready to go, Thorn?" he asked, expression tense.

I nodded. "Yep, definitely. Is everything okay?" In our world, it was worth asking that question. Even if most of the time I didn't enjoy the answer.

"Nope," he said swiftly. "I'll tell you in the car."

My chest grew tight, and my stomach swirled in the same instant. Nothing was worse for anxiety than having to wait for the bad news to drop. "Everyone's alive, right?" I whispered in a rush as I linked my arm through his. The receptionist called her goodbyes, but we were already out the door, Rhett rushing us along. His security hurried to get in front of us, and I had completely forgotten we had them with us until they fell into their usual positions on either side and slightly in front of us.

"Alive and well," he put me out of my misery. "It's band shit again."

Some of my panic died out. Not all of it, of course, because Bellerose was a pretty huge part of all their lives and that made it a huge part of mine now. Ironically.

I was the one who picked up the pace this time, hurrying us to our parking spot, and as Rhett held the door open for me, I all but dove into the passenger seat. Rhett's grim features softened a touch as he smiled. It was a nice smile. But there was no time to fall into him like I wanted to. Nope. I needed answers.

As soon as we were buckled in, security in their car behind, Rhett pulled out of the parking lot. I turned in my seat. "Spill."

He chuckled, and that eased just a little more tension. No one would laugh if it was really serious, right? "There's a new *Dirty Truths* post. Stating that we're going back on tour. Which is completely fucked up, considering what happened to Florence not even three weeks ago."

"Didn't you finish the last tour?" I asked, confused.

"We finished the North American leg of it," Rhett said. "But we had a whole bunch of international shows throughout the UK and Europe that were postponed indefinitely when you were kidnapped. Then with Flo's death, we decided to cancel. Tickets were refunded and everything. Or so we were told."

Relaxing into the seat, I stared out the front window, watching the icy landscape go by. "Who the fuck runs *Dirty Truths*? I mean, they seem to have more insight into our lives than we do. How are they always one step ahead or, at minimum, on the same step as we are?"

Rhett's fingers flexed on the wheel before he released a long breath. "We've been preoccupied with the other serious shit happening, but maybe it's time for us to show a little interest in *Dirty Truths*. Apply a little pressure to figure out who is running it."

"Grayson would be a good option," I suggested. Before reconsidering. "Actually, he already has too much to deal with, so maybe someone else."

"We'll figure it out," Rhett told me, taking another sharp turn that put us on the road to Grayson's. "In the meantime, we need to address this tour with Brenda and Big Noise. There's no fucking way we can head overseas with everything happening, and I'm more than happy to reiterate that loud and clear when we have our meeting."

As we pulled into the driveway, he hit the button to open the security gates and disarm the alarm system. We idled for a moment before it was clear to drive in. Our security didn't follow us through. They were housed nearby, on call for whenever Bellerose needed them. Conveniences of the rich and famous.

Conveniences and necessities.

Rhett parked and got to my door before I was even done unbuckling myself. When he swung it open, he reached in and lifted me from the seat, hugging me close. "How was therapy, Thorn? I should have asked that first."

Enjoying the warmth and comfort of being near him, I briefly closed my eyes. "It was good today. We delved into more of my past, and she warned me that it might make the nightmares worse for a little while but will eventually lead to more healing. This is a marathon, not a sprint, and there are no shortcuts to, hopefully, laying the past to rest."

"Makes sense," Rhett said softly. "The past is what keeps me awake, and I'm starting to think this therapy thing could be exactly what I need to let some of that shit go too."

Lifting my head from his chest, I stared into his clear green eyes. No signs of drugs or alcohol in his system for once. "I do think it could really help, even if you are making amazing progress on your own."

Shadows darkened the planes of his face briefly. "I have good and bad days. But most with you are good, so let's keep it that way. You can be my therapist, therapeutic exercise, and healing process. I'd be okay with that."

Fucking musicians. They had a way with words. It, of course, went without saying that I was in *no way* qualified or equipped to be anyone's therapist, but I knew what he was saying. For now, he wasn't ready to take that step. Maybe one day, though.

We shared a brief kiss, and then he let me settle back on my own feet and took my hand as we entered the house. Unlike when I'd arrived with Gray yesterday, today there was a lot of noise.

The shouting kind of noise.

"...fucking way that you can force us to do this."

"Looks like Jace is in a fantastic mood," Rhett muttered. "Two guesses who he's talking to."

Straightening my shoulders, I braced myself for whatever we were about to walk into. "Is there any mood for Jace other than shouty, emo asshole? And I'm guessing... Angelo or Brenda."

Angelo and Jace might be besties again, but they'd always argued like hotheaded, testosterone-fueled assholes. I'd love to say that I'd been the cool, calming balm between them, but I was fairly sure I'd been the fuel for their fires.

When we entered the living room, my second guess turned out to be correct. Brenda was standing in the middle of the room, the bridge of her nose pinched between fingers of her right hand as she shook her head. "It's out of my hands, Jace. I have argued and gone over the contract with a fine-tooth comb. We literally cannot get out of this unless you want to be sued for millions of dollars."

Jace was on his feet too, pacing back and forth. Grayson was in the armchair, Angelo and Vee on the couch, and all of them remained quiet as they watched the showdown. Gray was the only one who appeared to notice us enter, the rest too focused on Brenda and Jace.

"There are clauses for emotional leave," Jace shot back. "And one of our fucking bandmembers dying should trigger such a clause."

Brenda released her nose and took a long breath. "I argued that as well, but you used that up the first time you asked for it to be postponed." She appeared to notice Rhett and me then, waving us into the room and indicating we needed to take a seat. "I'm glad you're all here," she continued when we sat. "I know this isn't the news any of us wanted to hear, and I've never seen a label be this pigheaded in these circumstances, but nothing I did or said dissuaded Big Noise from forcing this through."

I turned to Angelo. "Big Noise is Ricci now. Have you spoken to your father? Why is he hell-bent on forcing this international tour?"

Angelo was quiet for a moment, before he let out a long breath. "I haven't spoken to him, but I can already guess that he's looking for a return on his investment.

I'm sure the merger was expensive, and Bellerose is Big Noise's big-ticket band. This is all about money, and I promise, he gives zero fucks about you all grieving."

A dark laugh escaped me. "Don't we fucking know it. That man has never had a heart, and he sure as shit isn't about to find one today."

Rhett shifted forward in the chair, bringing me with him since his arm was still around me. "So, what are our options, then?"

Brenda looked around, and if I was going to guess, I'd say she was trying to find the booze. I really didn't blame her. "Option one: Do the tour, get it over with, *finish your damn album,* and we break ties with Big Noise as soon as possible. Option two: Refuse and see how far we can push them before they actually sue. Option three: I initiate a complicated legal proceeding in the hopes of getting this all stopped before you have to leave. We can cite exceptional circumstances that nullify some of the contract's terms and then hope like hell we get a sympathetic judge that hasn't already been paid off by Ricci corp."

Jace appeared to calm a little when he was presented with these options. Fuck knows why, because they all sounded bad. "What are the odds of winning in court?" I asked her.

Brenda's expression remained grim. "Honestly? Not

great. You know I squeezed them for the best contract possible, but this isn't something I ever saw arising. And if we push it into the courts, it's going to drag all of your names into the spotlight once more in a negative light. It could impact future record label offers, which is something to consider since you want to break ties with Big Noise."

As I'd thought, no great options there.

"How long will they be gone on tour?" I asked softly. "If they go ahead with it."

"Two months," Brenda said quickly. "It's a dozen or so venues, and they've already sold the tickets. They went up yesterday and were sold out by this morning."

Those bastards were putting the band into a position where they couldn't refuse without letting their fans down again.

"What about a bassist?" Grayson asked, the first words I'd heard from him since we returned home. "From what you said earlier, we'd have to leave early next week to arrive in time to deal with all the facets of an international tour. We don't have a bassist, let alone one that has had time to learn our set list."

Next week! Holy fuck. Would I be going with them? The idea of two months without seeing any of them had me wanting to curl up into a damn ball and sob my eyes out. But none of them needed that today, so I'd keep it together. For as long as I could anyway.

"Big Noise has been holding auditions and have three options for you to choose fro—"

"No," Jace interrupted. "I can already tell you that all three are a no. The only one I'll consider is Angelo."

He pointed to his old friend and then crossed his arms like that fucking settled it.

Angelo's face was blank as he remained still.

Brenda blinked before shaking her head. "Giovanni is never going to let him go on tour with you all as a part of the band. He hated that his son was into music."

Angelo nodded slowly. "Very true. If he could have physically removed it from me with a blade, I'd be sporting far more wounds. But in this case, I can probably argue my presence because this is now a Ricci asset. Despite our current estrangement, he's still a businessman first and foremost."

A look of pure surprise lit up Brenda's face. "You would actually consider it? Stepping into the band for this tour?"

I knew Angelo fairly well, and it was clear that this didn't exactly sit right with him. I almost gasped when he shifted his gaze from Brenda to me. Only me. The complete focus of an intense man, a focus I hadn't really felt until recently, bored into me. Until whatever it was shifted between us. "Yes," he said softly. "A one-time chance to be a rock star. I'd take it."

Brenda was so fucking relieved it looked like she might be crying when she rubbed a hand over her face. "Okay, I didn't expect that. But it's good. Fuck, shit. I need to get everything organized. Private planes will leave tomorrow with all your sets and gear, and yours will be ready to go on Wednesday. That gets you into Dublin around the time of your first concert. Big Noise has had this planned for a lot longer than they let on to us, and they're really dropping you in the deep end." The band didn't react to this, but I felt their tension as she continued. "You'll have to deal with the jetlag, but it'll work out." She clapped her hands together loudly. "Okay, I need you to pack a bag; the rest can be bought on the way. Make sure Billie has a passport, even if you have to pay someone to camp out at the office."

My heart did a stupid flip in my chest at the knowledge that Brenda assumed I would be going. But the passport thing did halt me. "It's the holidays," I said softly. "Is the passport office even open?"

"She has one," Angelo said shortly. "I organized it when we started our charade. Just in case…"

He let that sentence trail off, but it was clear to all of us what he meant.

Just in case we'd had to run.

And the rock star dream was shattering under the reality. Under different circumstances, two months in Europe might have been exactly the reprieve we needed from the reality of our world. But someone—or several someones—wanted us dead, and without the security of our home soil, they might just succeed.

fourteen

BILLIE

The band had a lot to sort out with Brenda and their legal team, not the least of which was Angelo's temporary position as the Bellerose bass player. I still couldn't wrap my head around how easily he'd accepted that role, but I had to guess he wanted to stick it to Giovanni. His father had crushed Angelo's dreams of being a rock star when he was eighteen; maybe now was his chance for a do-over. Even just for two months.

I left them to their business discussions and hurried song rehearsals, opting to head upstairs and watch a movie with Vee instead. She stayed quiet and thoughtful for the whole movie, then right as the princess kissed her prince in the final scene, she turned to me and announced she was tagging along with us on tour.

Somehow, that decision eased one chunk of tension in my chest, and I surprised myself by hugging her. Sisters in pain and all that, it wouldn't feel right to leave her behind.

After the movie, I crawled into Rhett's bed and fell asleep to the faint sounds of Bellerose classics. Jace was wasting no time putting Angelo through his paces to check that he was up to the job, and I didn't blame him. Angelo was *crazy* talented, though. Flo's legacy was in good hands with him.

Later into the night, my restless sleep faded as Rhett slipped into bed with me, his cold hands snaking under my t-shirt and making me shiver.

"You're freezing," I mumbled, snuggling tighter against him rather than pulling away. "Put your hands on my boobs; they're always warm." True story.

He chuckled but did as I said. Only he took the opportunity to play with my nipples between his frosty fingers, and that really woke me up.

"Aren't you sleepy?" I asked with a yawn, arching into his touch eagerly.

His lips found my neck. "I was. Now I'm not. Are you sleeping in my t-shirt, Thorn?"

"Of course," I replied, smiling into the semidarkness with just enough light to make out his face. "They're my favorite."

"Mmm..." He kissed my jaw, his hands tugging the shirt up. "It looks better on my floor." He lifted it over my head and tossed it across the room. "That's better." Hands back on my boobs, he kissed my throat.

A slash of light cut through the bedroom as someone opened the door, but it quickly disappeared again as the door closed. "Oh, whoops," Gray said in a heavily sarcastic voice, "this isn't my bedroom. How awkward." Then he proceeded to climb into bed with us anyway.

"Gray..." Rhett groaned with a frustrated edge. "We talked about this. You need to—"

"*Share.* I know. Message received, loud and clear." He slapped one of Rhett's hands off my boob and replaced it with his mouth. "See? Sharing." He winked up at me, then circled my tight nipple with the tip of his tongue.

I gasped, wetting my lips in anticipation. This night had just taken an interesting turn, that was for sure.

Rhett made an irritated sound. "That's not..." He

broke off with a sigh. "Look, I'm not *not* into this. Billie? Your call, babe."

Lips parted, I looked between them with wide eyes. "Seriously?"

Rhett squinted his confusion. "Of course. It's always your call. Are you ready to test the big, selfish baby's ability to play nice?"

Grinning my amusement, I shifted my attention to Gray, who was glaring out the corner of his eye at Rhett. "I'm not selfish, just making up for lost time."

"He makes a good point," I agreed, "so I think we give him a chance."

"Gee, thanks," Grayson drawled, but I yanked his face to mine with a handful of his hair, kissing him hard enough to lose my breath. He gave a sexy rumble against my lips, and I reached out to tangle my fingers in Rhett's turquoise hair. When Gray left my mouth to suck my nipple again, I eagerly accepted Rhett's lips against mine.

Yeah. I was into the sharing thing and always had been. Jace and Angelo were living proof of that.

"I suppose, just this once," Rhett teased, kissing down my throat as Gray's fingers toyed with the waistband of my panties. "But don't go freaking out, Gray, if our swords cross. These things happen in three-ways, and it doesn't mean I'm into you. Clear?"

Grayson laughed silently against my ribs, his breath tickling my skin, but his answering "Fuck off" was gruff and serious, like he was genuinely annoyed at Rhett.

"Shh," I teased, pushing Rhett down the bed. "Less shit-talking, more pussy eating, Silver."

Rhett spluttered a shocked sound, gaping at me in the dim light. "What did you say, Thorn?"

"Oh yeah, Billie has a filthy mouth in bed," Gray purred, his long fingers stroking my heated core over the fabric of my underwear. "You didn't know? You've been missing out."

I wrinkled my nose, fighting back embarrassment again. "Rhett..."

"Yep, no, I'm okay with this. I like it. Dirty-talking Billie... nice." Then he did as I'd ordered and slid further down the bed to position himself between my legs. Grinning up at us, he peeled my panties down while lifting my legs over his head, then arranged me spread wide open.

I whimpered as he teased me, running the very tip of his tongue down my center ever so slowly, but Grayson was quick to swallow my sounds with his deep kisses. Rhett licked me more deliberately, and I bucked against his face.

"Patience, Thorn," he chuckled, pinning my thighs in

place with his rough hands. Fucking guitarists and their finger strength. His lips closed around my clit, his tongue flicking it with a steady rhythm like he was listening to music in his head while he drove me to the edge of insanity and back, and Gray kissed me utterly breathless and weak.

Gasping, I nipped Gray's lip between my teeth. "Gray," I moaned. "I want to taste you."

"Yeah?" he mused, his thumb brushing over my already puffy lower lip.

I nodded eagerly as Rhett slid his long musician's fingers into my pussy and made me squirm. "Yeah. Please. Can I suck your dick, Gray?"

"Jesus *fuck*," Rhett muttered against my pussy, and Gray exchanged a wicked grin with me.

"You can," Gray agreed. "But not like this. I'd be worried about choking you."

Rhett scoffed. "Don't flatter yourself."

Nonetheless, Grayson scooted up to rest his back on the headboard and tugged his sweatpants down to reveal his massive erection, the tip gleaming with pre-cum already.

"Oh shit," Rhett coughed. "Shower *and* a grower. Good for you, man."

I couldn't hold back my laugh as I wriggled free and rolled over to my belly between Grayson's legs. Excited,

I wrapped my hand around his base and marveled how my fingertips couldn't touch.

"Quit checking out my dick and make Billie come, Silver," Gray ordered, reaching down to slap my ass way harder than necessary. I yelped but rose up onto my knees with my ass in the air like I guessed he wanted me to do.

Rhett followed the repositioning, fingers teasing my pussy from behind. "Yes, sir," he muttered. "Bossy."

Gray gave a moan as I closed my lips around the thick head of his cock, and Rhett took that as his sign to go back to work. He didn't hesitate as he tongue-fucked my pussy from behind, and I had a hard time choking out moans of my own with my mouth full of Gray's dick. Like, *really* full. I couldn't even get half of him in, and as it was that was seriously pushing the limits of my throat.

"Silver, I told you to do something," Gray rumbled a few minutes later, "and you haven't done it. Do you need help?"

"Fuck you, Taylor," Rhett muttered, coming up for air. "I was taking my time."

"Don't," he growled. "She can take it."

Oh *god*, my insides quivered at that. Rhett apparently agreed with his bandmate because he picked up the intensity. His face buried between my legs, he sucked and flicked my clit while his fingers pumped my pussy hard enough to make me almost lose my balance. His other hand kept a tight grip on my hip, though, so when I inevitably climaxed a scarce few moments later, he was able to hold me in place —really held me there and prolonged the orgasm like I hadn't even known was possible.

I moaned and quivered, but Gray had a grip on my hair by now and forced my face down hard into his lap, damn near suffocating me on dick. Not that I was complaining, but I was also pretty sure he got more teeth than he was bargaining for.

"Holy shit, that was hot," Rhett chuckled, finally releasing me. Gray did the same, letting me up for air as my whole body trembled like barely set jelly.

Gray stroked my hair out of my face, then wiped my wet mouth with a smirk. "How we doing so far, Prickles? Sharing nicely?"

I licked my lips, tasting him, and then smiled. "So far, so good."

"Good, then we'd better continue. Come here." He tugged me closer, guiding me onto my knees on either side of his hips as he positioned his tip at my entrance. "That's it, baby girl, nice and easy. You can take it all now." He firmly lowered me down onto his sizable shaft, not stopping until my thighs met his, and I gave a groan at how *full* that made me.

As Gray started to move beneath me, Rhett was right there, tilting my face to his and kissing me hard. Our tongues danced together, his lip piercing adding that extra texture to our kisses, while Gray leisurely thrust up into me from below like he had all the time in the world. Like I wasn't about to come again just from how tight the fit was. The angle he was striking was doing unspeakable things to my insides, too. Like his thick head was just rubbing back and forth over my G-spot without ever letting up.

"Gray!" I squeaked in protest as my orgasm continued to build, but he just held me firm, his hands splayed over my hips to keep me captive.

"Come for me, Prickles. Then I'll let Rhett have a turn."

Holy hell, how could I refuse an order like that? Something about that wording—letting Rhett have a *turn*—should have freaked me out. Or at the very least triggered my feminist instinct, right? Nope, I just found myself spiraling into a heady, skin-tingling kind of orgasm that made me scream against Rhett's hungry kisses.

"Good girl," Grayson praised as I writhed in his lap.

"You're so pretty when you shatter, Billie, like a damn dream."

"My turn," Rhett growled, grabbing my hips from behind. He lifted me straight out of Grayson's lap—and off his dick—then dropped me onto my back on the bed. Gripping my thighs in his hands he hitched my legs wide, then plunged his pierced cock deep into my still-pulsing cunt.

I cried out with pleasure, and Gray met my eyes with a grin from above my head. I was so fucking turned around I didn't even know which way was up, but who fucking cared? I was having a *fantastic* time helping the boys learn to share.

"Shit, Thorn," Rhett groaned as he pumped his dick into me, "you feel so incredible. This body is unbelievable. You think you'd wanna take more?"

"More?" I gasped, staring up at him with wide— excited—eyes.

Rhett's lips tilted in an evil grin. "Don't play innocent, Billie Bellerose; you know what I'm saying." To make his point, he pulled out, flipped me onto my stomach, then plunged back into my pussy. This time, though, his index finger circled my asshole at the same time.

I squeaked in surprise, even though I absolutely had known that was what he meant.

"Okay?" Rhett asked, checking for permission before taking things further.

"Yes!" I gasped, rocking back onto him.

He gave a small groan, then pushed that finger deeper while his hips increased in rhythm. "Fuck," he breathed, and I made all kinds of noises that I'd be sure to blush about later. "You like that?"

My response was just a muffled jumble of sounds as I bit the comforter and let my eyes roll back. Shit's sake, he was going to make me come *again.*

"She's close," Gray commented, and I glanced up to see him just inches away with his cock in hand. He met my eyes and stroked his slick shaft slowly, teasingly. "Make her come, Silver, then pass her back."

I couldn't even argue with that. Rhett's finger pumped in time with his dick, and a moment later I detonated. This time I saw stars and my legs went spaghetti weak. Not that anyone minded. With soft praises and sweet kisses, the guys rolled me onto my back, and Gray took up position between my legs once more.

"You guys are gonna kill me," I moaned as he pushed his thickness back between my swollen folds. "Death by orgasm."

"Worse ways to go," Rhett chuckled, setting up residence right beside my head while Gray hitched my legs around his waist.

I grinned a loopy, delirious grin. "True." Then I leaned over and took Rhett in my mouth while Gray set about proving a point by making me come *again*. Was that even possible? Surely not.

Somehow, the two of them proved that not only was it possible, but that I was capable of even *more* before they each reached the end of their self-control. My dirty mouth was back in force, and I begged them to come on my tits at the same time—something they were both too damn happy to oblige me in.

Eventually, we all collapsed in a sticky, sweaty, boneless heap on the bed. Our heavy breathing echoed through the room, and I couldn't remember ever being so fucking *satisfied* in my life. Sharing was definitely my biggest kink.

"Dammit," I whispered after I'd regained my breath.

"What?" Rhett mumbled, cracking one eyelid to frown his confusion.

I shot him a mischievous smile back. "You never fucked my ass."

Gray made a noise that sounded like he'd just choked, and Rhett's shoulder shook with laughter.

"Next time, babe," Rhett promised, leaning over to

press a sweet kiss on my lips. "With lube. I promise. Me, not Gray. He'd cause the kind of damage that'd ruin all our days."

Gray just grunted in agreement. "True. You can warm her up for me on your pencil dick, Silver."

I scoffed because that was far from accurate, and Rhett reached over me to swat Gray's bare ass. Damn... was I into that? Yes.

The bed shook with Gray's silent laughter, but Rhett ignored him as he snuggled me into his arms, not even flinching at the mess still coating my chest. He just nuzzled his face into my hair, sighing like he was blissfully happy. Like I was.

"You're incredible, Billie Bellerose," he whispered.

I sighed with contentment. "I love how you guys say my name," I admitted. "Like it's more than a name. Like it's a prayer." I paused, thinking on that, then chuckled. "Good thing I got my Dad's surname. It just wouldn't sound the same if I were Billie Pionka."

"What?" Grayson asked, raising his head up to peer at me.

I yawned heavily, drugged out on way too many orgasms. "Mm-hmm, that was my mom's surname. Pionka. Mareika Pionka. Bellerose is a way better rock name, though."

Rhett hummed a soothing tune under his breath,

kissing my neck softly. "I don't care what your name is so long as you'll always be mine."

Happy tears pricked at my eyes, and I closed them to hold back any crying. I couldn't think of anywhere I'd rather be than curled up in the warmth of Rhett's and Grayson's love. Sleep came fast and easy, and for once my dreams didn't shatter into nightmares.

fifteen

BILLIE

In that moment between sleep and awake, I anticipated how glorious it was going to feel to be snuggled between two rock stars. My rock stars.

Rhett and Gray had absolutely destroyed my body last night, and the restful sleep after was exactly what I'd needed to wake refreshed and ready to deal with whatever bullshit was going to come at us today. Because we all knew there was going to be *all the bullshit.*

When I got my eyes open though, it was to find that Grayson was gone, his side of the bed cold and clearly abandoned for most of the night. Rhett was still wrapped around me, and I tried not to feel weird about Gray bailing during the night. Maybe it had been a little squishy in here with the three of us and his giant-ass body.

The boys had king-size beds, but we might need to invest in something a little more... custom.

"Morning, baby," Rhett said sleepily, dragging me closer and pressing his lips to the side of my neck. My eyes closed briefly as I enjoyed the snuggle, but a second later there was a bang on the door, and to both of our surprises, it was Angelo who called out.

"We have an early morning practice, Silver. You need to get out here."

Rhett's response was to groan, but he didn't shout back like he might have with Jace. "Be right out," he rasped, pressing his lips to my throat once more and casually kissing a path down to my collarbone and the swell of my tits. Angelo must have left because there was no more knocking, and I had just reached out to run my hands across Rhett's chest when he pulled himself up, his sleepy gaze meeting mine. "Unfortunately, they're right. If we have to go on tour with a new bassist, we need to utilize every second of practice. But I will be back for you later, Billie Bellerose."

I laughed, stretching myself in the bed so my tits

popped up in a perfect teasing pose. "I'll be here waiting for you, Rhett Silver."

His strangled groan sent shivers through my body, but somehow we both managed to leave the moment with just a brief kiss, and then he was off to shower. I left him to it, knowing that I shouldn't interrupt their practice time. It was important that this international tour went well, and knowing Angel would be stepping up on stage with them had me breathless to witness it.

My past and my present would collide in ways I'd never expected.

When Rhett emerged, he was, sadly, dressed, covering up all those glorious tattoos and piercings. It did make resisting him a little easier though, and fucking hell, I should be satisfied after last night. But if anything, all the sex and orgasms just had me wanting more. What we'd done together had destroyed me in ways that felt almost new. With Jace and Angelo... we'd been teenagers fumbling around with our sexuality. Rhett and Gray were far from inexperienced teens, that was for fucking sure.

"Are you showering now?" Rhett asked me, perching on the side of the bed. "Or sleeping in?"

I already knew my body was far too worked up to sleep, so I pushed myself up to a sitting position.

"Shower, definitely." I shot him a slow smile. "So you know where I'll be if you get lonely."

Rhett shook his head, looking like he was about to strip his clothes off in the next second. "You tempt me like no other. I might just come looking for you, Thorn, so be fucking ready."

Dropping my legs off the bed and standing tall, I swayed my hips as I strolled toward the bathroom. "I'm always ready, Zep," I shot back over my shoulder. "Always."

The damp heat on my inner thighs could attest to that, and since the boys had come on my chest last night, there was only one explanation for me being so wet still. I was ready for round two.

Or was it three? I mean, it was round seven for orgasms...

Whatever.

Rhett's groaning laughter followed me into the bathroom, and when I closed the door, I could still hear him for a few seconds before the sound faded. Seemed he was going to be the good boy today and go out to get some practice in. Probably for the best. Last thing I needed was Angelo barging in here and dragging him out by his mohawk.

Adjusting the water to the near scalding temperatures I enjoyed for my morning showers, I stepped under the stream and closed my eyes, enjoying the sensation of water running over me. I'd wash myself soon, but this was my favorite part of a shower, when I just took a second to exist.

I lost myself in the moment, and it was only when a small blast of cool air hit my ass that I realized I wasn't alone in here any longer.

Okay then, maybe Rhett wasn't going to be a *good boy* after all.

"Thought you needed to practice," I murmured, about to turn, but his strong grip on my hips kept me from shifting. Rhett pushed me forward to the tiles, and I was splayed against the hard surface in the next second. "Fuck," I groaned, rocking back against the hard length that was pressing against my ass.

"All fucking night," a low voice snarled. A low, familiar voice that was definitely not Rhett's.

What the actual shit? That motherfucker.

This time I bucked harder, but it wasn't with the same intentions as before. Jace kept me pinned with his bulk, the hot water beating down on both of us.

"All fucking night you screamed for them," he snarled, leaning down near my ear. "Just like you used to for me and Angel. That was *our* role in your life, not Rhett and Grayson's."

His fingers were tracing across the curve of my ass,

and I was near sobbing—not from fear or worry but from the feel of his touch once more. As his fingers slipped down my ass crack, he curled them so they slid up into my cunt, stroking me in harsh movements. "What did I warn you about letting others touch what's mine."

"Fuck," I choked out, the water blinding me and filling my mouth and nose. "I'm not yours, asshole."

His fingers stroked deeper, and my entire body trembled. "One part of you is lying," Jace said with a dark chuckle. "Your mouth or your cunt?"

The trembling increased, and I was about to come against my will—traitorous body—when Jace slowed his strokes. "Oh no, baby. You don't get to come yet. You get to suffer like I have for the past twelve hours."

"It wasn't twelve hours," I spluttered. "Like, one, tops."

He scoffed. "One last night and the night before and the time you disappeared with Grayson. There have been so many *one fucking hours* that I'm not sure you can suffer enough just in this shower. I think you need nights of suffering."

"I had fucking years," I shot back with a sad sob. "Years."

Jace paused, some of the pressure against my back easing. I managed to spin in his hold, wanting to face him, even though I knew it was a terrible-as-fuck idea to stare at his face, not when I needed to resist his thrall.

"We lost years because of you, Bellerose," he shot back at me. "We lost time and a baby and a true fucking love. All because you were a coward."

In some ways he was right, and I just didn't have the energy to argue with him any longer.

"I'm sorry, Jace," I said softly. Knowing it was a mistake to touch him, but needing to anyway, I put my hand on his chest. "I made a bad choice, and I've regretted and paid for it for eight fucked-up years. Can we please let it go, just for now? I'm not going anywhere."

This time his scoff had less bite. "I'll believe that when I see it."

Every part of me was determined to prove him wrong. "What are you really doing in here?" I asked, my hand falling from his chest. "What do you want?"

His hands were under my ass in the next beat as he hauled me up and pressed me back against the wall. "I need to fuck you," he said, dropping his head into the crevice of my throat, lips pressing against my skin, followed by his teeth, nipping me hard. "I need this out of my system so I can play music."

He thrust up, and even without foreplay I was wet

enough that he slid inside me without too much pain. Our groans were lost in the water streaming over us, and when Jace lifted me so he could thrust up again, with more force this time, I whimpered and barely held onto my scream. He said he was fucking me out of his system, but for me, every time we were together like this, it just made it that much harder to separate myself from Jace.

From the feelings that would never go anywhere.

The love and hate were so close for us that sometimes it was the same.

Jace's powerful hands held me motionless, so all I could do was dig my nails into his shoulders and hold on as he slammed into my pussy over and over, hard tiles against my back and an even harder man between my legs.

I tried not to come. I tried to resist with every part of my body, but it was an impossible task as the swirling intensity in my stomach unraveled. My screams were louder than I intended, and now everyone would know exactly where their missing lead singer was.

Since they were supposed to be practicing now.

"Mine," Jace said roughly, releasing his hold on me so it was only the wall at my back and my legs around his waist that kept me from falling to the tiled floor. He placed both hands on the wall above my head, and his hips moved so fast, fucking me with enough force that I couldn't even catch my breath between thrusts.

Soft, pleading words of encouragement fell from my lips, which only seemed to spur Jace on faster. "You will come for me again," he demanded.

"So much for making me suffer," I managed to say.

Jace shook his head. "I've figured that giving you this and then taking it away once more is how you suffer. Now fucking come."

I obeyed near instantly, body bucking against his as those cries turned once more to screams. He let out a low groan of his own, and I swore to fuck he whispered my name as he finished inside me, thrusting in a few last brutal strokes.

Before the swirling pleasure in my body had remotely subsided, he was sliding free and lowering me to the ground. His touch was gentle as he left me sprawled on the shower floor, and when he turned and left without another word, I almost wished he'd just dropped me. That would have hurt less than him treating me like I was a casual fucking booty call.

I understood why Jace was trying to fuck me from his mind, purge me from his soul, and exorcise the demons of our past. I absolutely understood, and I wasn't even mad about it.

Not when we had so much history to work through.

The true question of it, though, was would I survive his form of therapy?

At least with what was left of my heart and soul intact.

sixteen

GRAYSON

L eaving Billie's bed while she slept so sweetly between Rhett and me was one of the hardest things I'd done in a long time. Harder, even, than I'd realized, as the hollow pit of regret deepened in my gut with every mile I put between us.

But it was the right thing to do. I couldn't—wouldn't—lie there with her and bask in her affection while suspicion and dread filled me from within.

She deserved better than that. Hell, she deserved better than *me*, but I was so completely enamored with little spiky Billie Bellerose that I found myself driving halfway across the country to try and clear my conscience. All to be with her.

On my way out I'd seen Angelo sitting in the kitchen looking like hell and told him quietly that I'd be gone a few days. He'd given me a questioning glance but kept those questions to himself. I never thought I'd get along with a spoiled mafia prince, but our days of torturing bastards together had forged a bond. We understood one another. So he just nodded and promised to keep Billie safe while I was gone.

We had security—bodyguards and the like. Of course we did. Jace and Rhett were total fucking morons when it came to threat assessment, and with how famous the band was, we'd be idiots to dismiss them entirely. Angelo was better, though. Knowing he had my girl's back had given me the confidence to leave her that morning and reassured me now, almost twenty hours later, as I pulled into the parking lot of a seedy biker bar.

My phone buzzed with a new message from Angelo, and I opened it while ignoring the ones from Jace and Rhett.

Ricci: She's asking where you are. What do you want me to say?

No need to explain which *she* he meant. It wouldn't be Brenda or Vee. There was only one girl I'd fucked senseless all night while sharing her with one of my best friends. Hell, Rhett wasn't just a friend, he was a brother. Shit, what did that make us now? Brother-boyfriends? Ugh, a few nights of mind-blowing sex and I was thinking like a chick.

I exhaled heavily, glancing at the bar through my windshield. There were a couple of patched MC guys standing out front, smoking and talking shit. This was the last place I'd thought I'd visit after I'd walked away from my uncle's cartel all those years ago.

Taylor: Just... that I had some shit to sort out.

The reply was almost instant and exactly what I expected.

Ricci: Twenty hours and that's the best you came up with? Typical fucking drummer. I'll handle it, you uninspired fuck.

I huffed a laugh and shut my phone down, stashing it in the center console so I wouldn't lose it in a bar fight, should one eventuate during this visit. The odds seemed in favor of that happening, so I'd rather not have Bellerose business fall into bad hands.

Pushing Billie from my head, I loaded my Glock with a fresh clip and added a spare to my pocket. Then I checked the mirror to make sure I'd shrugged off every shred of softness that my girl had manifested in me. This wasn't the place for weakness, and these people wouldn't hesitate to leverage any whiff of vulnerability they caught.

Satisfied that I looked enough like the killer I was, I climbed out of my car and clicked the key fob to lock up. Then I strode confidently across the gravel parking lot to the bar.

As expected, the bikers at the door moved to block my entry with no-nonsense expressions.

"I'm here to see Bones," I told them with a flat glare. "He'll want to see me."

The smaller of the two men gave me an unimpressed up and down. "Oh, you think? Who the fuck are you?"

"Unimportant," I growled back. "Why don't you let Bones decide for himself, huh?"

The guys glanced at one another, then the bigger one shrugged. "Let him in. Could be fun."

I stifled the urge to roll my eyes. They seemed to think I was going to be leaving in a body bag just for requesting an audience with their president, but that wasn't in the cards for me today. Not when I had Billie's sweet kisses to get back to. I'd get the information I needed, then leave... by whatever means necessary.

The small guy reluctantly stepped aside, and I pushed past them to enter the bar. My eyes needed a moment to adjust to the dim light inside, and I swallowed the urge to gag at the smell. Two dozen sets of suspicious eyes turned my way, but the big guy from the door followed me in and clapped my shoulder.

"Prez is in the basement," he told me with a gold-toothed grin. "That way." He pointed me toward a door highlighted with a neon sign that flashed *Fuck Around* with an arrow pointing down.

Keeping my mouth shut, I ignored all the patched dudes staring at me and crossed to the door. Not hesitating, I yanked the door open and proceeded down the narrow staircase into the basement of the bar.

The lights flickered annoyingly as I entered the room, and I squinted around quickly to assess any possible threats. There were a handful of tough looking dudes, but far fewer than upstairs in the bar. In the middle of the basement, a boxing ring was set up, and inside it I spotted Bones—the Grave Robbers MC president—beating the ever-loving *shit* out of some guy.

His opponent was barely recognizable as a human, he was that messed up. As I drew closer, he dropped to the ground with a brutal right hook from Bones, blood splattering all over the stained mat. Bones then proceeded to kick the shit out of the nearly dead man, his steel-toed biker boots no doubt breaking some ribs in the process.

Saying nothing, I waited patiently until Bones was satisfied he'd inflicted enough pain. Then he stomped aggressively on the man's skull, and I didn't flinch. It was concerning how easily this all came back to me, but that was a worry for another day.

"Who the *fuck* is interrupting me while—" His furious bellow cut off abruptly when he recognized me, and his whole body froze for a moment. Then he quickly masked his shock with a lazy smile and bark of laughter. "Ho-ly *shit*. What is this, the Ghost of Christmas Past come to remind me of my sins?" He leapt out of the boxing ring, his lithe muscles dripping with blood as he approached.

"Something like that," I muttered.

Bones roared another laugh and clasped me in a rough hug, smearing me with blood and making my teeth grind. Affectionate fuck was always testing my limits. "I don't know what I did to deserve this visit, *Maker*, but fuck, it's good to see you! Jim-Bob! Go fetch us a bottle of Scotch."

He guided me over to the seating area on the side of the ring where he spectated when fights were on. Pulling a packet of rolled joints from his pocket, he offered me one. I accepted because, shit, I needed to calm down.

"Good stuff," I commented after the first drag, letting the musky smoke fill my head.

Bones gave a toothy grin. "The best. You should try

my coke; that shit is *smooth*. You'd be into that these days, right? Now that you're a big-time *rock star*." His tone was mocking and sarcastic, but there was no heat of betrayal. That was why I'd come to him and not a closer contact. Not *everyone* had been cool with my shift into the public spotlight, and plenty of my former associates saw my fame as a good excuse to rip me off. Or try to.

I grunted a noncommittal response and took another long drag of the joint. It really was good shit, but I probably shouldn't get too wasted. I still had to drive all the way back to Naples in time for our flight to Dublin on Wednesday.

"So, I assume you're not just here for a friendly visit." Bones cut straight to the chase after his guy delivered the Scotch that neither of us was likely to drink. He waved a hand to dismiss the extras from the room, giving us privacy to speak.

I shook my head. "No. I heard a name recently that has been needling at my memory, and I can't place it. Hoped maybe it'd mean something to you..." After all, Bones had cut his teeth in the Kahulu Cartel right alongside me. We'd trained together as kids, shared beatings at the hands of my uncle, and completed more than our fair share of *favors* for the cartel together. He also had an eidetic memory and was able to recall events and conversations from his whole life as though they were happening in real time inside his head.

It was a secret he didn't share with many, and a huge factor in his success as a crime lord of his own making. Even if he did still entertain a business relationship with my uncle.

Bones lifted his brows with undeniable curiosity. "What's the name?"

I rolled it around in my mouth for a moment, but that sick sense of dread and recognition was still attached to it. I needed to know.

"Mareika Pionka."

Bones nodded. "I know it."

I waited, but he didn't elaborate. Frustration and anger burned in my chest, and I gritted my teeth to hold back the desire to punch my old friend right in his smug fucking face. "And I assume it'll cost me something to get more than that?"

Another toothy grin from Bones. "I wouldn't be much of a businessman if I let the opportunity slide, now, would I?"

I released an exhale from behind my teeth. "What do you want?"

He shrugged. "Depends what *you* want, Grayson. How much info are we talking here?"

The more I asked, the more he'd want in return. All I

needed was the one burning question playing in my mind. "I need to know what my connection is to her. I've gone over it a thousand times and can't place it as anything more than uncomfortably familiar."

He nodded his understanding. "Makes sense. Alright, I'll tell you that much, and you make me some money tonight." He waved his joint at the boxing ring where the dead man still decorated the stained mat. "Fight my champ, cream him, and I'll accept that as payment for this little shred of your past. Deal?"

I quirked a brow in disbelief. "That's it?"

Bones's grin was like that of a hungry shark. "That's it. I love you like a brother, Grayson, but I've also seen your temper snap before. I'm not stupid enough to push my luck."

He was right about that. I nodded. "Deal."

More smiles. "Good. Mareika Pionka. She was one of your last hits before Ailani cut you loose. From memory, I think it was a house fire?" He shrugged like he was hazy on the details when we both knew he was crystal clear. "Pretty sure I heard after the fact, months later when I went snooping—you know how I like to know things—the daughter was home at the time of the fire. Nearly died of smoke inhalation and lost her baby in the process. Nasty business, that, but you'd already moved on with your new life and probably never saw the aftermath, huh?"

No. *No.* That was *not* the answer I'd wanted. Not even slightly. The finer details came screaming back into my mind, and I whispered a curse as I dropped my head into my hands. Guilt and despair drained the life out of me until I was sure I'd curl up and die right there on the floor.

"Fight starts at ten tonight," Bones told me with a clap on the shoulder. "See you then." He stood and started to saunter away, then called over his shoulder. "Always a pleasure, brother! Let's not leave it so long until next time."

Fuck. I was so fucked. Billie would never forgive me for this, and I couldn't blame her. Nor would Jace, for that matter. That knowledge didn't stop my heart from shredding into bloody ribbons, though. It was over, and I'd never regret anything more in my whole cursed life.

seventeen

BILLIE

Grayson had been gone for *days*. No word, no note, not even a phone call to say *Hey, Billie, thanks for the awesome three-way and letting me toss a load on your tits. I'm alive, by the way.* Nope, none of that. Just silence.

The one comforting fact was that he was also ignoring Rhett and Jace. Angelo had been in contact with him; I knew that for sure because that sneaky fuck couldn't lie to me even when he tried. On the first day, when I'd woken to find Gray missing from my bed, I hadn't thought much of it. Then he was absent from their band practice, and I'd started to worry.

Angelo eventually told me that Gray had spoken to

him before leaving the house in the early hours of the morning, and said he was *fine*. That was it. *Fine*.

By the time we were leaving for the airport and he still hadn't reappeared, I was officially losing my damn mind with concern, all the worst-case scenarios playing out nonstop. I'd quickly moved past assuming he was weirded out about our three-way and had officially settled into conspiracy theories that flip-flopped between him realizing he wasn't attracted to me and going out to fuck his way through a slew of Bellerose groupies to suspicions that the Wilsons or Altissimos or Riccis had abducted and murdered him. By now his body could be fish food at the bottom of Naples Harbor, and we would be none the wiser.

The only thing reassuring me was Angelo's continued insistence that I was being dramatic and Gray would be back *soon*. Whatever that fucking meant.

Thankfully, and making me feel a touch more sane, Rhett and Jace were just as shitty about the whole thing. By the time we strode across the tarmac to the private jet Big Noise had provided, none of us were talking. Every time we did, it ended in an argument because we were all so cranky and on edge.

Vee had tried her best in the car to make small talk but soon gave up with a huff of frustration.

"Who the fuck are they?" Jace snapped as we

approached the aircraft, pointing at the dark-suited men circling the plane with small flashlights. Clearly not airline employees.

Angelo quirked a brow. "My people."

"Yours?" Rhett challenged. "Or your father's?"

"Mine," Angelo replied in a cold voice. "You think I'd take chances after that setup at a Big Noise building before Christmas? I'm not that fucking stupid, Silver. They're sweeping the plane for tampering and explosives. We won't take off until it's been cleared."

That was reassuring. I hadn't even acknowledged that was a fear until he'd taken care of it.

"Thank you, Angel," I said quietly as I passed him to ascend the stairs.

"You're welcome, Bella," he whispered back.

Jace had boarded the plane ahead of me, so it was his angry shout that warned me we weren't the first passengers to arrive. My heart leapt to my throat, and I shoved past Jace to launch myself at Grayson.

"You're back!" I exclaimed, clinging onto him like a spider monkey. He didn't hug me back, though. He just stood there and *let* me hug him until I awkwardly released him and stepped back. "Where the fuck have you been?"

He wouldn't meet my eyes, his gaze shifting past

me to take in the rest of the band. "I had to deal with some things. Sorry."

My jaw dropped. His face was mottled with bruises and a butterfly stitch decorated his hairline, but that was all the explanation we got? He'd had to *deal with some things.*

"Are you fucking serious right now?" I demanded in a strangled voice. "Do you have *any* idea how—"

"All clear!" Angelo called out, striding into the cabin without realizing what he was interrupting. "Plane is good to go."

"Okay, great!" Brenda popped out of the cockpit and placed her hands on her hips to glare at everyone. "Sit your asses down; I'm giving the control tower the go ahead for takeoff. I can't come with you to Europe— baby needs his mama—so I've personally selected a new tour manager to fill in for me. That's Hannah." She pointed down the cabin to a woman I hadn't even noticed until now.

She was small, blonde, and surrounded by files, tablets, and other work material. She stood and waved, but no one on the plane even acknowledged her. "We don't need another fucking manager," Jace shot back at Brenda. "The last one almost destroyed us as a band."

Brenda leveled her best *pissed off* momager stare at him. "The last one was a temporary tour manager, and he was appointed by the misogynistic managers of Big Noise. Hannah is nothing like Tom, and she will be an asset to you in trying to navigate an international tour. She holds three degrees, has sixteen years of experience, and speaks eight fucking languages, so you will treat her with, at minimum, respect."

Jace returned Brenda's glare, and while he didn't agree to her terms, he also didn't argue. The next few minutes were filled with chaos as bags were loaded, seats taken, and the preflight checks done by the multitude of staff for this private jet. Hannah moved along briefly and met all of us, and I found her cute Southern accent completely at odds with what I expected from a sixteen-year tour managing veteran who spoke multiple languages.

That taught me not to judge a book by its adorable cover. There was a shark hidden in her baby-blue eyes, and I hoped that shark was here to destroy those threatening Bellerose. And not the band itself.

Surely Brenda would have been extra-selective in a replacement, knowing everything the band had been through.

"See you all in two months, though I might try and get across once or twice," Brenda called from the doorway before she exited the plane to allow for the final secure and cross-check of the cabin.

When it was time to taxi out, I was strapped in next to Rhett, Vee and Angelo were in the seats across the aisle from us, with Jace and Grayson behind them, just out of my easy view. I'd have to actually turn my head fully to see the drummer, and as badly as I wanted to do that, there was no point in us exchanging cold glares across a plane. I would just have to wait until we were able to move about the plane, and then I'd figure out how to kick his ass without him retaliating and murdering me with his ninja skills.

Grayson was someone I'd never worried about betraying me, but there was a sinking sensation in my gut now. The way he was acting wasn't adding up, and I had a feeling when I learned the truth, another piece of myself would be destroyed.

The pilot announced our departure and gave us an update on flying time and the conditions for our journey. It was supposed to be a smooth flight, outside of a little initial turbulence as we left American airspace. If only he knew that turbulence was more likely to be inside the fucking plane.

I'd only been on a plane a few times as a kid and couldn't really remember what happened from here. The drama with Gray had distracted me from my initial stress over this new experience, but as the plane moved into position at what looked like the head of a very long black tarmac, some of those swirls in my stomach shifted from Grayson worry to flying-in-a-plane worry.

"You okay?" Rhett asked, reaching out to grasp my hand. "Have you flown before?"

No one had asked me that until this second because it probably didn't occur to famous, rich rock stars that there were poor people who could barely afford a bus ticket, let alone a plane. "As a child, but I honestly can't remember anything about it. Are we waiting to take off now?"

He squeezed my hand tightly. "Yep. They wait for their turn, mostly to make sure we're not about to crash into another aircraft on the way up. The initial thrust will throw you back into your seat a little, but we'll be up in no time. I've got you, Thorn. No need to panic."

"Right," I breathed. "Easy as. So, what do you think is really going on with Gray?"

Rhett's hold on my hand tightened again, his only reaction to my random conversation switch. I just really needed the distraction from my unease over flying, and what better distraction than my unease over a lover acting like a stranger.

"I honestly have no idea," Rhett said softly, shifting his head just enough that I knew he was staring at the drummer. "It's not in his personality to freak out over sex or this sharing dynamic we have going on. That wasn't the first time you two fucked, so it can't be anything like that, and I also don't see him losing his shit over discovering that he's completely in love with you. Which the bullheaded asshole is."

Our relationship right now couldn't be farther from *love* if it fucking tried.

"Could it be a personal problem from his life before Bellerose?" I wondered. "I mean, he's ignored all of you as well. Maybe the timing of whatever happened to him just happened to coincide with us being in bed together."

I was grasping at any excuse, but the truth was, until Grayson told us himself, we would always be guessing.

"He's too old to ignore us because personal shit is going on in his life," Rhett said shortly. "All it would have taken was a brief call or text to explain what he was doing for us not to worry, and we'd have left him to it. Whatever the reason, he still needs his ass kicked."

"Motherfucker," I muttered, but the rest of my rage was cut off as the engine sound increased, and I could almost feel the plane gearing up to take off. Rhett's warning about the initial thrust allowed me to keep my calm when it happened, and I only closed my eyes for a few seconds as the ground first started to fade away outside my window.

My worry over Grayson muted as I watched our ascent, the clouds such an incredible sight out the window. It took longer than I expected for us to stop ascending and finally level out, and when that happened, the seatbelt-sign light disappeared and people began to move about the cabin. Hannah made her way to the front bathrooms, the flight hosts started to bang about in the kitchenette, and I felt myself relaxing into my seat. I'd been tenser than I realized until I'd finally allowed myself to relax.

"How was that?" Rhett asked. Our hands were still clasped together, and I couldn't think of anyone else I'd rather take my first adult flight with.

"Better and scarier than I expected," I said with a laugh. "It's incredible to see houses and land turn into tiny Lego landscapes, and then the vast expanse of water… makes you feel kind of small and insignificant."

Rhett ran his thumb along my palm. "You'll never be insignificant, Billie. No matter how small you feel. The most precious parts of the world are often found in small packages."

This motherfucker. He was going to kill me one day with his poetic kindness.

"Thank you," I whispered. "Fuck. Don't get me crying before I yell at Grayson. He'll think I'm sad then, and I'm mostly furious as hell."

Rhett's laugh was low and soothing. "Sweetheart, every man knows that if a woman is crying while she's yelling at you, she's reached maximum pissed off, and you should either run or shut the fuck up. Both, really."

"Both is the best," I agreed, my own laughter spilling free. It felt nice to joke again after the past few days of feeling stressed and sad.

Two factors that could have been resolved with one conversation.

A conversation I was about to fucking have.

eighteen

BILLIE

R hett let me go with a "Good luck and shout if
you need me." I really hoped I didn't need
him, because that would mean this conversation had taken a terrible turn.

Angelo met my gaze as I moved along the center
aisle. "You okay?" he asked me.

I nodded. "Fine, just need to have a conversation.
You know how it is."

He didn't say anything else, but his expression was
grim as he followed my progress, and when I turned
away from him to look for Grayson—who was not in
his seat any longer—I somehow knew that the mafia
prince's eyes remained on me.

196

Jace had his head buried in his phone as I passed, and the fact that he was also ignoring me didn't bother me as much as Grayson. I knew why Jace was an asshole. This was completely out of character for Gray, and that was what scared me the most.

The back part of the plane was unfamiliar to me, and I was surprised to see a closed door that didn't look like it was attached to a bathroom. Turning the handle, it opened easily, and I found Grayson sitting on the end of the bed. Of course, Bellerose's private plane had a fucking bedroom.

Why was I even surprised?

"Figured you'd want some privacy," he said shortly. "To talk."

He was cold. Cold in a way I'd never felt, except maybe the first night I'd walked into their hotel suite. His gaze then had been impassive, and he'd said very little, but I'd felt the weight of his stare. That Grayson almost felt like a dream compared to the flesh-and-blood man I knew now.

A bad dream returning to life.

"Why do we need privacy?" I asked, surprised at how steady my voice was because I sure as fuck didn't feel steady on the inside.

"I disappeared like a fucking thief in the night,

didn't contact you, and now am acting like a heartless asshole."

I blinked. "Uh, yeah, that's pretty much the gist of it."

There was silence after that, and when it became clear he wasn't elaborating—despite knowing exactly what the issue was—I snapped. "What the fuck, Gray?" I snarled, voice rising with each word. "What the fuck happened in the few hours between us fucking and you sneaking off? Why couldn't you just send me a message to let me know you were okay? I had to hear it from Angelo. Angel-fucking-O. When did you two even become such good friends? I mean, what the actual fuck? Nothing's making sense."

He let me rant and rave, and the expression on his face never changed, which only made me rage harder. My fists had clenched at my sides at some point in my speech, and I was so close to throwing fists that I had to start backing away to calm myself down.

Part of me understood that my rage was about more than just Grayson disappearing for a few days. This was a deep-seated issue that I had with abandonment and being let down by people I loved, but that was a problem for Dr. Candace. A problem she wasn't going to have time to fix before Grayson received the full force of my trauma.

When I ran out of steam and he was still just sitting on the bed staring at me, I sucked in some deep breaths. My rage wasn't making a dent in his cold exterior, so I decided to try a different tactic. "Just tell me," I said hoarsely, letting my pain seep out in a different way. "I can take it. Whatever it is that happened, I can take it. An old girlfriend came back, and you still love her? You have a secret baby that showed up? You realize you hate sharing me and would rather I disappear? I mean, I don't really know shit about your life, so it could be any or all of the above. Which is..." I wanted to say fine, but I couldn't lie that badly, so I changed the subject. "I can deal. You just need to tell me the truth, and I'll leave you alone."

The first crack in his armor appeared as he straightened, a clear jaw tic going on as he fought for his next words. "That's the last thing I want, Prickles." The words were low, but even with the noise of the jet engines, I heard him clearly. "You are"—he shook his head, clearing his throat—"the best fucking person to stumble into my messed-up world. There is no past love or past anything. There is only you, and you are all I give a fuck about." He ran a hand through his hair, and I was surprised to see his hand shaking. "I always knew my past was going to destroy my future. I knew it, even as I fought against it, but I never thought it would be like this. I never saw you coming, and for that, I'm so fucking sorry."

I took a step closer to him, the unease that had been plaguing me since, well, probably since Grayson had disappeared on us, surging to new heights. "What happened, Gray?" I whispered. "Tell me so we can work through it together."

He stood then, ducking his head so he didn't hit the roof. Our dynamic changed near instantly, and when he stepped closer, it triggered that tinge of fear that never completely disappeared around Grayson. "I want you to know that if I could go back, Billie," he rasped. "I would change everything." The swirls of unease grew stronger. "I'm not a good man, but for you, I would have tried. I'd have tried for something different."

He was going to destroy me. He *was destroying me.*

"Gray, you're scaring me," I whispered. "Just tell m—"

I was interrupted by the pilot's voice coming over the speaker. "We've put the seatbelt sign back on as we navigate the next pockets of storms. Please take your seats and buckle up."

Our argument had been so all consuming that I hadn't even noticed that the flight was growing rougher. As I had that thought, the plane did a little drop in the air, and I almost stumbled into the side of the bedroom wall. Grayson reacted instantly, reaching out and steadying me.

One of the airline staff appeared in the doorway then, a dark-haired woman about my age. She was clutching a few wine glasses she must have picked up on her way. "Can you please take your seats," she said, her words urgent. "The pilot said this pocket is a nasty one."

There was another drop in the cabin then, along with the rattling of the plane, which sent us all stumbling. Grayson kept me upright, but the dark-haired chick didn't have her own rock star to hold onto, and when she crashed into the doorframe, she unfortunately used the hand clutching the wine glass to steady herself.

The shatter of glass was loud, and with the continued turbulence raging around us, panic overtook my mind. That metallic scent of blood hit me next, and in that instant, I knew that I was about to have an episode. Before I had a chance to even try and focus on my techniques to prevent a flashback, the darkness overtook me, and I collapsed against Gray, the scent of smoke filling my senses.

Holding my belly, I sobbed before choking on smoke. When I made it out onto the landing, I headed for the stairs, sticking close to the side of the hall. Smoke thickened here, and pressing the damp cloth to my face, I lowered my face and headed for my parents. I could smell copper, like old blood, and I hoped they were okay and not injured. As I had that thought and started to move faster, a shadow caught my eye.

A shadowy figure.

I attempted to call for help, but all that emerged was a dry rasp. A sound that would never be heard over the rage of the fire. And I couldn't be seen through the smoke surrounding me. "Help," I tried again, but my throat was just too dry. The shadow had light feet, moving nearby but not so close that I could reach out and try to grab them. I wanted to sob, but there was no moisture left in my body to do so.

The shadow passed me once more, and when it reached the stairs, where the fire was burning the brightest, I caught a glimpse of a man, broad-shouldered, completely covered in black.

This was no firefighter.

He turned as he descended, taking one more look around, the darkness covering most of him except... the hair. It was longer... familiar.

My screams jolted me out of the flashback, and I found myself stretched out on the bed, Grayson holding me so that I didn't roll off and hurt myself. The moment I opened my eyes and saw his face, the moment I stared into the dark depths of his broken expression, I knew the truth. I knew that fucking hair.

Grayson had been there that night. The night my parents died. The night the fire started.

The night my baby died.

Grayson had been in my house, and he was the reason for everything.

"Prickles?" he said softly, loosening his hold. "Are you okay?"

Shock held me immobile as I tried to process. As I tried to breathe.

"The flight attendant is fine," he continued, "just a small cut on her hand. And the turbulence is already easing."

When I lifted my hands, they trembled so hard that I felt like I was literally rattling. Somehow, I got them before me. Somehow, I pushed against his chest. "Get away from me, murderer," I choked out, voice hoarse from all the screaming. My chest rattled as hard as my body as I sucked in a breath to get the next words out. "You. Fucking. Murderer."

Another scream escaped me as I lost control of myself, fighting his hold with everything I had, and it was only when Jace burst into the room that Grayson released me and stepped back.

"What the fuck happened?" Jace roared, looking

between me and Grayson as he dropped down beside the bed to wrap an arm around me. "What's wrong with Rose?"

I got myself up to a sitting position, random cries spilling from my lips, and I couldn't stop them. Somehow, between those gut-wrenching sounds, I managed to say, "Grayson killed my parents."

Jace turned in almost slow motion and stared at me, and it was all too much. The past and present, they were closer than I'd ever expected, and as my memories shattered once more, I gave into the darkness that pressed at the corners of my eyes.

I let the trauma drag me under, and part of me hoped—a small part of me—that maybe this time, I wouldn't wake up.

nineteen

JACE

When Billie passed out, I set her gently on the bed before pure rage had me leaping to my feet, and I punched Grayson in his hard-as-hell face. "You fucking bastard. You killed her parents? How the fuck could you hurt her like that? Billie, of all people." I wasn't rational. Rational me knew that Billie's parents had died long before Grayson met her, but the rage I felt didn't give a shit.

Grayson shoved me back. Normally, I'd take that as a warning not to push him any further, but I was beyond reason. Seeing Billie so broken was fucking breaking me. I slammed my fist into his face again, and blood spurted from a new gash on his cheek. When Gray swung back, I let it hit my chest, knowing that I could take it. He was a big guy. But so the fuck was I, and I had lethal rage on my side.

"Hey, what the hell," Rhett shouted, trying to get between us before he managed to yank Grayson out the door. "We're on a fucking plane. You can't beat each other up."

"I'm going to kill him," I snarled, starting forward but Angelo got there in the next beat, interfering like the nosy fucker he was.

"Bro, shit," he said as I struggled against his hold. "What the hell is going on? You both need to calm down."

"Fuck you," I shot back. "Grayson did something to Billie. She said he killed her fucking parents, and now I'm kicking his ass."

Grayson shouted something back to me, but I couldn't make it out over the roaring in my ears. Rhett wrangled our drummer from the room, then I heard him open the bathroom door and shove him in. "Clean yourself up," he told Grayson. "Don't come out until you've calmed down."

"Why has Billie passed out?" This came from Vee, who was hovering near the doorway, smart enough to know that she shouldn't venture in. "Is she okay?"

Like the mention of her name called her back to us, Billie shot right up on the bed, her eyes wide open. She stared around like she'd seen a ghost, small whimpers falling from her lips.

"Billie," I said, moving back to her as I wiped away the blood trickling from my lip and down my chin. Gray must have gotten another hit in that I'd missed in my jacked-up state.

I still couldn't feel anything with all the adrenaline pumping through me, but I'd know about the injuries soon enough. That fucker packed a mean punch.

Billie's eyes locked on mine, her lips trembling so hard that her next words were difficult to understand. "He killed my parents," she wailed. "He was there; I saw him in the fire."

That triggered me back to my previous rage. "He started the fire?" I bit out. "Do you remember him starting the fire, Rose?"

She just kept shaking her head, crying and sobbing. Her lips were moving, and as I leaned in closer, I heard her mumbling, "Our baby. Our baby. Our baby. Our baby."

In my anger over Billie's state when I raced into the room, I'd forgotten one very large detail in all of this. The fire that killed her parents. The fire that almost killed Billie.

It was the very same fucking fire that *killed our baby*.

Red tinged my sight as I raced away from her, heading for Grayson once more, this time determined to actually murder him. I knew my bandmate had a bad past, and I'd never given a shit so long as he didn't pose a danger to anyone I cared about. Over the years, he'd proven to be the opposite of a danger. He was a protector, and I respected his skills.

But that was fucking done now.

"Jace, no!" Angelo snapped, reaching out to grab me, and when he couldn't hold me, Rhett jumped in as well, the two of them wrestling me back into the bedroom and slamming the door behind us. Vee was on the other side still, but she didn't knock or try to enter.

"You need to calm the fuck down," Angelo said as he attempted to lock my arms behind me. *Good fucking luck, asshole.* I'd been wrestling with him for years and knew his moves well enough to counter them without much thought. "Bella needs you to calm down."

There was very little that could have cut through the white-hot burn of fury that was fueling my every move. Mentioning Billie was apparently one thing that would. I stopped fighting them. I just fucking stopped and focused on the bed once more.

She was shaking hard, rocking back and forth, her lips still moving.

Brushing my well-intentioned but asshole friends off me, I hurried across to the bed, and sliding my hands under her ass, I lifted her slight frame up and against my body. I cuddled her close and shifted us back on the bed so I could rest against the wall. "You two fuck off," I snapped. "This is not your trauma. It's ours."

Angelo stood at the foot of the bed. "It's mine too, and you know it."

Fucking fuck. He was right. *Our baby.* Rose might believe the baby was just mine, but we'd been in a trio relationship, so it was Angelo's too.

Rhett lessened the tension when he lifted his hands and shrugged. "As long as you both put your focus into Billie, and not into the other stupid shit that usually consumes you, then I'll leave and make sure Grayson isn't out there dismantling the plane one punch at a time."

"We'll focus on Billie," Angelo said, his eyes locked on the near-catatonic woman in my arms.

Our woman. Since the fucking day we'd met her.

Even if back then it'd been just the innocence of best friends.

Rhett left quietly, and Angelo kicked off his shoes, crawling in on the other side of Billie. I shifted to lay down so she was between the two of us. We rolled into her, locking our arms over the top of her, keeping her safe like we did when we were younger.

"Bella, love. It's going to be okay," Angelo murmured, before he spoke in Italian, whispering words of comfort and love. Words that fucking hurt to hear since it had been too damn long and it felt like we were stepping back to happier days.

Days that burned through my brain. Through my soul.

I didn't move, despite the urge to run the fuck away again knowing that this moment was going to shatter the fragile barriers I'd put up to keep myself safe. To keep myself from ever feeling what I did that day nine years ago.

Billie's sobs increased, but some color returned to her cheeks as we continued to hold and rock her. "Our daughter. Our little girl died," she cried.

My chest hurt, caving in from the pain and pressure. "I know, baby," I whispered, tightening my hold until the three of us were almost one. "I know she did, and it breaks my heart that we never got to meet her. To hold her. But I promise you she was and is loved."

"We loved her, and we love you," Angelo murmured. "Our *piccolo*."

Billie's shaking calmed just a touch, and her

murmured cries faded as well as she sank in between us. Just let herself go into our hold. "We do love you," I whispered near her ear. "Love has never been the problem."

"Our love got me through so much," she whispered back, and the fucking relief I felt that she'd returned to us enough to have a conversation was huge. "But I don't know how to get through this. I honestly don't know if I can."

She loved Grayson too, and I wished I'd snapped his damn neck. I'd been afraid that Billie would break my band members' hearts; I'd never thought it would be the other way around.

"Grayson grew up like me," Angelo said, his hold not easing at all. "In a bad family. One that forced him into situations he probably didn't want to be in. I'm not excusing what happened, but maybe you'll feel better if you hear his side of the story. He didn't know you then, Bella. It's no excuse, of course, but he was just doing his job."

Her choked sob echoed through the room, moisture dripping onto my shoulder from the tears she continuously shed. "I know you're right, but all I feel is pain and anger. I never dealt with Penelope's death, you know. That's why I need fucking therapy now. And this is just triggering that unbearable pain all over again, not to mention the loneliness and betrayal I felt when I grieved her alone."

My anger now was directed at myself. "We can't go back in time," I said gruffly, "but I sure as fuck wish I could. I'm sorry, Billie. I'm so fucking sorry."

She turned into me, and now the vise in my chest tightened until I couldn't breathe—especially as she wrapped her arms around me and sank deeper, her head tucking into my neck, like she used to do when we were younger. This was how I'd comforted her, and with Angel at her back, it was like opening a time capsule.

"I miss us," she sobbed again. "I miss this, and I miss our baby. There were many nights I contemplated taking my own life, you know, to escape the pain and misery."

The thought of Billie not existing in this world was too much to even consider. I'd never have survived it, I knew that for a fucking fact.

"I'm glad I didn't," she whispered sleepily. "I wouldn't want to miss this moment."

Her hand moved, and I saw that she was reaching back to take Angelo's as he shifted to spoon her from behind. "We will keep you safe, *amina mia*. Close your eyes and try to rest. Flashbacks and trauma episodes are exhausting, but you don't have to face them alone."

She released some more sobs, but she was calmer again. "Keep me safe," she whispered, and then not even a minute later, her breathing evened out and I knew she was asleep. I used to be a fucking expert at the minute changes in her breathing, and it looked like I hadn't forgotten.

Angelo and I didn't move, remaining in what was actually a comfortable silence. "You've never called her *amina mia* before," I said softly. "It was always *amore mio*. What does that mean?"

His next words were even softer than mine. "I called her what she owns."

"Your heart?" I guessed, fairly sure that wasn't right.

Angelo took a moment to respond. "She does own that, for sure, but more than that... she's my *la mia anima*. My soul."

Wasn't that the fucking truth. Heart and soul. Life and death.

Billie owned us, and she always had.

twenty

BILLIE

Most of the flight passed with me curled up in the big aircraft bed, snuggled between Angelo and Jace as they slept heavily. Sleep, filled with trauma and agony, only lasted a short time, then I woke and just lay there, listening to my first loves breathe. I felt some joy and peace in this moment, even if it was temporary.

In truth, I didn't remember everything that had happened before I fell asleep, either, just snippets of conversation and the warm feeling of *comfort* tempering the acidic burn of betrayal and hurt.

The bedroom door slid open with a quiet sound, and I lifted my head just enough to lock eyes with

Grayson. The man who'd killed my parents, *killed my baby*, and said *nothing* while charming his way into my pants.

"Get out," I ordered him in a cold, quiet voice. I didn't want to wake Jace and Angelo when I suspected they needed this rest even more than me.

Gray just frowned like he was disappointed in my attitude. "Billie, we need to have a conversation."

I curled my lip. "No. We should have had a *conversation* months ago. That boat sailed, sank, and disintegrated already. Get. Out."

His jaw tensed, but he didn't lose his cool. Gray never did, did he? Always so cool, calm, and collected. Always in control.

"Whatever you think you remember, Billie, I seriously doubt it's the full picture of what happened that night. Don't you want to hear my side?" He was trying to appeal to my sense of reason, but I was way past that point. Fuck logic. Fuck reason. I trusted my gut, and it told me I wasn't imagining things.

"All I need to hear from you is the answer to *one* question," I hissed, my glare like venom. "Were you there that night?"

He didn't flinch. "Yes."

Like a knife made of pure ice, right in my chest. "Then that's the only part of *your side* that matters. Get out, Gray. Pretend we never met, never fucked, never fell in lo—" I cut myself off with a choking sob. "Just get out. I can't even look at your lying, murdering face."

He held my gaze a moment longer, his expression utterly unreadable. Then he gave a small nod as he swallowed. "If that's what will help you process, then I'll respect your wishes. For now. But when you're ready to hear the rest of the story, I'll be waiting."

I scoffed. "Don't hold your breath; you'll be waiting a long time."

"If that's what it takes, so be it. I'm not going anywhere." His stare intensified like he really wanted me to believe him. As if I ever could again. "I won't force the answers on you, but just know that there's more to this whole story than even I realized until this week. But for my part in your pain, Prickles, I'll be eternally sorry."

He retreated out of the little bedroom, closing the door again behind himself, and I collapsed back into the bed with silent tears tracking down my face. Neither Jace nor Angelo had stirred during my quiet argument with Grayson, and I didn't want to wake them now.

What had happened to bring them together with me like this? My hazy memory brought up tear-filled statements of regret and love, but my head was a throbbing mess. Maybe I needed an emergency session with Dr. Candace. I'd spoken to her during the week about continuing our sessions via Zoom while we were on tour, and she'd agreed. Thank fuck.

As soon as we got to the hotel in Dublin, I'd send her receptionist a request.

Maybe she could help me work through Grayson's betrayal. Because as hurt, scared, angry, and heart-broken as I was, I didn't think I knew everything. I was in shock, with memories of choking on smoke, and terrified. I was smart enough—somewhere in my subconscious at least—to know that my "memory" might not be trustworthy. Or at least not what it seemed.

That was why I'd thrown Grayson that lifeline. *Were you there?* Yes. He'd confirmed he was, so... what other explanation was there? He'd already admitted to killing people for his family in the past. What if my parents were just a hit?

My stomach clenched with anxiety, and a groan slipped out of me when the plane shook slightly. The last thing I needed, on top of my flashback and panic attack, was to get motion sick.

A quiet tap on the door had me sitting up again, except this time it was Vee's pretty face that greeted me.

"Hey, you," she whispered, her eyes full of sympathy. Normally I hated feeling pitied, but right now I just felt... justified. Validated. Like I wasn't totally overreacting. "We're about to land; they asked us to return to our seats and buckle up."

I glanced down at the sleeping princes on either side of me, then gave Vee a tired nod. "Okay. I'll wake them up. Just give us a minute?"

She smiled her understanding and closed the door again. The last thing I wanted to do was wake Angelo and Jace up, but I also didn't want us all to die if the landing had more turbulence. So... it was the lesser of two evils.

I woke Angelo first, barely even shaking his arm before his eyes snapped open and he sat up in one smooth, if confused, motion. Then his gaze rested on me, and the tension ebbed away.

"Bella," he mumbled, his voice thick with sleep.

"We're landing," I told him quickly, not dwelling in the awkwardness of our mini-reunion. "We have to return to our seats and put on seat belts for safety and... stuff." Okay, rambling was a defense mechanism.

Angelo stared at me, puzzled, then glanced down at Jace, still sleeping on my other side. A soft smile touched his lips, then he groaned as he pushed to standing. His leg was still definitely hurting him, and I made a mental note to ask what he was doing about rehab. The walking aid might be gone, but that didn't mean he was all healed up.

"Jace," I murmured, shaking his shoulder. He didn't stir, so I did it again. Then he just snaked out an arm and hooked me around the waist. I gave a squeak of surprise as he dragged me down into his embrace, tucking me into his body like a small spoon.

It was so tempting to stay right there that I actually entertained the idea. But then we'd probably have one of the airline crew in here dragging us back to our seats, which would ruin the mood.

"We're about to land," I told him as his arm around my waist held me tight. "They need us in seats, Jace. You gotta wake up."

"Mmm," he mumbled, "'kay. In a sec."

I laughed quietly. "No, now. Come on, Sleeping Beauty, time to wake up."

He took his time, yawning and snuggling harder against me before I mustered the willpower to push him away. "Fine," he groaned. "I'm getting up."

Just as reluctant, I sat up and climbed out of the bed. "Um... thanks, I think. For..." I waved a hand in the general direction of the cabin, where Grayson was. "I don't totally know what happened after my flashback, but... I know you guys had my back. So thanks."

Jace rose to his feet in an enviably smooth motion, then crossed the small space to where I hovered awkwardly beside the door. "Billie," he murmured, his hands smoothing down my upper arms in a comforting gesture. "I'm sorry. I've been a dick to you ever since Rhett dragged you into that club in Siena."

I offered a half smile. "Yeah. You have."

He wrapped his arms around me, letting his hug say what I knew he meant: He wanted to move on from the past and start fresh. So did I.

"We're commencing our descent into Dublin; please ensure you're seated with safety belts fastened and tray tables folded away. Let's get this bird on the ground without any more incidents." The pilot sounded annoyed, and I didn't blame him. Hopefully, the flight attendant who'd cut herself was okay.

Jace released me from his hug, and silently we returned to the cabin. I deliberately avoided looking at Grayson, but my spine prickled with an awareness of his gaze. Too bad. The moment we got off this flying tin can, I was surgically removing him from my life. Somehow.

"Are we good?" Rhett asked softly as I took my seat beside him. His gaze was searching, his body language cautious, as if I was a ticking time bomb about to detonate.

"Yep," I lied. I was far from good, but for the sake of stopping another fistfight, it was the only answer I could give. I extended my hand, searching for his, and he linked our fingers together once more. "Do you ever wish you could just take a vacation from your own head?" My question popped out before I could put a leash on it, but Rhett, of all people, would know what I meant.

He sighed, slouching down in his seat and guiding my head to rest on his shoulder. "More often than I can count," he admitted. "But never when I'm with you, Thorn."

Crap. I was crying again.

Rhett just kissed my hair and held my hand, letting me silently sob against him as the plane lowered in altitude and finally delivered us with a jarring bump onto the Dublin runway. Forever the protector of my heart.

twenty-one

BILLIE

To my relief, Dr. Candace was happy to schedule me an emergency appointment over video chat when our time zones overlapped. She helped me dial back from *murderous rage* and ended our chat with me settling into a slightly less bloodthirsty *heartbroken and hurt*. Despite how good she was at never showing personal bias about my crises, I got the distinct impression she also felt that I'd be better served talking it through with Grayson rather than pinning all my faith on a blurry repressed memory from a deeply traumatic night.

Okay, it was more than just an impression. She pretty much said that word for word, which made me grumble about how being a mature adult was overrated.

Comfortingly, though, she validated the fact that I didn't *have* to hear him out. That my hurt feelings were totally okay, and no one needed to push me into dealing with him until I was good and ready. The sentiment reminded me of how patient and calm Grayson had been when I'd told him never to talk to me again. If I'd been dealing with Jace, he would have hit me over the head, tied me up, and forced me to hear his side whether I wanted to or not.

Grayson wasn't so hotheaded or insecure. He had a confidence that made me uneasy... because a guilty man wouldn't have that. Would he?

After my session I opted to stay at the hotel and watch movies that night rather than hang out with the band during their rehearsal at the concert venue. Vee stayed with me, and we made it crystal clear that we wouldn't leave the room, let alone the hotel. Security was thicker than on the last tour, and I was well aware it was Brenda's doing. She wasn't taking chances with our safety, since she couldn't stop the tour entirely, and I appreciated that.

Rather than sharing with Rhett like usual, I shared a room with Vee that night. I needed space to breathe and reflect, but neither Vee nor I particularly liked the idea of being totally alone. So Rhett had organized us a room with two queen beds and sent up room service with popcorn, candy, and sodas while they were at rehearsal.

"He's a keeper, that one," Vee commented, reading the little note that had accompanied our snacks. "'Enjoy the movies, Thorn. You know where I'm sleeping if you need late-night snuggles.' *Winky-face*." She smirked. "Is that code for sex?"

I chuckled, shrugging. "Who knows with Rhett." But I was mostly joking. I knew what he meant. "Rhett also struggles with nightmares," I told her in a more serious tone. "Or more like he just can't go to sleep in the first place."

Vee's lips twisted in sympathy. "That sucks. Trauma response?"

"I think so," I agreed. "He doesn't talk much about his past, but from the little bits the guys have said, I think he conditioned himself never to sleep deeply, like he was constantly waiting for something awful to happen."

Climbing onto her bed, my new friend gave a sad sigh. "That's horrible. He always seems like such an easygoing, no-fucks-given kind of guy. Like a sexy, human golden retriever."

I frowned slightly. "He'd never come across like

that to me. I'd always seen the pain in his eyes, the shadows at his back. I'd recognized him as a kindred spirit from our first meeting, and he'd joked in the past that we must have known each other in a different life. It really did feel like that, but it was likely just our common damage putting us on the same wavelength.

"Okay," I said, trying to lighten the mood. "If Rhett is a golden retriever—which I disagree with, by the way—then which animals does that make the rest of them?"

Vee made a show of thinking it through, then snapped her fingers. "Alright. Jace is a panther or some exotic kind of jungle cat. All sleek and pretty but with claws and teeth that would fuck you right up if you tried to boop his snoot."

My laughter surprised me so much that I choked on the sip of soda I'd just taken. That description of Jace was shockingly appropriate. "Good one," I croaked between coughs. "What about Angel?"

"Racoon," she said without hesitation.

My eyes rounded. "Seriously?"

She nodded with conviction. "That man has the soul of a trash panda: adorable as fuck but scrappy and mean and will scratch your face off if you try to take shit away from him. Even when the things don't belong to him in the first place." She gave me a pointed look, and my cheeks heated.

My uncertain relationship with Angelo wasn't something I was ready to talk about—and definitely not to his gorgeous, kindhearted wife. So in an attempt to keep the conversation light, I automatically just asked the next thing that came to mind. "Gray?"

Then I cringed. Just saying his name made me sour.

"King Kong," Vee replied, oblivious to—or strategically ignoring—my mood shift. "Created for violence and destruction, built for killing, but with a heart of gold. He would do anything to protect his Ann Darrow, even if he only has the relationship skills of an overgrown ape."

Wow. I dropped my gaze to the bedspread. "Fuck," I whispered. "Now I'm crying again." Tears ran down my cheeks, despite my efforts to hold them at bay, and Vee launched herself across the space to hug me.

"I'm sorry, Billie! Don't cry. I was trying to be funny. I'm hopeless at this." She petted my hair as she talked, and *that* brought a smile to my face.

"It's fine, I'm fine; let's just talk about anything *but* Bellerose for a while. Have you been in touch with Giana at all?" I hadn't forgotten her girlfriend, who'd been sent into hiding after Vee narrowly escaped her family.

She gave a sad shake of her head, returning to her own bed once more. "No. I wanted to, of course. When I saw the tour schedule, I thought maybe... But she's safe right now, and I want her to stay that way, at least until things get worked out with the Riccis and my father. It's just his style to have her raped and tortured to hurt me. I can't risk that."

I wrinkled my nose in disgust. "Are all mafia families so..."

"Cruel? Power hungry? Misogynistic?" She offered all the words I'd been thinking, and I nodded. "Yep. Pretty much. They're all run by men who have been raised to believe that *no one* is superior to them, no one is even equal. Power is *everything*, and fear is the best motivation. What better way to control your lesbian daughter than to threaten rape?"

Bile burned in my throat. "That's disgusting. You're his *child*."

Vee shook her head. "No, I'm his failure. I had an older brother, who was my father's glory. The *male heir*. When I was only four years old and Matty was twelve, he got shot and killed by a rival gang trying to move in on my father's business deals."

I sucked in a gasp, my heart breaking for the world Vee had been raised in.

"Despite my father's very best efforts—and believe

me, he tried—no other boys were born to his line. It was just me. So his only option was to arrange an advantageous marriage that could strengthen the family in another way." Her smile was warm and not at all resentful like I'd have been. "I definitely hit the mafia marriage lottery with A."

She had a good point there. "What will you do once this is all over? Will you start a new life with Giana somewhere?"

She tipped her head, considering, then gave a small headshake. "No. The mafia is in my blood. My future is in Siena, for better or worse. I just have to hedge my bets with A and hope he can bring positive changes."

I hadn't expected that, but just because it wouldn't be my choice didn't mean she was wrong. Just that she was a whole lot braver, and stronger, than she looked.

We settled in for our movies and both fell asleep covered in popcorn. When we woke up late the next morning, I had crushed popcorn embedded into my cheek and moaned about how much it hurt while Vee laughed at me.

She wasn't going to the concert—too afraid Ricci goons would see her and report back to the Altissimo leader—but she helped me get dressed and ready to go. Part of me just wanted to crawl back into bed and continue our girl-bonding, but I couldn't miss this concert. It was Angelo's first appearance as part of Bellerose, and anticipation fluttered through me with every breath.

I refused to miss the concert, but I didn't need to hang around any longer than necessary. Not while my fractured memories still screamed at me that Grayson had killed my parents, tried to kill me, and did kill my baby in the process. So I skipped sound check and had security deliver me to the venue right as they were running on stage after the opening band.

Rhett spotted me in the wings as he reached his mark and immediately ran back over.

"Uh, aren't you supposed to be starting?" I spluttered, pointing to where Jace was picking up the mic and asking the screaming crowd "How you doing, Dublin?"

Rhett just smirked and cupped my face between his hands, guitar loose at his back, hanging by the strap. "Hey babe," he said in a husky voice. "I missed you."

The way he kissed me almost made me forget where we were, and my body melted against him for a moment. Then the harsh thud of Grayson's drums jerked us back to reality, and I gave Rhett a push. "Go," I ordered with a laugh. "Make music, Zep. You're a rock star, remember?"

He dragged his lip piercing between his teeth,

giving me a hungry look, and cupped his dick to rearrange things. "To be continued, Thorn!"

"Definitely," I agreed, but he was already jogging back across the stage with his guitar in hand.

"Ah, there he is. Rhett Silver, ladies and gentlemen..." Jace drawled the intro into his mic while the crowd hooted and hollered. "Fashionably late, but better late than never, bro."

Rhett just flashed a toothy grin and extended his middle finger at Jace. Fucking rock stars.

Jace gave Angelo an intro, which saw the screams reach a deafening pitch, then he called for a moment of silence in respect for Flo. More than a few sobs were heard then, and my chest tightened with grief. She'd deserved better than the ending she got. I could still see her murder in my mind clear as day, how effortlessly that knife had slipped across her throat. The blood. So much blood.

Wrapping my arms around myself, I sat on an equipment case to watch the first song Bellerose launched into. It was an old one and one I'd heard them practicing at Grayson's house earlier in the week, but it sounded all wrong.

"What the fuck?" someone asked from nearby, and I glanced over to see the new tour manager, Hannah, scowling at the stage. She flicked a glance at me, then sighed. "Damn it."

I frowned. "What?"

"They're all out of sync. Grayson started quicker than they usually play, and Angelo isn't keeping up. Rhett and Jace are just confused, trying to smooth it out. They're a fucking mess, and I can't say I'm shocked after that flight." Her pointed look said she was holding me at least partly responsible for the state of Bellerose tonight. She wasn't angry or accusing, but facts were facts.

Unsure what exactly I could do to help, I just tucked my knees up and tried to enjoy the music. But now that she'd pointed it out, I couldn't stop hearing their mistakes.

After a few more songs, they seemed to level out and find their groove, and the vibes throughout the venue picked up markedly. But then on "Sweet Destruction" they lost it again. Grayson was a picture of frustration as he belted out the percussion, and Angelo almost seemed to be competing with Rhett for attention. It was cringe-worthy, and I wasn't the only one who noticed.

Jace apparently reached the end of his tether, because when that song ended, he announced that they were taking a quick break. It hadn't been planned into the set, but he just put the mic back on its stand and walked off stage, leaving the crew to frantically run around dimming lights and cutting sound.

They'd exited the stage to the opposite side, so I couldn't hear what he was snapping at the rest of the band. Based on his furious gestures, though, I had a fair idea. He glanced across the stage, locking eyes with me, and whatever he was saying trailed off.

I shrugged and gave a sympathetic gesture. Like... *I'm sorry your band is a shit show, but Gray is the one at fault here, dude.* Nevertheless... *pull it together, Jace! This is your band; kick some asses, and get everyone on the same page!*

He held my gaze for an intense moment, then smiled and nodded. *Thank you,* he mouthed, and confusion rippled through me. Thank you for *what*? Jace had already turned back to the band and snapped orders with a whole excited vibe to his movements. They *all* looked my way, and a trickle of anxiety ran down my spine. What the fuck just happened?

"Jace!" I called out as they all returned to the stage. I had a bad feeling.

He flashed me a grin. "I've got this, Rose," he called back. Then he signaled for the crew to raise the lights once more, and Grayson started tapping out a rhythm I didn't recognize. Was it a new song? Something he and

Rhett had worked on while I was in the hospital, maybe?

Then when Rhett joined in, recognition flooded through me like a tidal wave. My jaw dropped, and disbelief sucked all the air out of my lungs.

"This is new," Hannah commented, frowning her confusion. "I like it, but Brenda never mentioned they were revealing a new album track."

I raked my fingers through my hair, gripping the strands in fury. "They're *not!*" I protested in a horrified voice. "That's not their fucking song!" It was mine. The one I'd started at our trailer in the woods. The one I'd *specifically* told Jace he couldn't have.

That *motherfucker!*

I was going to kill him. Jace Adams, RIP. Death by Billie.

twenty-two

ANGELO

Jace was lucky that I had an ear for music. It only took me a few seconds to find my place in his *random new song that I'd never fucking heard.* For once, tonight, I was thankful to not be the lead guitar. It would have been a disaster. Way more of a disaster than some of our songs had already been.

But despite the few fuckups we'd experienced tonight, it had also been one of the best nights of my life. The intensity of stepping out onto the stage in front of thousands of screaming people—people who were screaming *my name*, since apparently word had gotten around already about my involvement via some blog site—was more than I'd ever imagined.

I'd spent a lot of time picturing how my life would have gone if I'd just followed Jace and my dreams. My visions had looked a lot like this, with music, concerts, screaming fans... and Billie waiting for us in the wings.

The *Billie* part was always the most bittersweet memory and dream. Billie, Jace, and I... we were a trio, stronger together, and it fucked with my head so much that we'd lost years by not recognizing the real truth of that. Apart, we'd each been living half a life, and that had never been more obvious than now. Now that we were back together.

When we finished the song, it was clear that Jace had just unveiled a brand-new hit. The crowd lost their mind, screaming for us to play it again, begging, even, as they all but dropped to their knees across the entire stadium. A buzz crossed my skin, the hairs standing up on my arms at the pure electricity of this moment.

"Thank you, Dublin," Jace shouted into his mic, always the showman. "That's our new single, "Desperate to Save," and it will be our first debut off our next album. If you want to hear it again, you know where to find it."

The screams were deafening, and my fingers moved across the strings, adding music to the cheers. The others joined me a moment later, each band member with their own personal touch, and fuck... we actually made beautiful music together when we weren't at each other's throats. Even Grayson looked more relaxed, easing the death grip he'd had on his sticks all night.

Rhett picked a direction and morphed us into another Bellerose hit—one of their older numbers, but definitely a crowd favorite—and this time none of us missed a fucking beat. We'd found our groove, and now it was like we'd been playing together for our entire lives.

Jace caught my eye, and I swore to fuck that big bastard's voice got even smoother as he fought for composure. He was emotional. I was fucking emotional.

This was the fruition of dreams that had been built by boys, and we were now men.

When the concert was done, the buzz in my veins was like nothing I'd ever felt before. When we swept off the stage after the encore, the crowd's screams continuing as if there were no end in sight, I was the first to reach Bella. After handing my bass off to a stagehand, I had her up in my arms in seconds, as I wrapped myself around her and let out a whoop. "Holy fuck," I burst out. "Holy fucking fuck."

As I swung her around, the pain in my knee was nonexistent under the adrenaline slamming through me. Billie let out a low laugh and smacked me on the shoulder. "Stop, Angel! You'll make me throw up if you keep that up. Not to mention you're still injured."

I slowed, even though my pulse raced inside of me, and I pulled back to see her beautiful face. Beautiful, tired, and filled with all the sadness in the world. "You were amazing," she said, before I could ask her if she was okay, stupid question as it was. "I have waited a lifetime to see you both on stage like that, and it was, honestly, more than I ever dreamed."

"For me too, Bella," I told her, adjusting my hold so I could keep her against me but also wipe away the single tear that escaped the corner of her eye. Leaning in, I pressed my lips to her cheek and whispered, "Do you want me to kill him? I know people."

A snort of sobbing laughter came from her. "You idiot. You *are* people."

It didn't escape my attention that she hadn't exactly turned my offer down regarding Grayson's demise, but I knew her well enough to realize that, despite her anger at him, she loved that dangerous asshole and it would destroy a part of her if he were gone from this world. For that, and out of my own respect for him, I wasn't going to interfere. At least not yet.

Billie wiggled against me, and I reluctantly released

her. Since waking in the hospital, I'd lost my ability to separate myself from her, and our time on the plane had only made it worse. It felt like she was mine again, and fuck if letting her go, especially when she jumped straight into Rhett's arms, didn't tear me up inside.

A hand landed on my shoulder. "It's okay, bro. I know the feeling." Jace's smile grew bigger. "And while I enjoy seeing you suffer, I also suffer, so I'm not going to rub it in."

"You'll be rubbing one out tonight," I snarled, feeling a slide of anger in my gut.

"Don't I fucking know it," Jace groaned, before he shook his head and stopped looking Billie's way. "For real, though. Thanks for tonight. I've never let myself think about us being on stage together, because I already had too many shattered dreams. But fuck... it was better than I'd expected."

His words brought back my excitement, and as I rubbed a hand over my face, I attempted to pull myself together. "It was everything. My father will probably try to murder me for this, but I would do it all the exact same way again, no matter the consequences."

"We'll figure out something regarding Giovanni," Jace said, his expression souring. He'd never liked my father, and the feeling was mutual. But Jace was no longer a punk-ass kid. He was rich and famous, and he had a lot of resources as well. It wasn't an even fight, but with me by his side, the odds were a hell of a lot better than we'd ever had.

Something to consider once we'd finished this tour.

The celebration backstage picked up until it was near deafening. Billie was right in the middle of it all, some of the dark clouds in her eyes fading as she grew more excited—helped in part by Grayson stalking off and disappearing not long after leaving the stage.

"Party tonight!" Jace shouted, a bottle of Champagne in his hand as he shot the top off, sending the liquid bursting free. "VIP is set up in Club Lovin'. The limos leave from the hotel in two hours."

He chugged from the bottle before handing it to me, and despite my absolute fucking distaste for this fairy piss of a drink, I took a swig. I was a rock star today, and those bastards were messy and free.

For the first time in my life, I was going to be the same.

When we left the venue, fans lined the drive out, and when our SUVs sped away, people were screaming and trying to jump over the barrier. "Holy shit," I said, shaking my head. Jace, Billie, and Rhett were in the same car, and they just laughed. "Is it always like this?"

Jace dropped his head back, a broad smile on his face as he took another drink from the bottle. "Every fucking time. It's like a shot to my heart and my fucking dick."

Billie snorted. "Well, that explains the first night I came back to your band suite. That chick had vocals that gave you a run for your money." She let out a low laugh before her voice grew breathier. "*Jace, oh Jace. Fuck me, fuck me you fucking rock star.*"

Rhett laughed so loudly that it drowned out the end of Billie's words, and Jace just shook his head. "What can I say, groupies love some cock. Jace's cock, to be more specific."

"The fact that you speak about yourself in the third person," I added drily, "tells me that you've been famous for too long. Someone needs to beat that shit out of you."

"You can fucking try, asshole" he shot back, and instead of wanting to beat him, I was resisting the urge to hug him. Having my best friend back, even if his ego was the size of the stadium we'd just played in, was knocking my emotions around.

Jace finished the bottle then, dropping it to the ground before he opened a small panel in the middle of the car. From there he pulled a decanter and four crystal tumblers. "We need to toast tonight," he said, dropping a shot of whiskey into each. "This was a long time coming, and we actually killed it."

"I should kill you," Billie said shortly when she grabbed her glass. "You used my fucking song without my permission. I expressly told you that you couldn't."

Jace swiveled in his seat to meet her glare. "What? We had a moment. You totally gave me permission."

Billie spluttered on her first sip of the expensive whiskey. I'd already tasted it, and it was smooth, so her reaction was all about Jace's comment. "What moment? You looked at me, and I offered my commiseration and told you to sort your fucking band out."

"Exactly," Jace exclaimed. "Sort it out. And I did, so thanks for your help. Congratulations, you wrote another number one."

"You'll get the full songwriting credit," Rhett added, leaning forward to get his glass. "Because our girl is one talented-as-fuck composer."

Some of Billie's anger faded as she smiled in his direction. "I really do love that side of music. I can't imagine going out on stage like you did, though. I'd probably die of fright."

Rhett lifted his glass, and all of us followed suit, clinking them together. "Nah, that's the best fucking part. Like flying without drugs. There's no feeling to compare." He paused for a second, before he shot Billie a wink. "Except maybe being insid—"

Jace growled and punched his bandmate, his

whiskey sloshing around the car, but no one appeared to care as they tussled. Billie just shook her head and shifted to the side to let them have their moment. We both sipped our whiskey, and I was relieved that the Champagne had been ditched. At least for now.

"Never a dull moment," I commented, and Billie's smile was filled with memories and amusement.

"You have no idea. No freaking idea."

I didn't, but part of me hoped that, for just a little while, I would.

When we arrived back, our security's cars boxed us in so that they surrounded us as we emerged into the secure underground parking lot of the hotel. Down here, there were no fans around, but they still didn't take any chances.

I'd already scoped out the place, and it looked clear from my angle, which didn't mean my gun wasn't primed and ready to go if needed. I didn't trust anyone else with security for me or those I loved, and if I knew him at all, Grayson had already done his own sweep of this parking lot.

We were as secure as we'd ever be.

"Meet you back here in an hour," Jace told everyone when we reached the shared living space of his suite. "Club Lovin' is prepped and ready for us."

Rhett scooped Billie up and hauled her off to his room, shouting as he went, "Don't wait up for us!"

Jace shouted after him. "I'll drag you out by your fucking balls, bro. Don't be late."

"Always trying to get your hands on my balls," Rhett laughed as he slammed his door shut.

Muttering under his breath, Jace wandered into his room, and I went in search of Vee. Ensuring she was safe was my responsibility.

The security stepped aside when I reached her door, and I entered without knocking. Vee was sprawled back on the bed, and she jumped up as soon as I entered the room and closed the door behind me. "A!" she screamed, throwing herself at me. I caught her with ease, accepting her hug and dropping her back to the floor. "Billie video-chatted me during some of your songs, and it was incredible. I'm so damn proud of you."

Fuck, I was starting to understand what Rhett meant about flying without drugs.

"Thanks, Vee. It was amazing. I'm not going to lie, it was a high I've never felt working for my father."

Vee led me to the bed, pulling me down to sit with her. "I've been thinking about that a lot tonight," she said softly. "About how happy you've seemed over the past few weeks. This is where you belong, Angelo. This is the life you should have always been living." She paused briefly, before looking up at me from under her long eyelashes. "With Jace and Billie."

I couldn't even argue with her. "Yeah, but sometimes that's all we get, the dreams of what should have been, versus the reality that we must live."

Vee shook her head, a stubborn expression I recognized very well crossing her features. "I refuse to accept that. I, personally, love the mafia world. And I think I'd be damned good at running the family, with a hell of a lot more brains than is currently being used. You, on the other hand, do not have the stomach for it. You do what must be done, but it doesn't fill your blood with passion. *This* is your passion, right here, with Bellerose. I will figure out how we can have both. I will figure it out, A."

Hugging her to my side, I released a long breath. "Maybe there is a way. If we're smart in how we force hands and reveal secrets, we might be able to rearrange the top level of our families—rearrange to our advantage."

Vee clapped her hands together before she leaned up to press a kiss to my cheek. "My thoughts exactly. We have a small reprieve now, hiding out in Europe. They'll think they've won, but I say we use this time to make some plans of our own."

My wife had not been arrogant when she said she had the skills to take over as the head of our family. Not that they'd *ever* let a woman hold the role, but I knew no one more suited. Beneath the beauty and kindness Valentina could display, there was a coldly calculating and intelligent woman. She didn't mind getting her hands dirty, and she could outshoot me any day of the week. Those old fucks controlling our lives had no idea what they'd unleashed by trying to kill her and destroying the last threads of her loyalty.

No idea at all.

twenty-three

BILLIE

Tonight was like living a dream. A dream from a million years ago, when I'd been so sure my future was with Jace and Angelo in all ways. As their best friend, lover, wife... their forever.

Of course, forever had turned out to be much shorter than I'd ever expected, but tonight it almost felt like none of those years apart had happened. If it weren't for this shit with Grayson—who had fucking disappeared after the concert, and despite my anger, I still hated not knowing where he was—then I'd be the happiest bitch in Dublin tonight.

"You ready, baby?" Rhett called through the door, and I popped the last coat of scarlet over my lips and gave my reflection a once over. I'd chosen a short and fitted, to every curve, red dress tonight. Like, Christmas-red, so bright that no one would miss me in the crowd. It was freezing in Dublin, so I added over-the-knee black boots and a long black jacket that I'd ditch when we got to the club.

My hair was curled and tousled down my back, and I'd gone much heavier than usual on my makeup, from dark eyeshadow to bright red lips that matched the dress. I was dressed to destroy, and I was well enough versed in therapy now to know there were multiple reasons for needing all the extra armor tonight. Reasons I was not interested in exploring, because I really wanted to let loose and have a good time.

"Ready," I announced, opening the door. I left the mess of makeup and hair products next to the sink, knowing Rhett wouldn't care because he had almost as many products as me. Mostly for his hawk.

When the door swung fully open, he was framed in it, and I almost laughed at the comical way he froze as his mouth fell open. "Jesus," he breathed. "Billie. Are you trying to fucking kill me?"

A genuine laugh burst up from my chest, and it was weird to feel happy after so many days of sadness. It reminded me that, on occasion, it was okay to push sadness aside and enjoy these moments. Life was too short not to.

"You look fairly delicious yourself," I purred, taking in his boots, dark, ripped jeans, and black Bellerose band shirt, which was tight enough to showcase his muscles. Stepping closer to him, the heels of my boots clicked on the tiles, only to be silenced when I made it onto carpet. Rhett was still a decent shot taller than me, so he ducked his head and pressed his lips to mine. When he pulled away, leaving me a little breathless, I was happy to see that my no-smudge lipstick was living up to its promise.

"Is everyone ready to leave?" I asked.

Rhett took a second to answer, his eyes dragging over the fit of my dress before he exhaled loudly and ran a hand over his hawk, messing it up a touch. "They're ready," he finally said, "but I'm starting to think that a party right here sounds so much more appealing."

Fuck, this boy was really good for a girl's ego.

"Plenty of time for that later," I reminded him, pressing closer again. "Tonight, I want to drink and dance and forget about the past few days." And years.

"You got it, baby," he said, wrapping one arm around me so that he was half carrying me toward the door. "Dancing is the next best thing to fucking. I'm going to enjoy both."

Shit, so was I.

When we made it out into the main hall, I was surprised to see Vee standing there alone. Well, as alone as one could be with a dozen or more security standing along the hall.

She was dressed in a knee-length black dress, which was as tight and fitted as mine, but without the attention-grabbing color. Her dark hair was perfectly curled, her makeup heavy, too, and I as I gave her a hug, I said, "You look fucking gorgeous, but aren't you worried about being seen out?"

She returned my hug with force. "I've recently decided that life is too short to stay in hiding," she said quickly, before she leaned back and took in my outfit. "You look stunning! These boys are going to have their hands full keeping you safe tonight."

Jace, who'd stepped out of his room in time to hear that, let out a husky laugh. "A task we've been doing since Billie was fourteen and grew tits."

Asshole. "If I recall correctly, the only ones interested in my tits were you and Angel."

"That's what we wanted you to think," he murmured, stepping closer to me. Vee moved out of his way, and then it was just Jace before me. Rhett remained a few steps to the side, giving us this moment.

My head spun at Jace's presence, as per usual, and I attempted to force myself to look away from how delicious he was. Attempted and failed. Like Rhett, he was dressed all in black, right down to the boots that made him look even taller than usual. He wore dark, distressed denim jeans and a fitted, long-sleeved black shirt that he'd pushed up on both forearms, so we all got the view of his perfectly toned and tanned skin. That and the tousled blond hair gave contrast to the all-black ensemble.

Bastard used his sex appeal as a weapon.

Both painful and beautiful to orbit within.

When he leaned in and pressed a kiss to my cheek, I held my fucking breath like a teenager. "That's going to take some getting used to," I breathed as he pulled away, leaving a tingling spot on my face where he'd touched.

"We've got time," he reminded me, our gazes holding for a long moment as a lifetime of emotion flashed between us. Whatever had happened on the plane after my breakdown had completely turned Jace's attitude toward me... toward us... around. This was *my Jace.*

It terrified me to fall into it, though, because I wouldn't survive the fall out of it. Not again.

When the tension had my knees weaker than ever,

he finally allowed me some space, turning to get the others organized. "Come on, we need to head out. Grayson is going to meet us there."

Rhett returned to his spot on my right side, and Angelo emerged from Vee's room, freshly shaven, wearing a white button-down shirt and black slacks over shiny dress shoes. You could take the man out of the mafia but apparently not the other way around. Like Jace, though, he had that shirt rolled up along his forearms, and if a little drool escaped me, the sexy men in this room were the ones to blame.

Angelo didn't look like a rock star tonight; he looked like a sexy, dangerous businessman, and I was equally as into it. "Bella," he greeted me, "you are stunning. Red has always been your color." He leaned down to kiss my cheek as well, choosing the opposite side Jace had and leaving me with a burning brand on both sides of my face. Tonight was either going to be one of the best nights of my life or it would completely destroy me.

Instinct told me there would be no middle ground.

When we headed for our transportation, our security surrounded us, and I found myself thinking about Grayson. Jace had said he was meeting us at the club tonight, and I wasn't sure how I felt about it. On one hand, I wanted to know where he was and that he was safe; on the other, I wanted to enjoy this night and his presence was going to make that fucking hard.

Rhett reached out and took my hand, and I returned his squeeze. "My mission for you tonight, Thorn," he said softly as we reached the doors of their private elevator, "is to turn your brain off. It's one thing I love about you, the way your mind works, but sometimes it stops you from just enjoying the moment. The past and pain will wait for tomorrow; I promise you it will. Tonight is a celebration."

He was right, and I was determined to give it my all. "As long as you're with me," I said, beaming up at him because he just made me that fucking happy, "I'm going to have the best night."

He let out a low groan, leaning down once more to kiss the hell out of me. The cold chill of his piercing and the hot swipe of his tongue had my legs weak by the time we made it into the elevator.

Vee shot me a slow smile when I was able to focus again, and I also noticed that I had more than just Rhett's attention. Angel and Jace were watching me too, and suddenly, this small box felt even smaller.

Thank fuck the security guards were staring at the door and not witnessing all the testosterone floating around back here. Vee shuffled her way closer, wrapped her arm around me, and nudged Rhett out of the way a touch. She turned and whispered, "I know I'm gay, but this tension is doing things to me that I can't explain. It's like... I envy you this attention, and I'm also intrigued to see how you manage the four of them."

"Three," I shot back. I had no idea how I could ever get to this spot with Gray again. Then I cringed at how easily I'd just claimed Angelo.

Vee chuckled. "Whatever you say, gorgeous. Whatever you say. There's a reason they're called Bellerose. They belong to you."

They belong to you.

Damn, those words were going to live rent free in my head for a really long time.

The ride to Club Lovin' went quite smoothly, with everyone focusing on music, alcohol, and the small joint that Rhett produced from somewhere and passed around the limo. By the time we spilled out, heading for a private side entrance with a dozen or so security around us, I felt relaxed and buzzed at the same time.

My worries were firmly secured in the back of my mind, and the aim for the night was to keep them there.

The club was packed when we entered. Security and staff led us up to the private balcony area they had secured for Bellerose. A lot of their roadies were already there, but I didn't see any sign of Hannah. I wasn't sure if the temporary tour manager would be into this scene or not. Brave of her not to be here to keep an eye on the band, though.

Maybe Brenda had warned her Bellerose wouldn't take lightly to interference in their personal lives and to focus more on keeping the tour schedule running smoothly.

Our table ended up being right near the edge of the balcony that looked over to the packed main dance floor. Lights flashed in the darkness, and the beat was heavy and pumping. My body moved to the rhythm, and I wasn't the only one, with Rhett and Jace already finding the beat.

A huge tray of drinks waited for us in the center of the table, which was built like a giant ice bucket, and I reached out and snagged a pre-mixed vodka, happy to see that it was still firmly sealed. The last thing I wanted to worry about was some overzealous groupies trying to drug us so they could have their way with my boys.

The boys of Bellerose.

Another phrase that lived rent free in my head, thanks to that fucking blog.

Rhett settled in on one side of me, Vee on the other, and as Jace and Angelo took a spot opposite to where I was, I sucked in a long drink from the glass bottle in my hands. The vodka warmed me immediately, and the extra sugar in this sort of pre-mixed version spiked in my blood so fast that it felt like the buzz was immediate.

The first drink went down so easily, and I was very content to snuggle in next to Rhett while quietly eye-fucking Jace and Angelo, who were deep in conversation about something. It was unreal to see them side by side once more, so different in looks and yet the same in many ways, from their height to broad shoulders to that devilish fucking glint in their eyes when they were touching me.

I didn't know the truth about my parents any longer—that fight from my flashbacks was filled with so many missed details—but I owed them thanks for choosing just the right house to move into. That house —and it's neighbors—would shape my entire destiny, and while some of that was heartbreakingly destructive, other parts of it were perfection.

"Wanna dance?" Vee said suddenly, linking her arm through mine and pulling me up before I could answer. "This is my favorite song."

The VIP area had a smaller dance floor that was filled with quite a few people already, some I recognized and others I didn't. Vee led me over, and as we got closer, I caught sight of a giant shadow perched against one of the pillars near the entrance.

Grayson.

His expression was flat as he watched me pass, and whatever fizzle of happiness the alcohol had produced vanished as the shadowy memories of the fire forced themselves into my mind.

Tearing my gaze away, I sucked in a few deep breaths, following Vee without conscious thoughts of dancing any longer.

"Don't show him that you're affected," she said firmly, pulling me around and moving her body in time to the beat. "Forget Grayson for the night, and feel this fucking song."

She lifted her hands up in the air, and I tried to relax my stiff shoulders. I still held the second drink I'd grabbed from the table, so I chugged it half down to kickstart my buzz again, and eventually, I was able to relax again.

"Fuck yes," Vee yelled, hands in the air as she closed her eyes and moved her hips side to side. "Can't believe I almost died and missed this."

I couldn't believe it either.

Following suit, I closed my eyes and drank more vodka until the bottle was empty and I was finally feeling the beat. Strong hands landed on my hips, and I spun to find Angelo there, stepping in to dance with his wife and me.

Yeah, it was as fucking weird as it sounded.

Only he didn't even look at Vee, the darkly enticing stare reserved completely for me.

Before I knew what the hell I was doing, I stepped forward and threw myself into his arms.

Just like I'd done back at Grayson's when Angelo first returned from hospital, I hugged him with every part of me, and his groan as he lifted me off the ground had heat blooming in my center.

Hotter than any alcohol could produce.

"Bella," he rumbled, his lips landing on mine.

Our last kiss had been in anger, but this one was filled with so many emotions.

Pain, hope, lust, and... love.

Just like with Jace, we might have been apart, but the love had never gone anywhere.

It was a forever kind of love, and I was in big fucking trouble with all these men.

How did one survive without their heart?

I had so many more to lose now.

twenty-four

BILLIE

My kiss with Angelo lasted only a few hot, stolen moments, but that was long enough to shake me through to my core. When the song shifted, we naturally drifted apart as our bodies moved to the beat, and soon I found myself dancing—and grinding—on Rhett while a roaming waitress handed us Jell-o shots. When I turned around again, Angelo was nowhere to be seen. Nor was Vee.

An uncomfortable ribbon of anxiety wrapped around my chest, but I quickly convinced myself they'd just gone to get more drinks. Or pee. Or something. Besides, I was buzzed enough that it was easy to forget and just *lose myself* in the moment. The music, the lights, the drinks... Rhett's hands. I was so addicted to his touch I forgot where we were, until a camera flash lit the dancefloor near my face.

"Shit," Rhett sighed. "We should go. Too many cameras in here tonight."

Jace was sitting alone at our table, a drink in hand and a scowl set on his face. When Rhett asked where everyone was, Jace just shrugged and finished his drink with one gulp.

"We done?" he asked, rising from his seat with that shitty expression still creasing his brow.

I was easily drunk enough to start a fight with him over it, but sanity prevailed as I remembered the camera phones turned our direction. So I bit my tongue and let them lead me out of the club with Rhett's arm possessively draped over my shoulders.

More flashes seemed to go off as our security pulled up with a car, but maybe I was just being paranoid. Maybe it was just normal club lights? Jace was on his phone, his fingers flying over the screen as he waited for Rhett and me to get into the backseat before sliding in on my other side.

"Told the others that we're heading back to the hotel," he announced as our driver pulled away from the club. This car wasn't the spacious limo we'd all arrived in, just a standard, blacked-out SUV, which meant I was squished up in the tiny middle seat with two big, tattooed, sweaty rock stars on either side of me.

Could I *really* be blamed for having flashbacks of our one and only threesome? I was only human, and a tipsy one at that.

"And we're already up on *Dirty Truths*," Rhett groaned, snapping me out of my sexy thoughts. Apparently, his mind was firmly elsewhere as he glared down at his phone screen. "This time they're crediting the pictures to someone else who sent them in, so it gives us zero hints who's behind the blog."

"What's the story?" Jace asked, opening his own phone. "Bellerose plays a crappy show, then goes out to party? Not much of a—" He broke off when the page loaded. "Oh, I see."

"What?" I asked, peering over at his screen. Then I sighed heavily. "Ah. That."

Someone had snapped a picture of Angelo and I locked in a passionate embrace in the middle of the dance floor, and it was slapped right alongside a contrasting—or complimentary—picture of me and Rhett locking lips. Considering my distinctive dress, it was pretty obvious both kisses were from the same night.

"Fuck's sake," Rhett muttered.

Jace said nothing, just shifted his moody gaze out the window. I thought for a moment that Rhett was angry at me, but the way he gripped my knee reassured me it was the blog post—not my kiss with Angel—that had him shaking with rage.

No one spoke for the rest of the drive to the hotel, and my drunk buzz was nearly gone by the time our driver pulled up at the foyer. Jace hopped out first, then extended a hand to help me. I took it, grateful that I could avoid flashing my panties to anyone who might be looking. I'd been in more than enough gossip articles to last me a lifetime without pulling that classic move.

At least I had panties on, though.

As we entered the five-star hotel lobby, a red-haired guy jerked his chin to Rhett like he knew him. Rhett made a small sound of surprise, then kissed my hair and told me to head upstairs with Jace. He gave us a little push in the direction of the elevators, and Jace touched a hand to the small of my back to keep me moving.

"Who was that?" I asked, frowning, as we stepped into the elevator that a bellboy held open.

Jace waited until the doors had closed, leaving us alone, before he replied. "Dunno. Weed dealer, probably."

His tone was hard and cold, like he was mad at me. I

wrinkled my nose and folded my arms under my breasts. "What's your problem, Adams? You were all forgiveness and *thanks for the song* earlier, and now you're acting like I just kicked your puppy."

His head swiveled, his eye twitching with outrage as he stared at me. Then he slammed his hand on the emergency stop button, and the elevator shuddered to a complete standstill.

"My *problem*?" he exclaimed, incredulous for some reason. "Is that a joke?"

I blinked. "Um. No?" I was missing something big here, I was almost sure of it. Maybe I was still a little tipsier than I thought I was, because my brain wasn't putting the pieces together.

"You're *unbelievable*!" he roared, throwing up his hands as he whirled to face me. Two steps forward and he was in my personal space, backing me up into the corner of the elevator. "Are you really that oblivious, Billie? You have no clue why I'm pissed off right now? None at all? You're a smart girl, Rose. Think about it."

I swallowed heavily, unable to tear my eyes away from his as he stared right into my soul. Wetting my lips, I tried to think rationally. When had he shifted from easygoing and relaxed to moody and tense? The blog? No, he'd already been grouchy before we got in the car. So it had to have been something at the club...

"You're angry that I kissed Angel," I said in a quiet, uncertain voice. It couldn't have been about Rhett, since he kissed me all the time and gave zero fucks who was around to witness it. But Angel... that was a new thing. Unexpected, but not in a bad way.

Jace made a feral noise. "Bingo."

My brow dipped, and my anger flared. "Why? What the fuck does it matter to you? Or are you just pissed that it was so public and now the blog is focusing on my love life instead of your *surprise* new album track? That you fucking stole, I might add."

Jace's face twisted with fury, and his fist slammed into the mirror behind me. "Jesus, Rose! You're not that fucking naïve, so don't play games. It *matters* because..." He trailed off with a sound of frustration, his searing gaze dropping away from my face as he bowed his head.

"Jace," I whispered, reaching out to touch his cheek and bring his eyes back up. "What is going on with us? I don't even know where we stand. Ever since..." *Ever since the plane, when you and Angelo comforted me like only the two of you could. When the three of us shared the pain of our collective loss and let go of some resentment over it...*

"You really don't know where we stand, Rose?" His voice was hoarse and pained. "I miss you. I always have.

And *fuck*, watching you kiss Angel like everything was forgiven, like the last eight years never happened, it made me so jealous I could have punched through the wall. Every time I have to watch Rhett touch you, kiss you, *love* you, makes me want to commit murder. Every. Damn. Time. And he's my best friend. Do you know what that does to me, Rose? I'm torn up inside, feeling homicidal toward these guys I consider my brothers, and you want nothing to do with me. We occasionally fuck, when the bickering gets too much, and then you act like nothing even happened. Meanwhile, I'm slowly losing my mind and my heart, and you..." He laughed bitterly "You just turn up looking like a fucking dream, then kiss Angel... instead of me."

My heart pounded so hard it was like I'd just run a marathon, my fight-or-flight reflex filling me with adrenaline as Jace spoke. My palm still rested on his cheek, and I couldn't tear it away even if I'd wanted to. But I didn't. I wanted to give in to the tension between us and show Jace that I cared more than he realized.

That thought *terrified* me, though. Threesomes and casual ménage was one thing. Falling utterly in love with four guys all at once? That was a whole different league. Hell, it was a whole different *sport*. Not to mention how destroyed I'd be if Jace broke my heart this time.

I stayed silent too long, and Jace blew out a frustrated sigh, shaking his head. "Forget it. Mixing weed and alcohol fucks me up; I probably won't remember any of this tomorrow."

That casual dismissal cut through me like a serrated knife, and I grabbed his neck before he could turn away.

"Jace, don't—" My protest cut into a gasp as his mouth slammed into mine. It wasn't what I'd intended when I grabbed him, but I also wasn't pushing him away. Not by a long shot. My back arched as his tongue dove into my mouth, like my body was actively trying to melt into him. But Jace kept his hands gripping the elevator rails on either side of my waist like he didn't trust what he'd do if more than his lips touched me.

It was infuriating.

"Jace..." This time I said his voice with a moan, and his control snapped. His hands gripped my waist, boosting me up until my butt rested on the corner of the handrails, bringing me up to his height for kissing.

I hooked a leg around him, pulling him closer, then gave a breathy gasp as his hardness ground against my core. He was already so turned on, and after everything he'd just said, after all the vulnerability he'd just exposed, my better judgment flew right out the window.

"Dammit, Rose," he groaned against my lips, his

body rocking against me like he wanted to make me come through our clothes. "We can't keep doing this. I want to fuck you so bad. Right here."

I licked his lips, then kissed him to reel him back in. "Do it," I whispered when we both separated for air. "Fuck me, Jace. I want to feel you inside me again." To encourage him, I quickly tugged his belt open and popped the button on his jeans. Fuck good judgement, I wanted my Jace back.

"Shit," he breathed, "I never could say no to you."

He slid his hands beneath my dress, hitching it up over my hips as I palmed his cock. With frantic motions, Jace tugged the crotch of my panties aside and plunged his fingers inside me, pumping them a few times as he locked his lips back on mine. He kissed me deep, his tongue matching the pace of his hand, then tugged my lower lip with his teeth as I groaned my encouragement.

A moment later he switched his fingers for his cock, not even bothering to take my underwear off. He just held the lace aside as he pushed in, and my whole body shivered with ecstasy.

"Oh fuck," I gasped as he filled me with his dick. "Jace, you feel so good."

He pulled out slightly, then thrust back in hard

enough to make me cry out. "Because, Rose, this pussy was made for me. Remember our first time?"

Christ. How could I forget? We'd been dumb kids, messing around with shit we didn't understand... like love and *forever*. But somehow, Jace had made it magical. It was the kind of shit I could never forget, no matter how much bad blood passed between us.

Moaning, I pushed his t-shirt up, revealing those washboard abs that had been on way too many billboards. I wanted more. I wanted him naked, in bed, all mine. But right now, I'd settle for what I could get. Not that it was a hardship.

"Maybe this needs to be my new plan," he grunted as he fucking *railed* me against the corner of the elevator. His teeth brushed over the delicate skin of my neck like he was considering ripping my throat out. "Fuck you so good you can't remember all the cruel shit I've said. Make you come so hard and so often all you think when you hear my name is how *good* I make you feel."

That sounded like a great plan. Foolproof. I liked the new plan.

"Rose, *fuck*..." Jace grabbed my ass with his huge hands, pulling me tighter against him and fucking me deeper.

The pleasure that had been curling through me from the moment we started kissing ramped up, the intensity so much it was making me dizzy. "Jace, I'm gonna come already," I gasped. "If your intent is to punish me, now's the time to walk away."

Please don't. Please, please, *stop turning your back on me. Just let us start to heal. One orgasm at a time.*

As if he could read my mind, he brushed a soft kiss over my lips as one of his hands drifted to my neck and held my jaw. "I'm done with that, Billie. You don't deserve punishment. Not from me. Not ever. All I can do now is apologize."

If his version of an apology was mind-blowing sex and an earth-shattering climax... he was doing a damn good job of it. I shattered to pieces a moment later, crying out against his kisses and thrashing in his arms. My orgasm triggered him, and with a few exasperated curses, he came a second later, his cock twitching inside me as he pumped me full of his release.

For a moment, we just stayed as we were, him buried deep inside me, my legs around his waist, and our foreheads resting on one another's shoulder as we gasped for breath. Then static crackled through the elevator car just a split second before a ding sounded from the speaker.

"Um, this is Joran from hotel security. We notice the elevator hasn't moved in quite some time. Is everything okay in there?"

My face flushed with heat, panic gripping my lungs as I pushed Jace away. As smoothly as possible, I tugged my panties and dress back into place as I slid to the floor.

Jace frowned at me while casually buckling his jeans. "Yeah, fine," he drawled, trying to catch my eye. I was mortified, though. It was pretty fucking obvious that *Joran from hotel security* knew exactly what had just gone down in here. A suspicion that was confirmed when I spotted a security camera in the corner opposite us with a green LED light on.

First I kiss Angelo and Rhett in a packed night club, and now I'm caught fucking Jace in the hotel elevator? They weren't the Boys of Bellerose, I was the *Whore of Bellerose*. Fucking hell, what had I been thinking?

I hadn't been. That was the problem.

Tense and ashamed, I silently pressed the stop-release button, putting the elevator in motion once more.

Jace gave a frustrated sigh, scrubbing his hand over his face. Then when the doors opened a moment later, he just stood there instead of getting out.

"Jace," I murmured, pausing just outside the elevator doors. "What are you doing?"

His head lifted, his eyes meeting mine with an anguished glare. "Heading back out. Maybe if I pick up a Bellerose groupie, I can finally fuck someone who doesn't look like she hates herself when we're done."

Not waiting for my answer, he smacked the door close button and I stood there utterly frozen in shock as he disappeared from sight.

I'd fucked up. Again. Story of my goddamn life at this point.

twenty-five

RHETT

The flight to Edinburgh was tense. Grayson, who'd only appeared a few minutes before takeoff, was right at the back, a silent watcher, leaving everyone else to their drama.

I wasn't sure what his plan with Billie was—he wasn't talking to any of us—but my brother would only exist on the fringes for so long. He was giving her time now, but it wouldn't be long before he forced her to listen to his explanation. One all of us were ready to hear.

Jace showed up completely wasted, half-carried by his security, and I would have smashed his fucking face in if he didn't already look all kinds of fucked up.

Getting back to the hotel room last night, after securing some quality weed, to find Billie sobbing into her pillow had fired me up. If Jace had been somewhere close by, there would have been a new fucking story for *Dirty Truths*.

"He went out for groupies because I screwed up," my little Thorn had sobbed, and while I very much doubted Jace was doing anything other than drowning his sorrows—the bastard was totally in love with my girl—I was still pissed on her behalf, especially since she was once again blaming herself for what was no doubt mutually questionable behavior.

She was curled up by my side now, and I adjusted the blanket over her, letting her doze. It wasn't a long flight today, just a touch over an hour, but Billie was wiped out. I made a note to contact Brenda and make sure that Dr. Candace had a video appointment set up.

Jace was a large part of the demons in Billie's past, and just when she was learning to deal with them wasn't the time to take ten steps back.

Fuck, I should really schedule my own appointment with the doc. Maybe I would ask Brenda for that.

Shooting off a text to our manager, who wouldn't get it until we landed, I relaxed into the seat and brushed my hand gently up and down Billie's hair.

Angelo, who was across with Vee, caught my eye and mouthed, "Is she okay?"

I shrugged because what the fuck could I say? She wasn't okay. None of us were fucking okay, but we were well used to existing within the darker slice of life and we'd always gotten through it before.

We'd get through this as well.

There was no other option.

Billie remained asleep, only waking when we touched down. "Shit," she rasped, sitting up and rubbing a hand over her face. "I was totally out of it."

Pushing back some of her tangled hair, I forced a smile. When life was at its darkest, you had to smile the brightest. Sometimes it even tricked your mind into believing that true happiness was just around the corner. "We'll be at the hotel soon, sweetheart. You can keep sleeping there."

She shook her head, before a yawn stretched her face briefly. "Shit, fuck. No, I'm awake. I want to see Edinburgh too. This is my first time out of America, and it might be my last. I don't want to miss anything on this whirlwind tour."

There was no fucking way this would be her last. I'd take her around the damn world as many times as she wanted. We had one last album owed to our record label, and then we could take some time off and reassess our priorities. Mine, for fucking one, was no longer Big Noise. If Jace didn't wrangle us up a better label, then I'd be going elsewhere.

When we landed, cars were on the tarmac waiting for us, and we were on our way to the hotel in no time. Not worrying about luggage or going through anything other than customs was a perk of this life. Billie was in the car with me, Angelo, and Vee. She had her face all but pressed to the window, watching the otherworldly charm of Edinburgh pass us by.

It wasn't hard to imagine this exact version of the city existing hundreds of years ago. So much history and so many ancient buildings could be seen, right up to the castle on the top of the hill. Our hotel was one of the nicest in the region, with an absolute world-class view of the castle from every window.

At least that's what Brenda had told us when she was going over our schedules just before we left.

Billie's face was filled with enchantment when she finally turned to me as we entered the parking lot. "Please tell me we can figure out a way to get out and explore this city. I absolutely have to know every freaking story and event that took place in these cobbled streets."

Angelo let out a low chuckle. "Never thought my

Bella would be a history buff. Didn't you used to fall asleep in history class at least four times a week?"

She glared for a beat, before it morphed into a resigned laugh. "Look, what can I say. Sixteen-year-old Billie was interested in *other things*. History really didn't make the cut."

I recognized that look on Angelo's face, and it was lucky that I'd figured out a way to be cool with our arrangement because he was a man who clearly knew what *other things* she'd been into back then. But their history together was the only factor that made me jealous. Not that nineteen-year-old me would have been any fucking good for the sweet-faced sixteen-year-old Billie. I'd been a messed-up kid then, and I would have brought that into her life. Now, I'd learned to keep the past locked down hard so it didn't destroy my future.

But if I truly wanted a good future, I needed to deal with the past in a constructive way. Not destructive.

Hence my text about Dr. Candace.

Brenda replied as we reached the set of rooms reserved for us.

Momager: Got it all set up, Silver. You will have the appointment after Billie. Proud of you.

That *proud of you* hit fucking harder than it should. My trauma needed Candace, that was for shit's sure.

Silver: Thanks, mom!

She hated it when I called her mom, so of course, I had to do it at least every second time we communicated via text.

Momager: *Fuck you, brat.*

She was totally a mom to more than just her new little crotch fruit. Even if she was only a couple of years older than Gray.

"Everything okay?" Billie asked, glancing down at the phone in my hand.

I gave a reassuring smile and smacked a kiss on her lips. "Absolutely. Brenda was confirming your appointment with Dr. Candace over videocall for this afternoon."

Her brows rose. "Again? Yeah, I guess I need it, huh?"

Squeezing her fingers, I sighed. "It seems to be really helping you, Thorn. You haven't gone all homicidal on Gray like I would have, and to be honest I'm really impressed with how you're working through your feelings." I hesitated, then remembered who I was talking to. If I couldn't tell Thorn, I definitely couldn't handle talking to a random therapist. "I asked Brenda to make me an appointment, too."

Her lips parted in surprise, then she wrapped her arms around me and hugged tight. That said everything I needed, that *she* was also proud of me for taking this step toward improved mental health. And that meant the fucking world to me.

Our security and the new *temporary* Brenda had so far been running things like a well-oiled machine, so there were no major delays in getting to our hotel rooms. The penthouse suite was booked for us, but as it only had three bedrooms, Grayson and Vee both opted for rooms on the floor below.

Angelo panicked at the idea of having Vee out of sight—there was a price on her head right now—but after a private chat with Grayson, he let the subject drop.

"Where's Billie going to sleep?" Jace asked, dropping down onto the huge sofa like he was some kind of ancient deity.

"None of *your* fucking business, Adams," Billie snapped back. "Don't worry; your bed will be free and clear for whatever fresh groupies you want to fuck tonight."

Jace's expression clouded with anger, his cheeks heating, and Angelo cast a curious glance between the two of them. Billie wasn't hanging around for a stinging comeback, though; she just flipped Jace her middle finger and retreated into the bedroom that one of the hotel staff had just delivered our bags to.

"Bro," I said with a sigh, shaking my head. "Why do you need to do that?"

Jace's eyes narrowed. "Do what?"

I rolled my eyes and headed into the bedroom, closing the door behind me. Angelo could deal with Jace's idiotic bullshit. In reality, it was in my best interest if he fucked things up with Billie because it meant I could keep her all to myself. For now.

It just sucked seeing her hurt and knowing it was my best friend causing that pain.

Jace was such a moron.

"Do you think we have time to go for a walk before my session with Dr. Candace?" Billie asked with a hopeful look on her face. "I feel like you can't connect with a city from a car, not like when you walk the streets."

I smiled, flopping onto the bed. "You have no idea how bad I want to say yes, babe. But it's not safe without a half-dozen security guards, and that in itself brings more attention. And... I just really don't want to risk your safety."

Her face fell with disappointment, and the urge to make her smile again nearly had me changing my mind. But after that article in *Dirty Truths* about her kissing Angelo... it was too risky. Brenda had blasted the whole band with a warning that Billie was taking some serious heat from the Bellerose superfans and not in a good way.

"I'm sorry," I said with sincerity, reaching out a hand to pull her closer. "Fame really does have its drawbacks. Maybe when this tour is over, I can bring you back here for a vacation. We can wear disguises and pretend to be normal people without the hype of *Bellerose* overshadowing every step."

Her smile warmed. "That sounds perfect."

For a couple of hours, we just chilled out in our room together, watching pay-per-view movies and ordering snacks from room service. Then I got her all set up with a laptop and webcam for her session with Dr. Candace.

"Did you want to stay?" she asked in a quiet voice as I pulled my shoes on to leave her in peace. My brows hitched in surprise, and she wrinkled her nose. "You don't have to leave, I mean. I don't talk about anything I wouldn't be comfortable telling you anyway."

I hesitated a moment, tempted. But ultimately, I shook my head. "No, you don't need me listening in and making shit awkward. My session is after yours, though, so I'll be back before you're done. Just going to go kick Gray's ass for his crappy drumming in Dublin."

That... and I needed to psych myself up for talking to the doctor myself. I still wasn't totally sure I had the nuts to go through with it... but I had to try. For Billie, and for myself. I owed it to myself to make the most of my opportunities, I saw that now. The best form of vengeance was happiness.

Hey, that might make a cool song lyric.

twenty-six

BILLIE

My session with Dr. Candace helped me come to terms with three heavy-hitting issues.

Number one: I had feelings for Angelo, and that couldn't just be ignored endlessly. We'd kissed, and that toothpaste couldn't be put back into the tube. The only way to move forward without making things sour between us was to address the situation. Maybe it was just a lingering crush on the memory of him. Maybe he didn't feel the same way. But the only way to know for sure was to ask.

Number two: Jace was a petulant, spoiled brat. He was also more than likely lying his ass off about fucking a groupie last night, purely to make me jealous. Mature? God, no. But drastically better than him actually fucking a random girl after our elevator quickie.

Regardless of Dr. Candace's much more mature advice, I decided I had a couple of options on how to handle *this* problem. And I knew myself well enough to know I'd be unlikely to take the high road. Low road was infinitely more satisfying.

Number three: I needed to clear the air with Grayson. Right now, we were just hanging in limbo, constantly tense and avoiding each other, but that was no way to continue. It was already impacting their music, and at the end of the day as Dr Candace had pointed out, a big part of me knew he wasn't as guilty as I'd initially assumed. If I truly believed he'd murdered my parents and tried to kill me, I wouldn't still be here. I wouldn't be traveling with him, staying in the same hotels, attending his shows. I'd be sitting in a police station, giving evidence and demanding justice.

Also, I had already fallen in love with the big, grumpy fuck. That was why it'd all hit me so damn hard, and I was really struggling with heavy doses of guilt for dividing my heart so many different ways.

Rhett had returned right on time as my session

finished, but when I made to leave the room and give him privacy, he'd grabbed my hand.

"Stay?" he asked in a tight voice. His brow beaded with sweat, and a tiny tremble shook his fingers where he clasped mine. His eyes were huge and round, pleading. "Please, Thorn? I want you to know all my damage, but I don't want to tell this story twice."

Shocked, I gave a nod and sank back down onto the bed. I would stay, offering support, but I wanted to blend into the background so I didn't distract him from Dr. Candace's guidance. Rhett flashed me a relieved, thankful smile, then took my seat in front of the computer and webcam.

After introductions, I watched Rhett slowly relax. Dr. Candace had a calming energy, even over the video call, and Rhett was responding to her a hundred times faster than I had. Then again, no one was *forcing* him into treatment; he was here willingly because he wanted help.

I admired that.

Sometime later, after Dr. Candace had gently eased him into talking about himself, she redirected the chat to ask the question burning at the front of my mind.

"Do you want to tell me about why you booked this session, Rhett? As lovely as it is to meet one of the men healing Billie's heart, I suspect there is more on your mind."

Rhett shot a glance my way, and I offered a reassuring smile back. "Yeah. Ever since Billie started these sessions with you, it got me thinking that maybe I should deal with some of my... damage." He took a deep breath and blew it out in a heavy sigh. "I guess... my concern right now is that maybe I'm being too needy and possessive with her, when I know it's not fair to the other guys."

My jaw dropped, but I bit my tongue before voicing my protest. This was his session; I was just here for support. Nothing more. So I needed to keep my opinions to myself until he was done with Dr. Candace. Then I'd show him exactly what I thought of his concern.

"Billie, hon, I know you're there, and I appreciate you keeping quiet," she said through the laptop speaker, and my cheeks heated. She knew how hard it was for me to bite my tongue. With some gentle, open-ended questions, she prompted Rhett into spilling his story.

Even with his first sentence, I knew this was going to hurt just to hear. And then when I thought about innocent-child Rhett living this life, it gutted me.

"My grandfather is Jeremiah Townsend."

A chill ran down my spine. *I knew that fucking name.* Most of America knew that name. Rhett's grandfather was a cult leader, notorious for some stomach-churning crimes for which he'd magically been acquitted, time and time again. I'd never met him—thank fuck—but even from seeing him in the news there was no question in my mind; Jeremiah Townsend was evil incarnate. Something Rhett only confirmed as he continued.

"I don't know how familiar you are with Townsend Community," he murmured, his attention on the laptop screen rather than me, "but it's a cult, thinly veiled by a made-up religion built off of a dystopian fiction novel that Jeremiah's father wrote."

"I'm aware," Dr Candace replied, her voice so carefully calm I had to admire her. "Did you grow up there?"

Rhett jerked a nod. "Yes. In his home. My mother was one of his *chosen ones*, treated like a favorite pet and punished just the same. Like a dog." He paused, his eyes flicking to me ever so quickly. "She tried so fucking hard to protect me, but it was like an ant trying to resist a boot. He's... he's the reason I don't sleep easily."

"He hurt you," Dr Candace stated. It was an observation, not a question.

Another sharp nod from Rhett. "At first he just focused on her. I'd wake up to find him right there in the bed beside us—" He broke off with a choked sound, shaking his head at the memory. "As I got older, I tried to protect her. Tried to fight him off. Then he made it his mission to break me... Boys like me, ones who resisted his brainwashing, held no value in his church. Not if we couldn't be controlled to do his every wish without question, no matter how sick and twisted."

He paused, reaching for the bottle of water I'd left beside the computer earlier. I said nothing while he took a sip, nor did Dr. Candace.

"Eventually, after a lot of pain, I just figured out how to not sleep. Not deeply, anyway. The smallest sounds wake me up, and when you live in a house with eighteen other people, there is no shortage of sounds. So I grabbed five or ten minutes, here and there, just enough to stay sane. Sort of. But it meant that when *he* came for me, I was prepared for the beating."

"That must be a hard lesson to forget," Dr. Candace said when Rhett paused for longer. "I can imagine there is also no shortage of sounds on a tour bus to keep you permanently on edge. How'd you end up in Bellerose?"

Rhett glanced my way again, and I scooted closer to offer him my hand. He took it without hesitation, linking our fingers together.

"I made it my mission to get out of the community. I bided my time, laid my plans, got everything fucking *perfect*. We were going to escape, just run away with nothing but the clothes on our backs. There was nothing for us there and nothing we wanted to take. A homeless life on the streets had to be better than the atrocities of Townsend Community." He frowned, clearly remembering that time in his life, and my fingers squeezed his with reassurance.

"Who is *we*, Rhett?" Dr Candace asked.

His focus returned to the laptop screen. "My mother and I. She wanted to get out; she wanted to leave *with me* and start a new life out of Jeremiah's reach."

"What changed?" she asked, hearing the past tense of those statements just like I had.

Rhett swallowed hard, his face pale as he remembered. "We got caught. Someone that she trusted sold us out to Jeremiah, and he caught us on the edge of the compound."

I needed to force my breathing to stay calm when inside I just wanted to burst out crying. Poor Rhett. He'd been through so much... Was it any wonder that he struggled to sleep? Or that he'd had a burning need to protect me from our very first meeting when I ran into him, scared and bloody, in an alleyway in Siena? Fucking hell, he was so much stronger than I'd ever realized to have been through so much and not let it twist him into something ugly and cruel.

"For the first time in as long as I could remember, he didn't reach for his belt," Rhett continued, locked in his memory now. "He just laughed at us. Fucking laughed. I was so confused, expecting to be killed on the spot. But he just stood there, his thumbs looped into his fucking belt buckle, and told us to go... if that was what we really wanted."

Ice formed in my gut. Now I understood his reaction when it seemed like I'd *chosen* Angelo—a man who seemed very much like an abuser—over him.

"She changed her mind?" I asked in a hoarse whisper, lost in his story alongside him. "She chose to stay?"

Rhett gave me a pain-filled nod. "I think... she'd never planned to go through with it. He had her too deeply indoctrinated. Too well *trained* to ever betray him." He gave a bitter laugh. "Turns out the only reason he let me leave—the reason he'd never actually killed me over the years—was because it's against the Townsend Chronicle to murder a child of his own blood. Except he isn't my mother's biological father—her mother married Jeremiah when she was just a baby. He's *mine*."

My stomach clenched tight, bile rising in my throat as I processed. His mother's father—biological or not—had fathered him. I seriously doubted it was consensual either. Fucking hell... *Rhett*. My heart broke for him.

"Wow," Dr Candace responded before she caught herself, and Rhett flashed a sad smile.

"Didn't expect that, huh? Yeah. Me either. He stood there after telling me this and said I was free to go, if I wanted, but then I'd be dead to the Townsend Community. I couldn't take *anything* with me. Not my clothes or shoes, not even my name. There was no fucking hesitation for me; I stripped everything off right then and there and spat at his feet that I'd gladly leave my name behind. But then I looked at my mom, and she... she wouldn't look at me. She just stood there, cowering under Jeremiah's hand. He gave her the same offer, told her she was *free to go*... but she started crying when he said she'd be dead to the community. Dead to *him*." He slouched in his seat, long, tattooed fingers rubbing at his brow. "She stayed. I left. The end."

I knew that Dr Candace wouldn't leave the session like that; she'd extend the time and talk to him more about the impact this has had on his life. But right now, I just wanted to punch something, more than I ever had in my entire freaking life.

Sliding off the bed, I leaned over and gave Rhett a quick kiss. "I need to run to the bathroom," I said quietly. "Keep talking; I'll be back. And Rhett? I'm so glad you left. You're the strongest person I've ever met, and I love you."

His conflicted gaze locked on mine, searching my face for signs that he'd scared me away, I had to guess. So I kissed him again, hard, totally ignoring the doctor on video chat.

"I'll never leave you, Rhett Silver. Never again. You have my heart and soul."

With that promise, I slipped out of the bedroom and made it all the way to the sofa before I cracked and started crying.

twenty-seven

BILLIE

I t wasn't that I'd ever thought my relationship with Rhett was shallow. It had happened fast, absolutely, but it was one of those connections where you meet and instantly feel as if you've known each other forever. There was none of that weird, awkward-new-relationship stuff, and we'd just fallen into *comfortable* in an inexplicable way.

So, no, it wasn't shallow, but I was well aware that we hadn't *known* each other for a long period of time, and it had been quite a hectic situation from the first moment, so our discussions of personal shit hadn't gotten to the level of people who had known each other for years.

Hearing about his family. His past. It opened up a new layer to the bond between us, between our shared trauma. Once he'd finished up with Dr Candace, and I'd pulled myself together enough to return to the main room, I wrapped my arms around him and held him on the bed.

I held him together just like he'd done the same for me so many times.

My knight. My perfect fucking knight.

"You think of me differently now?"

It was the first question he'd asked in ages, and it almost startled me to hear his voice in the super quiet room.

"No!" I said way too loudly for this conversation, but emotions were suddenly bursting from me. "You are one of the most amazing, strong, incredible people I've ever known. I thank the universe every damn day that I stumbled into your alley." His hold tightened on me, his head burying against my shoulder as he held onto me like I was keeping him grounded. "You escaped the sort of situation that very few could, and you went on to become one of the most famous and desirable men in the world. I'm so proud of you for opening up to the doc. That takes a strength I don't think I would have had in the same circumstances."

I felt moisture on my skin, and even though he

wasn't making a sound, I felt his cathartic release. Or at least I prayed it was cathartic.

"It's time for healing now," I whispered, rocking him back and forth. Eventually, his breathing evened out, and I knew he'd fallen asleep. I stayed with him for a long time, silently crying, staring at the ceiling, and wishing that this world wouldn't keep hurting the people I loved.

At least this time we were all together. This time we would fight the darkness as a team, not alone. That had to make a damn difference.

Fuck, I already knew it made a difference.

With that in mind, I decided that I had to chat with Grayson. I waited until Rhett was awake so he wouldn't wake alone. "You going to shower before sound check tonight?" I asked him.

His smile was gentle as he rubbed a hand across his face—a face unmarred by grief, as perfect and handsome as ever. "Yeah, need to pull myself together." He pushed up and pressed his lips to mine. "Thank you for staying with me. I honestly... Fuck, I honestly feel a little better, and I never expected that."

Therapy, it had a way about it. Especially with the sort of caring, insightful therapist Dr. Candace was turning out to be. "Whenever you need me," I replied,

"I'm there. I'll walk through the valley of the shadow of death with you, Knight."

He quirked an eyebrow. "Knight?"

I nodded. "Yeah, you're my knight in shining armor. You are the very definition of the title, and it's how I've always thought of you."

His next kiss was devouring, and I moaned against his mouth, my body pressed into the bed beneath him. "You are fucking perfection, Thorn," he rasped against my lips, "and my biggest regret today is that I don't have time to fuck you for the next three hours. Rain check?"

Another groan escaped me as my lower half jerked against him, needing some relief. *Calm your tits; we don't have damn time.*

"All the freaking rain checks," I breathed. "Now, take a damn shower before I tie you to the bed."

He was tempted. Very tempted, if the look on his face was any indication. But unfortunately, with huge rock concerts, you couldn't really play hooky, so he dragged himself off to the shower a few minutes later. "I'm going to try and talk to Gray," I called after him, and his smile was gentle when he turned back to me.

"Let me know if I need to beat his ass, baby girl. Just say the word."

He'd do it too. Take on the giant to avenge my honor. *Knight* fit him in so many ways.

"Love you," I called after him.

"Love you more," he shot back, before quickly ducking inside the bathroom and slamming the door so I couldn't respond.

Bastard.

Pulling on jeans over my panties, and making sure my shirt was in place, I left the room determined to find Gray. I was about to text him to suggest a meetup, when I realized there was no need. He was sitting in the living room, staring at the door I'd just exited as if he'd been waiting for me to.

"Everything okay with Rhett?" he asked, immediately on his feet. He moved fast for a big guy.

"Not really, but I think it will be," I replied, before swallowing roughly. I wanted to try and have this conversation openly and without anger. At least until I got his side of the story. "Wait, how did you know that something might be wrong with Rhett?"

"He mentioned therapy, and I know how that shit destroys you after years of repressed trauma. I've been worried about him." His gaze traced over me quickly. "And you."

Fuck. Right.

"I was actually looking for you," I said softly. "I think it's time we talked."

The relief that crossed his face hit me harder than I'd expected. The last few days had been hell for me, but clearly, it'd been the same for Grayson. That relaxed more of my anger toward him, and channeling Dr. Candace, I opened myself up to hearing whatever Gray had to say... all the while desperately hoping that there was a really good explanation for my memories of that night.

"Should we sit?" he suggested, waving to the chair he'd just vacated.

I nodded but didn't take the spot beside him—firstly, because his close presence usually ensured that I was less than focused and, secondly, because we weren't there yet. Maybe we'd never be, depending on what was said next.

"I'm so sorry that I disappeared after our night together, Billie," he started, and I blinked at what felt like an odd opening. This wasn't at all about the sex, and we both knew it. "I can only imagine how you felt and what you thought when I up and disappeared for a few days after the sex. I need you to know, before we get into the past, that my time with you has been some of the greatest moments of my life. That night included." For some fucked up reason, that did make me feel a tiny bit better. It eased the part of me that had been stressing over this multi-relationship and whether it would prove to be too much for the men in my life.

Grayson apparently was okay with the sharing, so now we just had to see if I was okay with the other shit.

"I've got a past that would probably turn your therapist's hair gray," he continued, "and I won't be opening up to her anytime soon about it. But today I need to explain some of it to you. To explain who I used to be and how far from that person I am today."

The nerves racing through my gut had me on the verge of vomiting, but I forced myself to stay calm. I would not fucking interrupt this, no matter what I had to do.

"As you know, my family is part of a large cartel that rules most of Hawaii and, for the last two decades, some of the mainland. I was born into it and, for most of my life, was their reaper. *The Maker.* The one who existed in the darkness, fulfilling their hits and taking care of anyone who fucked with the family business."

Fulfilling their hits. That one felt like a very pointed statement.

"I was there that night, Billie," he rasped, his eyes dropping as he breathed deeply. "But I never knew that was your house or that you had any connection to that job, not until you mentioned your mom's name. I told you that I've never looked into your past, and I meant it. But when you mentioned that fairly unusual name, it triggered a memory. A familiarity. I took off to find an old acquaintance who would be able to remind me why that name felt familiar."

Bile rose in my throat. "Why were you there that night?"

I mean, the reason was obvious, but I needed him to say it. No confusion. I had to know exactly why Gray had been there that night and what he'd done.

"There was a hit on your mom, Billie." Short, blunt, earth-shattering statement. My mom, a fucking boring-ass accountant, had had a damn hit on her? Make it make sense.

"Why?" I breathed. "Why would she have a hit? She was a normal housewife and an accountant, if also a somewhat neurotic mother." Except there had been that conversation between her and Dad. The one that had sounded a lot like she wasn't exactly *normal.*

Grayson shook his head. "I don't ask questions about why. Or at least, I never used to. I got my assignments and carried them out. Think of me as your mind-less, cartel killing machine."

A shiver traced down my spine. I'd always known Grayson was dangerous, but the picture he painted of himself in his past life didn't gel at all with the man I knew today. "You would never let someone control you like a damn puppet," I bit out. "I can't believe it."

The skin around his eyes tightened as he lifted his gaze to meet mine once more. "I wasn't completely mindless, but from a very young age, I'd known the punishment for disobeying orders. In the end, it was easier to stop fighting."

He must have fought eventually, though, because he'd gotten out. Like Rhett, he'd figured out how to change his circumstances in the most difficult of lives.

"So, there was a hit ordered on my mom, and you showed up that night... then what?"

"When I got there the door was locked, so I picked the lock and let myself in."

"It was locked when I tried to get out," I breathed.

He nodded. "Yeah, I always left the scene—"

The rest of his sentence was cut off by a door slamming open and Rhett hurrying out. A beat later, Jace appeared from the opposite room, and Vee and Angelo arrived from the floor below. "You got the text from Hannah?" Jace said in a rush. "We're fucking late, and if we don't move our asses, we're in for a huge fine."

Fucking hell. Grayson didn't move, despite the urgency in those around him. "You go on ahead without me," he said stiffly. "I need to talk to Billie."

"Not a fucking chance," Jace said, shooting me a

dark look. "Your shit can wait. Apparently, we need to be inside the venue by 5:00PM or we will be locked out completely with the roadblocks going up around it. This is literally our last chance."

Motherfucker. I still had no real answers about what role Gray had played in the death of my parents and the fire. My memories weren't accurate; I'd already sensed that. Dr. Candace had also warned me that repressed memories didn't always return accurately and that it was very likely I pictured events and their timing incorrectly.

But these things wouldn't be cleared up until I found another moment alone with Grayson.

"Get dressed, Billie," Jace bit out. "You'll be at the concert tonight so we can keep an eye on you and ensure that you've got enough security."

"What about me?" Vee asked. She'd been in the club last night, so it stood to reason we weren't hiding her any longer.

"You can come too. But you literally have five minutes to dress and whatever othershit you need to do."

Jace waved us off, and I was up and off the couch in seconds, racing toward the room with my makeup and clothes in it. Three minutes later I wore black jeans and a black band tee of Rhett's, and my hair was brushed and wavy down my back. Some slapped-on makeup completed the look.

This was the best they were getting on such short notice.

When I entered the living room again, Angelo and a couple of security guards were all that remained. "I'm here to make sure you get to the cars safely," Angel said, holding out his hand to me.

I took it without hesitation, enjoying the feel of his strength encasing my fingers. "Thank you," I said with a smile, thinking about our kiss last night on the dance floor. It had been on my mind more than I'd like to admit, even with all the other drama and trauma going on.

"I'm in love with you, Bella."

We had just stepped into the elevator, the security fanning out around us, and I made a comical gasp before he'd even finished that sentence.

"I've never stopped," he continued. "Never. You are part of my soul, and even though I was forced to marry Vee, I always wanted it to be you. It has always been you."

"You walked away from me," I whispered.

He shook his head before leaning down so he was whispering right near my ear. All our security guards signed NDAs, the sort that bankrupted you *and* your kids if you broke them, but I still understood his need to keep this private. "I had to protect you from my family. They would have had you killed without a fucking moment's hesitation, and I was too young to protect you in any other way."

My soul hurt at the pain all my boys had had to live through thanks to fucked up families.

"Vee was a gift, you know," he continued in that same whisper. "A woman who needed the same sort of relationship as me. A fake one. Because we were both in love with another."

I was gripping his hand so hard that it had to be hurting him, but he never made a sound.

"You know that it's different now, right?" I whispered back.

He shifted his head so I could see the slow smile on his full lips. Lips that I really wanted to kiss again, lest they stop haunting my dreams. "I was always good at sharing, Bella. To a certain extent. If you have your chosen harem of men, then I'm just hoping there's a place for me in it."

Fuck. *Harem.*

That word freaked me right out, so I chose not to focus on it at all.

"You have a place in my world," I told him. "You always have."

He gave me exactly what I needed when his lips met mine, tongue sweeping out lazily to brush along my own, and I barely managed to swallow my groan.

The elevator dinged a second later, and we had to pull apart and head for the cars. The others were already inside, from what I could see, waiting for us.

"Will you go on a date with me, Bella?" Angelo asked when we were nearing the SUVs. "Let's do this properly this time."

A date? Had I ever been on a proper date?

"I'd love that," I told him, tendrils of joy pushing through the heavy clouds that had been hanging over me for days. Clouds that wouldn't go anywhere until this Grayson uncertainty was put to rest, one way or another. But at least there were small moments of light.

At times, these *lighter* moments were all that got me through.

twenty-eight

GRAYSON

So close. I'd been so fucking close to telling Billie everything that'd happened that night... the night of the fire, the night that she'd lost her parents and her baby. Fucking hell, the guilt over her losses weighed on me like a lead jacket, but I couldn't turn back the clock.

Frustration belted through my drumsticks as we crashed into our first set of the night, but this time I let it flow free. I wasn't fighting my emotions or running from them. I wasn't holding back tonight, and it made a massive difference in our music. Everyone knows the drummer is the heart and soul of a band, so if I was off, we were all off. When I was in the zone, though...

"Holy shit, we're on *fire* tonight!" Rhett yelled over at me in a break between songs. He'd switched off his mic, and Jace was schmoozing the audience like only Jace could. The feverish excitement on Rhett's face was something new. Since his therapy session, he'd been walking with a lightness to his step, like he was finally able to breathe freely. I envied him but also knew that one *completed* conversation with Billie would make a world of difference.

It wouldn't alleviate my guilt entirely—nothing could change my involvement in her worst trauma—but I was aching to try and soothe her hurt. If my version of events could bring her some kind of closure —even if it meant she *hated* me for it—then that was what I needed to do. When she was ready. I could be patient and wait for her to re-engage the conversation.

Music poured out of us, the new sound of Bellerose totally elevated by all the pain, loss, and *love* that we now shared. It helped that the Edinburgh audience was totally wild, one hundred percent with us on this journey.

About a third of the way into our show, we got a quick break while the roadies rearranged the stage, so I gratefully accepted a sweat towel and bottle of water from one of our crew.

"Gray... that was lit," Angelo commented with a nod. "Respect."

I nodded back, swallowing my mouthful. "You too. Quick learner, huh?"

His smirk was secretive. "Apparently. Helps that some of those classic Bellerose tracks used to be Snake Soup originals."

My brows rose. "Shit. Yeah, I forgot Jace brought a lot of that first album with him... Well, thanks?"

Angelo just shrugged, grabbing his own sweat towel to mop his face as he moved to talk with Jace. Rhett gave me a nod but had his arm firmly around a smiling Billie, so I couldn't blame him for not letting her go.

With a sigh, I finished my water and quickly dashed around the corner to take a piss. In my ear, the stage manager gave us a two-minute warning, so I had enough time. The single stall was occupied, though, and I hammered on the door with my fist.

"Hurry up!" I barked.

The door opened a split second later, and a coked-up looking groupie girl stumbled out with a giggle, sniffing. One of our road crew followed her with a smirk, adjusting his jeans.

"'Sup, man?" he drawled when he saw me there. "Sick set out there."

Ignoring him, I pushed into the cubicle and locked the door. It was none of my business who our crew wanted to fuck, but they knew not to use the closest pisser to the stage.

The one-minute warning hurried me along, and I finished up, giving my hands a quick wash, then paused when I saw an empty coke baggie on the side of the sink. The logo printed on the bag seemed familiar, but I couldn't place why. Something about it struck a bad feeling, and the last time that'd happened was when Billie mentioned her mom's name.

My knowledge of European drug traffickers had never been incredible in the first place, though, but maybe Rhett would know. I tucked it into the pocket of my jeans and hurried back onstage just in time for the lights to flare up once more.

"You good, bro?" Jace asked, away from his mic. There was nothing but concern in his eyes, and I nodded back. Despite all the messy shit we had going on with Billie behind the scenes, out here we were solid. We were brothers. With a half smile, I twirled my drumsticks and smacked out the beat to our next song.

Jace grinned and grabbed his mic to work up the audience once more, accompanied by my drum solo. I gave it heaps, improvising as he flirted with the ten thousand–strong crowd, then Angelo and Rhett joined me to launch into "On the Edge," one of the hits from our latest album.

My gaze shifted to offstage where Billie bounced along to the beat, a huge smile on her face. It was a huge contrast from the first concert she'd attended, when I'd given her headphones to drown out Jace's lyrics about how she'd broken his heart.

Knowing now what it felt like to fall for her... I got it.

We finished the concert on a high, and all exited the stage dripping sweat and buzzing with endorphins. Billie and Vee were waiting with excited congratulations, but it was Rhett who swept her up in his arms to spin her around. Of course it was. A dark look passed between Billie and Jace, making me curious about what their latest argument was over.

Angelo clapped me on the shoulder, then approached Rhett with a sly smirk. "Sorry, Silver, I need to steal Bella away."

Rhett hated to share. No matter what he *said* about being okay with it, he had a buttload of residual trauma from his childhood that meant he held onto things that were *his* with fierce defensiveness. Clothes, guitars... girls. He was all for a threesome, but god help anyone who tried to take his things away from him. Quietly, I was waiting for this polyamorous thing with Billie to explode, with Rhett as the spark *and* fuse.

"Fuck off, Ricci," he replied, surprising no one.

"Don't be a child, Silver. Bella promised me a date." Angelo folded his tattoo-covered arms over his damp Bellerose t-shirt. *Concert Angelo* had had to make some huge changes to *mafia Angelo's* wardrobe, and he looked like a totally different guy now. Edgier, and less murderous.

"Now?" Billie squeaked, wriggling free of Rhett's possessive grip.

Angelo shrugged. "Seize the day, Bella. Come on." He extended a hand, and she took it without hesitation. Their kiss at the club last night had really changed things between them. Jealousy burned in my chest, but the gaping chasm between Billie and I was entirely my own fault.

Just as they started to walk away, my gaze caught on a tattoo on the back of Angelo's arm. Frowning, I pulled out the empty coke baggie from the bathroom to compare the symbol.

Sure enough, it was the same scorpion in a spider web.

"What the fuck?" I muttered to myself.

"Hitting the hard shit, Gray?" Jace asked with a pointed look at the bag in my hand.

I shrugged because, in the grand scheme of things, none of us really considered coke to be *hard shit* anymore. "Hey, does this logo look familiar?" I showed him the bag.

Jace wrinkled his nose, thinking. "Maybe? I dunno; I don't pay much attention when I'm racking up lines. Rhett might know."

Our party-boy guitarist glanced up from the phone in his hand, then peered at the bag. "Dunno. Actually, it does seem similar to what I got in Dublin. Lemme check." He patted down his pockets and muttered a curse. "I'm all out. Hang on. Kristie! Come here!" He beckoned over one of the girls in our road crew who'd been on the original tour.

Kristie hurried over with an eager-to-please look on her face. When Rhett asked if she had any coke leftover from Dublin, she produced an almost empty bag from her bra.

"Hah! Knew it." He tossed the bag to me. "Same."

Jace arched a brow with curiosity. "Something we need to know, Gray?"

I frowned down at the two identical logos in my hand. "Maybe. Probably. I'll let you know when I have something more than a hunch, though." I tucked both bags into my pocket. "You guys going to party?" I nodded toward Vee, who was hanging out nearby while chatting to one of the groupie girls. "She probably needs someone to keep an eye on her if you hit the clubs."

Jace and Rhett exchanged a look, then Rhett shook his head. "I'm heading to the hotel; I'll take Vee."

"Guess it's just the Jace show tonight, then," our lead singer said with a forced grin. "Unless you're joining me, Gray?"

"Not tonight," I replied, then left them to it. I wanted to take a shower and change, but I also had a nagging feeling that I needed to investigate this link between the coke bags and Angelo's tattoo.

In the dressing room, I took my sweet-ass time showering—drumming was hot work, even in winter and the stage lights were scorching—then got dressed into clean clothes. By the time I exited the dressing room, most of the crew were busy with packing up all our shit. The tour schedule they'd forced us into was *insanely* tight, so our guys were being pushed to their limit to make sure all the equipment got packed, moved, and delivered to the next country and city in time.

Dressed in my usual black-on-black clothing, I slipped into the shadows to poke around. It couldn't be a coincidence that the same drugs were being sold at our Dublin and Edinburgh concerts. Or that Angelo mysteriously had the same design tattooed on his arm. It wasn't the official Ricci family symbol; I knew that one well. But it was clearly connected to an arm of their operation. An arm that had followed us to Europe... Something in my gut told me to snoop around a bit, so that's what I did.

An hour later, though, the whole venue was nearly cleared, and I was starting to think I was just being paranoid because I needed a project to keep my mind off Billie and my crushing guilt. With a sigh, I pushed open the fire escape door and headed out onto the loading docks. I'd shot a message to my driver to meet me around back, and he said he'd be there in five.

Everything was quiet when I got out there, but one of our equipment trucks stood waiting at the dock with the trailer door rolled up. A couple of "Bellerose Grass-roots Tour" equipment cases sat nearby, waiting to be loaded, but no crew were around that I could see. Which was weird. Our security was tight enough that nothing, not even equipment, should be left unattended. Ever.

Moving closer, I looked around. Surely there was someone here.

No one appeared, and the dock remained silent, causing a thread of unease to curl around my chest.

Needing to satisfy my own suspicious mind, I unlatched the closest equipment case and lifted the lid.

"Shit," I muttered, staring down at the massive quantity of cocaine, all packaged up in—I assumed—one-gram bags. All marked with the same logo.

Now it was starting to make sense. With a frustrated sigh, I boosted myself into the truck to see just how bad things really were. There were several more cases of drugs, not all coke, and the other cases were full of cash. Not nice, neat stacks, either. Nope, this cash was dirty, crumpled, rolled... it was the cash of drug deals.

"Goddamn it," I said out loud, tucking my phone into my pocket after taking multiple pictures as evidence. Now I was surer than ever someone had wandered off the job, but they'd be back any second. I didn't need to get caught up in *this* mess, so I jumped out of the truck and pretended to mind my own fucking business as I exited the loading dock.

I made it all of about ten paces outside in the dark when I stumbled across two rough-looking guys who were *probably* supposed to be guarding the truck. Instead, they were smoking a joint around the corner from the dock, and when I interrupted them, they panicked.

Shots fired. I disarmed them quickly, smacking their

heads into each other to knock them out, before I dragged both of them out of sight, into a side alley. I couldn't leave them alive to out my knowledge of this drug racket to Giovanni Ricci; I had no choice but to break their necks. Quick, clean, silencing them permanently. I stashed the bodies behind some dumpsters, knowing that I had no time now to deal with them. I'd come back later and ensure they disappeared permanently.

A horn sounded, and I wiped my hands on my pants, hauling ass to where I could see my driver approaching in the distance. It wasn't until I was safely in the backseat of the sedan, driving away from the concert venue, that I realized I'd been shot.

Fucking hell.

twenty-nine

BILLIE

How the fuck Angelo had time to plan out a date while also playing a concert, I had no idea. But he'd managed it, whisking me right from the concert venue to a restaurant in the basement of a stone building that had to be *hundreds* of years old. He seated me in a private dining room set just for two, then disappeared for ten minutes to shower and change somewhere.

When he returned, Angel, the new Bellerose bass player, was gone, and Angelo Ricci was back. I didn't want to say anything, because he was putting in so much effort, but I liked Angel better. He was authentic and raw and emotional... Angelo Ricci was cold and controlled.

Biting my tongue, I gave him a tight smile, and when the waiter came over to fill Angelo's glass, I let him refill my glass of wine.

"This is fancy," I commented, looking around the room. Dozens of candles lit the space with a warm glow, and fresh flowers filled the air with a delicate scent. It was like something out of *The Bachelor*, right down to Angelo's designer suit. "I feel kind of under-dressed."

He sat back, his eyes raking over my jeans and Bellerose band shirt. "You look perfect, Bella. You always do."

For some reason that heated my cheeks, and I nervously sipped my wine. At this rate, I'd be white-girl-wasted and talking to my imaginary crocodile before the night was over.

"So," I started, using the most original opening word of the decade, "this is kind of weird. Right?"

Angelo's smile was relaxed, and he apparently had no need to slam his wine like it was a drinking contest. Good for him.

"Is it really weird?" he asked with a shrug. "I feel like this is the natural relationship progression we should have had all along. Life fucked that up for a while, but we're back on track now. Back where we should be."

"You can't simply go back like that," I whispered, throat tight. Just call me Billie the Saboteur because I apparently couldn't let the fucking past go, kept bringing it into the present. But in my defense, Dr. Candace was really the one to blame. She was all, *You have to deal with the past to have a future,* along with some other very insightful but painful advice.

Angelo leaned across the table and captured my hand, his movement strong and sure, like he wasn't worried at all that I'd reject him. I had always admired his confidence, and in the few times it'd wavered, I'd loved being there to comfort and build him back up. "Bella, we're not going back in that sense. We're moving forward, which is the only direction one can truly take. But I will never forget the past. The times I shared with you are still some of my best memories, the moments that got me through a lot of hard shit."

The ball of pain in my throat tightened further. "But you left me," I choked out in a whisper. "Just... walked away."

His jaw tightened to match the tightness in my chest. "I had no choice, Bella. My father was going to have you killed to ensure I would comply with his wishes—wishes of who I had to marry and the role I would play in the Ricci family. At the time, I didn't have the power or the resources to stand against him, and it was too big of a risk, especially after the   "

He cut himself off abruptly, but I knew exactly what that last word was going to be: *fire*.

"You knew, even back then, it'd been deliberately lit?"

Angelo's hold on my hand tightened as he blinked at me for a beat. Clearly, he'd expected me to dissolve into tears and freak out talking about the death of my parents and child. Fuck knows I wanted to, but a larger part of me wanted answers. I'd spent the last near decade crying over the tragedy that shaped the rest of my life. I already *knew* it was arson, but I wanted to hear it from Angelo.

I wanted to hear who the fuck was truly responsible for it.

Even if Grayson had been the hand that lit the flame, his orders had come from above.

"Yes."

I didn't say anything, needing him to elaborate.

"The timing was too suspicious for me to think anything else, even though I've never been able to find any command going through Ricci or other connected families."

"Is Grayson's family connected to yours?" I asked him softly.

Angelo shook his head. "No, not in any true sense. Ricci and Kahulu are both criminal organizations and have crossed paths, but that's as far as it goes."

So there had been another player. "Maybe the Wilsons?" I tossed out the first possibility entering my head. "But why would they want to kill my parents? Mom worked for your father, right?"

Angelo nodded slowly, and I was grateful that he still hadn't released my hand. This was a tough conversation we were long overdue to have. "I never pushed too hard," he admitted. "You were alive and I wanted to keep you that way, but I promise that I've always been looking for information. Now that we know Grayson received a kill command, maybe he can send us in the right direction regarding what actually happened that night."

It was probably time for me to tell someone exactly what I remembered in my flashbacks. The details had slowly been resurfacing in dreams ever since the explosion at the record label. I was finally at a point where I felt like I was clearer on what had happened that day.

"The day of the fire I'd just come back from an ultrasound," I said quickly, wanting the conversation done, "and I heard my parents arguing. Dad was telling mom that she'd gone too far and that *they* were going to kill us all. That she wasn't dealing with white-collar criminals but the mafia. Mom kept assuring him it was fine and that she'd done it for us and the *cursed baby*."

Angelo's eyes were so dark that I couldn't differentiate pupil and iris. He looked beautiful, but also scary and dangerous as he stared into my soul. "She called it a cursed baby?"

I nodded, unable to speak for a second. "And the fire was that night," I managed to say.

There was no way it was a coincidence. "I need to speak with my father," Angelo rasped, anger still imprinted across his features. "For the first time, I think I'm ready to push the fucking issue. I swear, Bella, if I find out he ordered the hit that killed your parents and our baby, I'm going to put the Ricci boss six feet under."

Now it was my turn to squeeze his hand half to death. "Don't you risk your own life, Angel. Nothing will bring Penelope or my dad back, nothing. And if my mom was the cause of the fire, then she got exactly what she deserved. I won't lose you as well to this senseless fucking war."

Angelo and Jace were my constants. Constants that changed from friend to lover to enemy, depending on the day. But constants all the same. To lose them would be the death of myself, and I'd had enough death and loss already to last multiple lifetimes.

"Leave it with me, Bella," he said, and that didn't reassure me at all. Before I could yank his stubborn ass across the damn table—or at least attempt to—and demand that he stay safe, the waiter returned with some bread and oils for dipping. Angelo released my hand so that there was space in the center of the table for food, and I kind of wished we were anywhere but here. I'd take hand holding over bread any day. Or both, maybe. Yeah, both would be nice.

"Are you ready to order, sir?" the waiter asked, ignoring me completely.

Normally, that would piss me right off, but I had way too many other things to be stressed about. As much as Dr. Candace said I needed to deal with the past to move on from it, the past had such a hook into me that dealing with it wouldn't be a simple or easy task.

It was going to have to be cut free, painfully, leaving parts of me scarred and disformed.

"Bella?" Angelo said softly, and I cleared my throat, realizing he and the waiter were both staring at me. Clearly, I'd missed whatever had been said. "Are you ready to order?"

Right. Right. Fucking food. My stomach was so tight

I doubted I'd be able to stomach anything, but I was going to give it a try. For Angel.

"I'll take the gnocchi," I said quickly, having already read the menu while Angelo showered. "And a small side salad."

"I'll take the Ovation Lamb," Angel ordered, "with seasonal vegetables and mint gravy."

Oh damn. Instant food envy. That'd been my next choice... maybe he'd let me try it.

The waiter disappeared, leaving us to our conversation. But I didn't want to keep flogging that dead horse. We were on a date, not a joint therapy session, right?

"How did it feel being out on stage with Bellerose?" I asked him instead. "Is it weird for you?"

He sipped his wine, considering my question, then shook his head. "Not really. It feels... I don't really know how to explain it, but it feels natural. As though it was always meant to play out like this. Is it weird for you?"

I wrinkled my nose. "Yes. But no. It's like I keep getting memories of Snake Soup practicing in Jace's garage overlaid with the lights and glamor of a Bellerose concert. It's strange but in a good way. How is it playing with Rhett and Gray, though?"

Angelo's lips curved in a smile that was less reserved. "Can I tell you a secret?"

Surprise parted my lips. "Um, of course."

322

He ran his hand over his mouth, groaning with embarrassment. "I already know their music. After... everything, when Brenda got Jace his deal with Big Noise and I had to walk away from the music—and you both—I sort of stayed in the loop."

"You mean you're a secret Bellerose fan?" I pictured Angelo locked in his bathroom, lip-synching into his hairbrush, and the mental image was awesome.

He chuckled. "Um... sort of." He licked his lips, and I couldn't stop watching the movement. Was I turned on? Yes. I was human, after all. "Jace would kill me if he knew... but even though I never signed a recording contract, Brenda and I stayed in touch."

My brows rose. "You guys dated?"

His laughter was relaxed as he shrugged. "I mean, there was one moment, but no. I paid her to share any and all Bellerose information with me." He winced. "That sounds bad out loud."

It kind of did. But I was mostly confused. "I don't understand. You..."

"Paid Brenda to break confidentiality? Yeah. I paid well, too." He had the self-awareness to look embarrassed at this information.

"But why? That seems kind of masochistic, don't you think? Keeping tabs on the life you missed out on?"

He shrugged. "I guess. But I was convinced Jace

couldn't—or wouldn't—look out for his own best interests. After you broke up with him, after we let him think we were in a relationship that he had no part in, he was so fucking hurt. So self-destructive. I worried that someone in the music industry would take advantage of his mental state. So I got copies of contracts and deals and ran them through my own legal team before they were ever presented to the band. She also sent through early recordings of their songs, so... yeah. I know them."

"I'm so confused," I admitted, frowning. "Brenda doesn't seem like the type to let you do her job for her just to make a quick buck. She's way too girl-boss for that, and genuinely seems to care about the future of Bellerose."

Angelo winced. "Okay, yes... technically she didn't *only* do it for money. There was a heavy amount of, um, pressure applied to make her agree to the deal in those early days. Then over the years she grew to trust my intentions were good and we worked more collaboratively for the good of Bellerose."

I squinted. "Pressure? Like..."

"I threatened to kill her aging parents if she didn't agree. Then I used the paper trail of our transactions to keep her locked in after they passed. I never would have *actually* hurt them but, uh, she believed I would. So... yeah."

I blinked a couple of times, then nodded. "Yeah okay. Jace really would kill you... and probably fire Brenda, which would be stupid because she seems great despite this shady fucking arrangement you two had. That explains why you guys seemed so friendly."

"You look like you have something else to ask," he murmured, taking a sip of his wine.

I gulped my own, finishing it again. "Yeah. I do." Come on liquid courage, help me out. "Why... *Fuck*. Okay. Why keep tabs on Jace and not me? After all those years of radio silence, you became this scary stranger in my head. After all the rumors and gossip about the Riccis... that night when I saw you kill that guy in the alleyway, I was genuinely scared. I thought you would kill me too."

"I know," he admitted with a sigh. "I fucked up. Those first months after the fire, and after Penelope, I put a PI on you, just to make sure you were *safe*. But my father found out and threatened your life if I didn't cut ties. This union with Valentina meant too much to our families; the idea that my new wife would think I was cheating on her was too dangerous. So to *keep you safe* I had to cut ties. All of them. And I've never regretted anything more in my whole fucking life, Bella."

Emotion choked me, and I reached for my wine. The damn thing was empty, though, so I settled for a shocked, "Wow."

Our food arrived then, and the conversation shifted once more, thankfully, easing the tension and giving us both a chance to relax and flirt a little. It was a first date but also a continuation of our teenage romance. I was quietly confident that Angelo and I were finally on the right path together.

thirty

BILLIE

With the heavier topics of conversation behind us, and many glasses of wine consumed, things got heated. Our flirting turned to casual touches, and before I knew it, we were making out in the back of a limo like horny teens... which seemed appropriate for us, so I sure as hell wasn't complaining.

Somehow, I'd ended up in his lap, straddling him on the backseat of the moving vehicle as his tongue tangled with mine like we were made for one another. I moaned against his kiss, grinding down on his hard- ness and plotting how to get rid of the clothing between us. I *desperately* wanted to fuck Angel, and the hotel was too damn far away.

"Bella," he murmured against my lips, his fingers achingly close to my core but *not quite there*. "We should pause this."

The fuck did he just say? "Why?" Horny-tipsy me had no finesse.

Angelo's smile was slow. "Because this time we're doing this the right way. Dating, falling for each other again, learning *more* of who we are now."

It was a bit late for the *falling for each other* part, but I understood the rest. Even if I didn't particularly enjoy the cockblocking I'd just received.

My disappointment must have been more than a little obvious on my face, as he chuckled and palmed my cheek with his huge hand. "We have time, Bella. All the time. There's no need to rush."

"My vagina disagrees," I said matter-of-factly, and that just got another slow smile.

He kissed me again, a solid, toe-curling sort of kiss, and then deposited me back into the chair next to him. He kept a possessive hold on my thigh with one hand, while the other traced patterns across my body, so when the limo returned to our hotel and he kissed me goodnight at the door of my room, I was a desperately aching and needy mess.

"See you tomorrow, amore mio," Angelo said against my lips, and at least it appeared to be painful for him to leave as well, if the tense cut of his muscles under my hands was any indication. "Sweet dreams."

He moved away quickly, and I groaned. "Bastard," I muttered, and I got the pleasure of hearing his fucking laugh all the way down the hall until he made it into the elevator to go to his floor.

Slamming the room door open, I raced inside, hoping like hell that Rhett was sprawled out on the bed, ready and waiting. My high sex drive was perfectly designed for multiple men, and lucky me, I just happened to be dating more than one gorgeous, sexy rock star.

Of course, the room was empty, and when I checked my phone—which had been on silent for most of the date—it was to find a text that he was heading out for some food at one of the restaurants that they'd rented out for the band and crew. He'd left an open invite for me to join them, but in my current state, it probably wasn't the best idea.

Wandering from the hotel room, I tried Jace's door on a whim. No doubt he'd gone to the restaurant too, but curiosity had me checking. He had no issue using me for casual sex, so why couldn't I do the same to him?

To my surprise, the door swung open, and he stood

there in just a pair of soft basketball shorts, no fucking shirt, ink and muscles on display. He had a guitar in his hand, and it was clear I'd interrupted some music making.

The room behind looked empty, too, and I wasn't going to examine how relieved I felt to see him alone. "Rose?" he said, quirking an eyebrow. "Didn't expect to see you clothed and not wrapped around Angelo's tiny dick."

Only the smallest bite was in his tone, and for us, that was practically a pleasant start to the conversation.

"He's acting like a gentleman," I said sourly. "Something about doing this the right way this time, going on dates and getting to know each other as adults."

Jace's lips twitched, but he managed not to laugh. "Does he remember you at all? Our girl likes to be fucked on the regular, and you were never good at denial. Edging was basically like torture."

Yeah, facts were facts. "Firstly, please don't make me sound like an addict, I just have a healthy appetite for dick. And secondly, I don't remember you ever saying no." My tone was dry. "I mean, your dick went hard when a breeze blew in its direction. Angelo's too. I was the one who had to keep up with two horny teenage boys."

"Which you managed quite nicely," Jace said with a shrug.

Fucker. "I did, but since then I've gone years without a regular hookup. Angelo won't break me by dragging this out. I can hold out too."

"Then why are you here?" Jace shot back. "With those diluted pupils and flushed cheeks? I know that look, sweetheart, and let me tell you... no."

Not going to lie, I was floored. Even though we hated each other, Jace was always down to fuck. But he'd just rejected me too, and without the romantic gesture and explanation behind it that Angelo had attempted.

"No?" I repeated. "From what I've heard, you've literally fucked walking silicon dolls, and you're telling me no?"

I mean, I hadn't actually asked the question, but... whatever.

Jace pushed himself from the doorframe and stepped into my personal space. The guitar was between us, but I could still feel that electric energy from his body. "We have some shit to work out, Rose. We can't keep hate-fucking and then find a moment of peace and then hate each other again. This cycle has to end. I'm choosing to end it now."

I almost stumbled back, but his hand shot out and

caught me before I could fall. "You're done?" I whispered. "Done with us?"

His grip on me tightened momentarily, and the intensity of his blue eyes held me motionless as his jaw worked angrily. "Never, Rose! Never fucking done. But we're going to do things differently from now on too."

He released me then, and before I could pull myself together and say anything else, he stepped back into his room and firmly closed the door. It wasn't a slam, but the move made it perfectly clear that he was done for the night.

Done *with me* for the night, to be accurate. But not forever, and that allowed me to breathe deeply once more.

But seriously, who were these motherfucking assholes who thought they could get me all hot and bothered and then deny me in their stupid need to *do things differently*?

By the time I'd ranted and raved my way into my empty hotel room, I'd worked off some of the steam, and a long hot shower was calling my name. After shooting off a text to Rhett telling him I wouldn't make it to the restaurant, I slunk into the luxurious shower stall and let the water beat over me. After some time, my hand slid down my stomach, then lower until my fingers pressed to my aching clit.

The shower relaxed some parts of me, but others would not be eased without a little extra assistance.

It took me only a few minutes to come, Angelo's and Jace's faces in my mind as I muffled my moans against my free hand. It had been a long time since they'd shared my body, but I remembered it like it was yesterday and I wanted new memories. If we were doing things differently now—with some of my horniness eased, I could appreciate their gestures a touch more—maybe this time we could find true happiness.

Or at least an ending that was a little less fucked than our previous one.

Back then, we'd been just kids fooling around, not really knowing what to do. Already, the threesomes I'd had with the boys of Bellerose were in a whole other realm of amazing. Adult threesomes. I was dying to try out more risqué combinations.

A polite tap on my door grabbed my attention as I toweled my hair dry, and I went to check the peephole. One couldn't be too cautious.

Vee was there with a frown creasing her pretty face. I opened the door for her and gestured her inside before resecuring the safety latch.

"Is... everything okay?" I asked, waving for her to sit on the bed while I tossed my hair towel aside and hunted for a brush.

Her answering smile was forced. "Uh-huh. Why?"

I quirked one brow. "You seem tense, Vee. Is this about my date with Angelo?" Which would be logical, since they *were* married.

She wrinkled her nose. "Kind of, but I don't really want to add to your already overflowing stress, Billie. I just... also don't want to hide shit from you, because we're sort of friends now. Aren't we?"

"Yes, I think so. Whatever it is, I'd rather hear it now than find out later." But still, angst and unease churned in my belly to the point of cramps. My imagination was already running wild on what she was so reluctant to tell me.

Vee heaved a sigh, running her fingers through her perfect red waves. "Okay, so, I was bored and scrolling the internet, and I found this... *blog* site. I guess. It's all about—"

"Ah, let me guess. *Dirty Truths?*" Relief washed over me.

She nodded, still frowning. "That's the one. Anyway, someone snapped a pic of you and A heading into the restaurant tonight, and the comments..." She grimaced.

"That bad?" I asked, feeling gross. "I've been carefully *not* looking because it's easy to guess that Bellerose fans are ripping me to shreds online. The boys seem to think if they don't tell me, then I'll stupidly think it's not happening."

Vee's shoulders sagged as she exhaled. "Okay, fuck. Here I was freaking out and thinking you didn't know. They're *horrible* on there, girl. You're doing the right thing by ignoring it."

I shrugged. "Nothing said by some internet troll will change how I live my life, so why let it weigh me down? I know me, and I like me. Most days, anyway. Regardless of what the guys' *fans* think of our situation, it's really none of their business. And they have no clue what we've all gone through together, either. So when you look at it like that, isn't it kind of embarrassing for them to form such strong opinions with only a fraction of the information and no context?"

Vee nodded thoughtfully, her fingers rubbing her left forearm where a fresh pink scar remained from her vicious beating. "That is a good way of thinking about it, Billie. You're smarter than you look."

I spluttered a laugh. "Ouch. Thanks?"

Her eyes widened. "Oh my god, no! I didn't mean it like that. I'm sorry!" But her apology dissolved into laughter when she saw I wasn't actually offended. "Okay, I feel better for telling you that, particularly as you already knew and I was stressing out over nothing."

"I'm just glad that's what had you all frowny. For a moment I thought you weren't okay with me pursuing things with Angel..." I glanced at her from under my lashes, still not *totally* sure.

Vee's smile was genuine, though. "Billie, babe. I always knew he'd find his way back to you one day, and I couldn't be happier. For both of you. A love like that... I'm jealous. As much as I care for Giana, I won't give up my world for her. Not like A would for you. Now that he's got you back in his grasp, nothing and no one could keep you apart, I am sure of it. If push comes to shove, he'll slit his own father's throat to keep you safe. Second-chance romance just hits differently, don't you think? So much more intense when you already know how it feels to lose that person."

Speechless, I just stared at her in total agreement.

"Anyway. I'll leave you to sleep." She stood up to hug me, and I returned the gesture. It'd been a *long* time since I'd had any close girl friends, but Vee was... more. She was starting to feel like family.

"Thanks, Vee," I finally croaked out when she released me. "It means a lot that you care."

Her smile was warm as she shrugged. "Of course. You're a good person, Billie. You deserve good things. And great sex, which I think you've got in spades right now." She flashed me a wink before exiting my bedroom once more, leaving me to bask in our little moment of friendship.

A lot of bad had come out of the last decade, but the good was there as well. The lonely, friendless Billie I'd been when I ran into Rhett in that alley felt like a dream. Or nightmare.

I barely recognized the *before Billie* now; this new life was so full of love and warmth that it drowned out the darkness. I mean, sure, there was still drama, like with Grayson, but for the most part, I'd found true happiness and contentment with Bellerose.

All that was left was to ensure no one took that away from me. Not ever again.

thirty-one

JACE

Fuck me dead. Saying *no* to Billie, then shutting the door in her face was officially the hardest thing I'd done in my entire life. No wait, scratch that. My *dick* was harder, which was why I'd kept the guitar carefully between us so she wouldn't call me on my bluff. Because I'd been one hundred percent bluffing. If she'd pushed just a little harder, I'd have dragged her into my room and fucked her senseless against the damn door.

I wished she'd pushed.

After closing the door on her shocked face, I stood there way too long waiting for her to try again. Then I replayed the entire conversation in my head like a girl with a crush, obsessing over what I could have said differently and questioning whether she'd missed my point.

Eventually though, I tossed my guitar back on the bed and groaned. My point—whether she'd understood it or not—was still valid. We couldn't keep hate-fucking in secret, then ignoring each other in public. I needed *more* from her... and surely, she felt the same?

Fucking hell. We had a long road ahead if we were going to ever move forward, and I couldn't help feeling like my constant need to touch her was only pushing us further apart. Her showing up like that only proved my point, didn't it? She hadn't looked at me like the boy who'd once held her heart in my hands. She saw me as a booty call. A quick fuck to burn off excess energy. Nothing more.

That hurt way more than I had been prepared for. Even if it was entirely my own fault. After all, in our last few months together, when had she ever initiated the sex between us? It was always me blowing off steam and walking away the minute we were done.

"Goddamn it, Jace," I groaned, rubbing my hands over my face and flopping down on my bed. "You're an idiot."

An idiot with a dick so hard it could cut glass. Billie had been so worked up I could practically smell her arousal. My imagination liked to think I still could. What would she do now? Rhett must not be here, or there was no way she'd have knocked on my door.

Damn Angelo to hell, what had he been *thinking* leaving her like that? It was fucking rude. More to the point, *how* did he manage to hold back when she was more than willing and eager? Billie was a siren who'd only grown more potent with age.

Getting comfy, I tugged my shorts down to grip my cock. Would she hold onto the need to fuck until Rhett got back? Or take care of things herself?

Stroking my fist up and down my shaft, I closed my eyes and let my mind wander. Knowing my Rose, I'd bet she'd take matters into her own hands. Maybe she was splayed out on the bed, legs spread wide as her fingers disappeared between those sweet thighs... Or was she in the shower, all slick and wet as she pretended her hand was someone else's? Angelo's probably. But what if it was mine that she imagined while pumping two of those delicate fingers into her sweet pussy?

"Rose..." I moaned as my hand worked my dick faster. In my head, she was moaning *my* name in the shower, her fingers working her clit with desperation and her nipples hard with need. "Fuck."

My balls tightened up, my release coming hard and fast as I pictured Billie's shudders and moans as she came. I'd felt her climax on my dick often enough lately that it took almost no creativity to conjure up the exact sensations and sounds of her pleasure while my hot load splattered over my abs and hand. What a mess.

"Shit," I breathed, panting hard as I lay there for several moments. Eventually I got up to shower, then afterward picked up my guitar to let some post-climax creativity flow. And holy hell, did it flow.

"You stand before me, shattered flower, but life blooms below. I see your heart, I feel your heat, I crave your scent. It calls me from the dark and tattered life I've built. "

The music poured out of me, my pen making a mess of my notebook as ideas tripped over each other. Then I needed to drop it all and frantically jerk my dick again because I couldn't fucking stop thinking about Billie. I needed to *fix* things with her because I wanted so badly to go crashing into her room and sink my dick into her perfect pussy... whether she was busy with Rhett or not. He could share just fucking fine.

A quick, heavy knock on my bedroom door jolted me out of my head right as I was coming again, and I gave a frustrated growl when I saw cum splattered across my lyric book. Fucking hell.

"What?" I barked, more than a little annoyed. It wasn't Billie again; she didn't knock that hard.

"Let me in," Gray snapped back, his volume quieter

than the words would suggest. To not wake the rest of the suite? "Quickly, Jace. We need to talk."

My first instinct was to tell him to fuck off— dangerous as that may be with someone like Grayson. But there was a tone in that command that had me hesitating. I'd only heard it from him a few times, and each had been when real shit was going down.

"Hang on," I yelled, snatching up a towel and quickly removing the evidence of my Billie obsession. The shirt I'd ditched earlier was still on the floor, so I yanked it up on my way to the door, pulling it over my head as I opened the door to find Grayson, pale as fuck, leaned against the wall.

"Gray, fuck!"

I pulled the door wider and hurried to help him inside. He started to shake me off, but then stumbled and accepted my help as I got him in the room. The door slammed behind us.

"What the fuck happened?" I snapped as we reached the couch, and he let out a groan and sprawled back.

"Got shot," he said shortly, before he appeared to shake off the pain and pushed himself up straighter, gaze meeting mine. "We need to talk, Jace."

No fucking shit. "You got shot?" I scanned his chest but couldn't see the origin of the wound. The dark material of his shirt hid a lot. "Where? Do you need a hospital?"

"These baggies of coke have been circulating the last two shows," he said, ignoring my questions. "I did some snooping tonight because that emblem on the baggies looked familiar, and I figured out why when I saw the matching tattoo on Angelo. It's part of the Ricci family assets, and I'm fairly sure that's why this international tour was pushed through."

"Where. The. Fuck. Were. You. Shot?" I bit out between clenched teeth, ready to rip his fucking shirt off and bear the consequences of touching Grayson without his permission. Stupid fucker was going to bleed out on the hotel couch if he wasn't careful.

He stood—at this point I could only assume he'd been shot in the head if his behavior was any indication —shrugged off his jacket, and then stripped the Bellerose shirt away as well. He took a second to examine the few areas he was clearly hurting. "Got me in the lateral abdomen," he said shortly when his assessment was done. "Nothing to worry about."

He went to pull the shirt back on, but I reached out and grabbed his arm. "Is the bullet still in you? Do you need a doctor?"

"It's a flesh wound, went straight through the

muscle. Going to hurt like a fucker when I'm drumming but otherwise nothing to worry about."

There was a fuck ton to worry about, but sure, bro. "Okay, tell me about what you saw tonight, then."

He didn't bother to put his shirt on, instead using it to press against the exit wound on his side, leaning into it. The entry point didn't look too bad, thankfully, only oozing a little blood. "I found a Bellerose truck that had a dozen or more equipment cases in it, and when I opened the first few, they were filled with drugs and cash. Giovanni is clearly taking advantage of our shows to mass sell his drugs to an international audience."

This didn't surprise me at all; Angelo's father was an evil piece of shit. "Explains why he didn't make a scene about Angel stepping in for bass. He clearly just wanted this leg of the tour to go ahead no matter what."

Grayson nodded, sweat beading on his brow. I hurried across to the minibar and snatched up a couple of bottles of water. Opening one on the way, I thrust it at him. "Drink this; you look like shit."

He grimaced but took the bottle. "Feel like shit too. Been too long since I got shot. I'm getting rusty."

Fucking hell. "You should always be rusty at getting shot, bro. That's how getting shot works."

Unless you had nine damn lives like Grayson apparently did.

"So, what do we do about this now?" I asked, frustrated that once again my life was out of my control, my future in the hands of another corrupt asshole only interested in using and abusing my band. "Giovanni won't hesitate to kill us if we make waves about this," I reminded Grayson. "He doesn't care, and he won't sweat the bad publicity. Big Noise is only a stepping stone for him. Not an end game."

Grayson nodded, and I was reminded that he'd been part of this life, similar to Angelo. "First thing, we need to tell the rest of the band. Billie and Rhett."

"What about Angelo?" I asked. "Surely, he'd have the best idea of how to deal with Ricci business."

Grayson nodded, readjusting his position as pain crossed his face briefly. "Yes, he would, but he's also in deep with his family. It's not that I don't trust him, because to my fucking astonishment, I actually do, but I'm not sure what side he might take here. Drugs are a big part of their business, and I think his suggestion will be to just let it run and ignore it."

He was probably right. "I agree. We should talk to Billie and Rhett first, and then we'll decide together what we want to happen and how we involve Angelo and Vee. They're the ones with the mafia knowledge, and we'll need that if we decide that we won't allow ourselves to be used to sell drugs."

We were no fucking saints, but this pissed me right the fuck off. Even more so that these assholes had shot Grayson without warning. At my fucking show.

Speaking of... "What happened to the guys who shot you?"

Grayson let out a humorless chuckle. "They met *The Maker*. We'll need to double back and clean that up, along with the evidence in the truck, before tonight is done."

Great. So we had two dead bodies alongside concerts full of Ricci drugs to deal with.

I really should have fucked Billie tonight because the way my luck was going, I might not make it to the end of this tour alive.

None of us might.

thirty-two

BILLIE

My screams were muffled by the pillow that I bit down on, trying desperately to control my volume as Rhett pounded my pussy from behind. He whispered praise as he gripped my hip tighter with one hand, his other busy with two fingers in my ass, pumping in sync with his cock. I was on cloud freaking nine, and it was all I could do not to wake the entire fucking suite up with my moans and screams.

"Let it out, babe," Rhett teased, his pierced dick stimulating my G-spot with every thrust. "They're probably tucked up in their beds right now, dicks in hands, jerking off to the sound of you getting fucked."

Oh *Christ*, that mental image did filthy things to me. "Dammit, Zep," I groaned, then took another mouthful of pillow as my inner walls tightened up and my orgasm started to crest.

With the most infuriating timing, someone pounded on the bedroom door, and Rhett paused, which in turn scared my orgasm off like a timid mouse.

"What?" Rhett snapped, glancing over his shoulder at the door.

"We need to talk," Jace replied, sounding vexed. Good. Fuck him for turning me down. It was all well and good for him to work out *his* frustration with quick hate fucks, but when I need the release, it was all "No, Rose. Not like this." Bastard.

Rhett grunted, giving me a little thrust that made me squeak. "Kinda busy. Come back later."

"Now, Rhett," Jace replied. "It's urgent." Then, because he was an arrogant prick, he just opened the door and let himself inside without waiting for a reply. "Oh."

I gave a strangled giggle because I was face down, ass up with Rhett on his knees behind me, dick and fingers deep in my body.

"Rude," Rhett muttered, his hips starting to move again. "Just keep your mouth shut for a minute, dick-head. She was right about to come again."

True. I really had been. Wait, were we just going to carry on while he watched? Apparently, yes. Rhett shrugged Jace's presence off and went right back to fucking me as though we hadn't been interrupted.

The added element of Jace *watching us* was too good to deny, and it barely took any time at all before my orgasm came rushing back out, and I screamed into the pillow as the intense, bone-shaking pleasure rippled through me and Rhett emptied himself deep inside my cunt.

"Nice," Rhett said, giving my ass a pat before I collapsed in a heap beneath him. "Oh shit, I didn't even hear you come in, Gray."

I froze. Gray was here too? Shit. It was one thing to rub Jace's face in it—he deserved it—but Gray and I were still on such rocky ground that I instantly felt awful. In a flap of motion, I wrapped myself up in the sheet as though I could somehow disappear entirely.

"Why are you covered in blood, bro?" Rhett asked.

"What?!" My panicked yelp was more of a shriek than intended, and then, of course, I couldn't find my way gracefully out of the sheets I'd just tangled myself in and had to squirm around a moment before finally freeing my face. Sure enough, Grayson was ashen-faced and shirtless, a wad of fabric pressed to his side and blood covering his hand.

"Because I got shot. But I'm fine," he grunted, leaning his shoulder against the doorframe. "This isn't *that* urgent."

"Grayson, *you've been shot!*" I yelled, gesturing wildly from inside my sheet burrito. "Why are you here and not at the hospital? You need a doctor! You need to—"

"I'm *fine*," he growled with more determination. "Rhett can stitch me up while you get dressed, Prickles. Just... take a breath." His brow dipped like he was worried about me. *He* was worried about *me*, yet he was the one who'd been fucking shot!

Rhett had already pulled on a pair of pants, and Jace was calling the hotel concierge for a medical kit, and I released my grip on the sheet burrito while I sat there on the edge of the bed staring at Grayson with tears in my eyes.

"Prickles. I'm okay." He said it softer this time, like he knew I was about to have a mental breakdown. I was still so mad at him, so conflicted and hurt about the part he'd played in my parent's deaths—and Penelope's —but the idea of him being hurt or *worse* made me distraught.

He shouldn't be comforting me, though. He was the one bleeding out after having probably just seen me coming all over his best friend's dick. I needed to pull myself together and get some perspective.

"Do I have a minute to take a shower?" I croaked, wetting my lips to keep from crying.

Gray met my eyes, his gaze full of concern. He nodded. "Of course. Take as long as you need."

Choked up, I scurried my sheet-covered ass into the attached bathroom and shut the door firmly behind me. Then I took a few deep breaths before turning on the shower. Call me crazy, but this didn't feel like the right time to be chilling out with Rhett's cum dripping out of my pussy. If it were just to antagonize Jace, different story. But when Gray was covered in blood, something serious was going on.

The hot water and soap also helped me pull my shit together so that I didn't start sobbing like a little bitch, and when I stepped out squeaky clean, I felt stronger. Calmer. Rhett had delivered some clean clothes for me while I showered, and I dressed quickly to rejoin the guys in the bedroom I had shared with Rhett.

Gray was stretched out on the bed facedown, while Rhett threaded what looked like fishing line through his flesh.

I gagged a little at the sight of it all, and Gray turned his face to look my way.

"Sorry," I muttered, wincing. "Sorry. That's just... Rhett are you sure you should be doing that? Isn't it better to call a doctor?"

"Yep," Rhett replied, his eyes on the task at hand. "It would be better. But you try telling rocks-for-brains that."

Grayson huffed. "It doesn't require a doctor. I don't need neat, tidy scars, and it's not life threatening. Going to a hospital would be a waste of everyone's time."

"Agree to disagree," Rhett muttered, but he continued to stitch Grayson's flesh, nonetheless.

"What happened?" I asked, shaking my head. "How did you get shot? Who did it? Why?"

Grayson grimaced in pain, and Jace indicated for me to sit in the little chair at the corner of the room while he stood.

"Giovanni is pushing drugs through our concerts," Jace announced. "Gray stumbled over the evidence and got shot for it. I can only assume the guy who fired the gun didn't realize who he was as that would really mess up the tour—and Giovanni's plans."

Rhett scoffed. "He'd probably just replace Gray with some other Ricci who conveniently plays the drums."

My jaw dropped. "Wait, do we think Angelo has something to do with this?"

None of the guys answered immediately, and my stomach flipped with anxiety.

"No..." Jace finally said with a sigh. He ran a hand over his hair, looking tired. "I don't think so. But we also think he might not see it as an issue."

"I'm kind of on his side on this, then," Rhett commented. "Drugs get sold at concerts. We know this; we've benefited from it ourselves and never given two shits who is doing the selling... Why do we care now?"

Jace scowled. "This isn't the same thing."

"Isn't it?" Rhett straightened up, giving Grayson a break. "If we're talking about those bags you had earlier, Gray, then I can verify the quality of product is perfectly fine. It's not some shady, back-alley crap cut with who fucking knows what, if that's our concern."

"That's not the point, Rhett. If Giovanni is—"

"Bro, chill. I get it. You hate the thought that the Riccis are using us to push their drugs into countries they'd normally be locked out of, but I just want to be clear about what we're *actually* worried about. And I don't think it's the drugs." Rhett shrugged, and I had to agree with him. It wasn't like the band itself was clean and sober, let alone their concerts.

Jace was fuming with outrage, though. "You really think Giovanni's goons care who they're selling to? I guarantee they don't give a shit how old the buyer is so long as they have cash. They could be selling drugs to *kids*, Rhett."

"Which is disgusting and sad as fuck, but don't sit up there on your podium and act like any other random drug dealer distributing at our show gives a fuck how old the buyers are either. You and I both bought drugs before we were eighteen, so cut the sanctimonious crap. You're pissed that we're being used, and that's valid. I am too."

"Agreed," Grayson rumbled. "So what do we do about it? Because their product and cash are being moved in *Bellerose* equipment cases, on *Bellerose* trucks. How many people will actually believe we had nothing to do with this? At minimum we get accused of being accessory to the crime but at worst..." He trailed off with a grimace.

"That would mean you guys would get criminal charges," I said quietly, wrapping my arms around myself. "We need to tell Angelo."

"I'd rather not," Grayson muttered. "He's still a Ricci."

"Exactly," I shot back, frowning. "If anyone can fix this, it's him. And don't bullshit me by saying he'd pick his family over us; we all know that's not true."

Rhett and Jace exchanged a silent, loaded look.

Then Rhett shook his head. "I still don't fully trust him, Thorn. Would he sell *you* out? No way in hell. The rest of us might be fair game, though."

"Bullshit," I spat. "I know him. So do you, Jace. And right now... with all of this?" I gestured to Grayson's freaking gunshot wound that Rhett had just finished stitching closed. "We're in over our heads. We need Angelo, and Vee too, for that matter. This is mafia shit; let the mafia heirs handle it."

None of them responded. Then Jace sighed and headed for the door. "I'll wake them up," he said as he exited, leaving me alone with Rhett and Gray.

Tension vibrated through me, and words built up in my throat, desperate to be released as I met Grayson's pained gaze.

"Rhett, can I have a minute alone with Gray?" I whispered, not tearing my eyes away from the wounded drummer.

Rhett quickly wiped up all the excess blood around his neat stitching, then peeled off his latex gloves. "Sure thing. I'll go sort out some room service."

He left the room, and suddenly the silence grew oppressive and heavy.

"Gray..." I sighed, moving over to kneel on the carpet beside where he lay. "We didn't finish our conversation earlier, and I can't keep going like this, with this big fucking question mark hanging over us. You could have died tonight, and the damn truth"— and my heart—"would have died with you. Things are getting crazy, and I need to know what happened that night. Save the details for another day; just tell me the key points. Please?"

He knew perfectly well what I was talking about. Not the drugs nor the bullet hole in his muscular flesh. I wanted to know about my parents.

"I didn't kill them, Billie," he told me without hesitation, and the relief those words brought me was enough to make tears roll. "I'm sorry, Prickles; I wish I'd connected the dots sooner. But I swear to you they were already dead when I got there. My uncle placed a hit on your mom, but he wasn't the only person she'd double-crossed. Someone else had gotten there before me, so I walked away and let my family assume we had completed the job."

Thank fuck. Thank *fuck*. I knew there had to be a rational explanation, one that didn't involve Grayson slitting my parent's throats. Sure, he would have done it if someone else hadn't got there first, but it was infinitely easier to forgive the intent than the action.

"The fire?" I asked, choking on my sadness and relief.

Gray frowned. "Already alight when I got there. I

was inside for barely more than a minute, just enough to see that your parents were dead and the house ablaze. I didn't hang around after that, just left. My intel said they would be home alone... If I'd known you were there—"

"I was supposed to be out that night," I whispered, shaking my head. Tears coursed down my cheeks, and I swiped at them with the heel of my hand. "Thank you for telling me."

Gray stroked my damp face tenderly. "I can give you more details, when you're ready."

I nodded, sniffing heavily. "I know. For now, it's enough to know you didn't kill them. You didn't light the fire that nearly killed me." In more ways than one. "Let's deal with this Ricci mess tonight and work on us tomorrow."

His tight expression eased noticeably, and a tiny smile of understanding softened his features. "Thank you, Prickles."

"For what?" I frowned in confusion.

"For giving me hope that there's still an *us* to work on tomorrow." His reply was so quiet but soaked in vulnerability, a rare emotion to see from Grayson Taylor and entirely unexpected.

Swallowing back my fresh tears, I gave a nonchalant shrug. "Of course there is. I'm still in love with you, Gray. That's what made this so hard."

His eyes widened, then he wrapped his hand around the back of my neck and pulled me closer for a kiss. "I love you, Billie Bellerose," he rumbled against my lips. "More than I even knew I could."

thirty-three

BILLIE

Angelo's response, when we'd caught him up to speed, was surprising to everyone except me and Vee. She and I understood how Angelo truly felt about his father and his place in the Ricci family, so to us it was no shock when he flipped over the coffee table in a fit of rage, shattering the glass top as it landed.

After *that* we'd needed to relocate into different rooms so housekeeping could clean up all the broken glass, and I'd fallen asleep in Rhett's lap while we went around and around in circles trying to decide what to do about Giovanni's drug operation.

When we boarded our flight to Berlin a few days

later, we were all zombies, dark circles under our eyes and coffee cups clutched in our hands like a fucking lifeline. It was an evening flight, and then we had the night "off" before a concert tomorrow. The exhaustion was worth it, though. Between rehearsals, changing cities, and playing a show in Manchester, we'd finally come up with a plan that everyone *sort of* agreed on.

It hinged almost entirely on Angelo and his crime world contacts, but I had full faith in him.

"I need to speak with my father," he told me in a grim voice as we all settled into our seats for takeoff. I'd opted to sit beside him because, despite how tired I was, I hadn't forgotten how nice our date had been... or how he'd left me so worked up. I wanted revenge.

I buckled myself in, then folded my legs. "Are you sure that's a good idea?"

He gave a small shrug. "Probably not. But I don't need to let on how much we know. He'll already be suspicious since Grayson circled back and made his men and drugs *disappear*. I want to get an idea what the bigger picture is. Drugs are such a small part of Giovanni's empire; I just know there's more going on."

"Do you think he will tell you?" I slipped my hand into his when he offered it, threading our fingers together. "The fact that he let you join the band and never said anything about this whole operation kind of says he doesn't trust you."

Angelo squeezed my fingers and sighed. "I have to try. Any information I can get out of him has to be useful, right?"

"Good luck with that," Jace muttered from across the aisle, already reclining his seat, despite the fact that we hadn't even taken off. Hannah, Bellerose's fill-in manager, settled in last, looking totally disinterested in all of us as she scrolled her phone. She'd turned out to be okay, keeping to herself for the most part. The only time we heard from her was when the guys were late for an appointment on the schedule.

Almost immediately after takeoff, the cabin lights dimmed, and everyone tucked in for a nap on the short flight across to Berlin. I didn't blame them and would have done the same if Angelo wasn't totally distracting me by tracing little patterns on the inside of my knee.

I held out as long as possible, until Jace's snoring filled the cabin and the seatbelt sign flicked off. Then I unlatched my seat belt and leaned over to kiss Angelo.

He met me with a low chuckle, his lips caressing mine with measured calm as he cupped my head in his hand. The way his fingers threaded into my hair meant he had all the control. Again.

Frustrated at being held back, I bit his lip a little

harder than playful, but he just grinned against my kiss. Of course, the infuriating fuck would think that was cute.

Giving a huff, I pushed away and flopped back in my seat with an undoubtedly sour expression on my face. Maybe he'd changed his mind about being into me and I was trying to force a square peg into a round hole. Maybe it was one of those things where he'd *thought* he was attracted to me, but then when we'd actually hooked up, he felt like he was kissing his sister.

Christ, now my cheeks were flaming with embarrassment at the direction my thoughts had taken.

"Bella," Angelo murmured in my ear, leaning over to kiss my neck just below my ear. "I'm trying *really* hard to be a gentleman and not just drag you into the aircraft bathroom to fuck. That petulant look on your face is not helping."

My lips parted in surprise, and I turned my face to meet his deep brown eyes. "Oh."

"Mmm," he replied, swiping the tip of his tongue over his lip like he was tasting my kiss.

I flicked a glance down. "How hard are you trying?"

His lips tugged into a playful grin. "So hard it hurts, Bella." He took my hand, giving a quick glance past me, then showed me just how *hard* he was trying. My eyes widened as my fingers curled around him as best I could through his pants. Goddamn, now I was thirsting after his dick even more than before.

I must have made a little whine because he chuckled again and removed my hand from his pants. "You see? I desire nothing more than to make good use of this flight and fuck you senseless, but I want to be more than that for you. I want us to take things slow and fall in love all over again, without the sex over-riding the romance. Is that okay?"

Ugh, when he put it like that...

"I guess," I mumbled, trying not to pout. The way I was sulking, anyone would think I hadn't had sex in a decade. But technically, I hadn't had sex *with Angel* in nearly that long, so... I was justified. Right?

Angelo grinned at me, probably reading my mind, and pulled a blanket out from the compartment beside his seat. "Here. Recline your seat and have a rest." He draped the blanket over me and helped me get comfy with both our seats reclined. One of the airline staff must have noticed everyone was napping, so the cabin lights dimmed down until they'd left us in near darkness.

No way could I sleep with how worked up and horny I was, though. Briefly, I debated waking Rhett up, but he was right beside Jace, fast asleep with his mouth open. It was so rare for him to sleep deeply that I could never wake him deliberately. So I gave myself a little mental scolding about being an adult and not *needing* to take care of things. But that didn't stop me from glancing over at Angelo again in the hope that he'd changed his mind.

Dammit. His eyes were closed, dark lashes fanning across his tanned skin. He'd left his hand on my leg, the warm weight against my knee reminding me how he'd mentioned fucking in the bathroom. Holding my breath, I slid a hand up my own skirt, intending to just... I don't know what. Maybe just cup my throbbing pussy to tell it to calm down. I didn't get that far, though, before Angelo's fingers wrapped around my wrist and his eyes snapped open.

"Bella..." he murmured.

"Angel..." I replied with a teasing grin.

He rolled his eyes, swatting my hand away. But he didn't stop there. His hand arrived at the place mine had been heading, and his long fingers stroked my heat through the thin fabric of my panties. A deep shudder of pleasure rolled through me, and a tiny whimper escaped my throat.

Angelo flicked my inner thigh, a small reprimand for making noise, and I bit my lip. Hard. Message received: Keep *quiet*.

When he was confident I understood, he continued.

Up and down the crotch of my panties, he stroked me with maddening touches until I was so worked up I must have been making my seat wet. If I could have made clothing disappear with the power of thought, my underwear would be ancient history.

"Shhh," he breathed, his finger rubbing my clit through the now very damp fabric. I squirmed, desperate for more, then brought the blanket to my mouth to bite on. Nothing else was going to keep me quiet—especially when Angelo tugged my panties aside and slid his fingers deep inside my pulsing cunt. I bit the blanket so hard my jaw hurt, then he was fucking me with his hand in quick motions that made me shake from head to toe.

When I came, he jerked the blanket out of my mouth so he could kiss me. I moaned quietly against his lips, and his tongue captured mine as I shuddered and convulsed, tightening around his fingers as my orgasm washed through me in a dizzying wave of relief.

"Better?" he whispered, releasing my mouth a moment later.

"Yessss," I replied on a heavy exhale. "And no. Now I want more." I was only partly joking.

He laughed softly, righting my panties for me before bringing his fingers to his lips. Then he held my gaze as he licked them thoroughly, and I all but came again. Damn it, I'd forgotten what a *tease* Angel was.

Groaning, I grabbed the back of his neck to pull him into another hot and heavy kiss, tasting myself on his tongue. I badly wanted to return the favor and rubbed him through his pants with my hand once more as he kissed me back, but I got the feeling I might wake the plane up if I decided to get on my knees and choke on Angelo's big dick right now. But then that got me wondering if it would be such a bad thing if we had an audience.

The only thing stopping me was the presence of the airline staff, Hannah, and Vee. As hot as it sounded to have Jace, Rhett, and Grayson witness me sucking Angelo's cock... I doubted Hannah and Vee would be into that. Nor would I. Talk about a buzzkill.

"Later, *amore mio*," Angel whispered against my kisses. "Later. This time I don't just want a quick hand job under the blanket; I want you stretched out underneath me, that beautiful body on display, and no distractions."

That *did* sound good. With effort, I took my hands off of him and settled back into my seat. I lay slightly on my side, as did Angelo, and for a while we just lay there staring at each other. Then a thought popped into my head that needed to be asked out loud.

"When Vee got hurt," I whispered, curiosity winning out, "you were so angry at me. You thought it was my fault because of the fake baby."

Angelo winced. "I'm sorry, Bella. That was wrong of me. It was my own guilt talking; I was so convinced she'd been hurt because of my own selfish, impulsive desire to keep you in my life. I was so wrong to try and share that blame with you."

"Understandable, though," I commented. "But that day, and a few times after, you've called Vee the same thing you call me: *amore mio*."

He nodded. "My love."

I remembered the translation from when we were younger. "Vee..."

"Is my wife," he whispered, his gaze steady and unflinching. "She's also the closest thing I have to a best friend and the only person I have ever shared my true self with... since leaving you and Jace. She and I do not share a romantic love, not like how I feel for you, Bella, but we still love each other deeply." He paused, his eyes searching mine. "Does that worry you?"

Did it? I wasn't one hundred percent sure. But... "I don't think so. I can see the connection between you two, the trust and understanding. I'm jealous," I admitted, wrinkling my nose, "but only because she got all those years that I missed out on. I get it, though. I really like her too."

Angelo stroked the backs of his fingers down the side of my face in a loving gesture. "She may have those years, Bella, but you have my heart. Always have, always will."

thirty-four

ANGELO

Billie Bellerose was going to be the death of me. When news of my untimely demise reached my father, he'd be told that I died of extreme sexual frustration. Of my own making, too. What the fuck I'd been thinking, getting her off like that on the plane, I had no clue. All I'd achieved was a boner so hard and unrelenting that I'd needed to slip into the bathroom after she fell asleep and rub one out.

When we disembarked in Berlin, Grayson glared daggers at me, and I just smirked back. Then sucked my fingers again. He'd seen what had happened in the dark of the plane, watching with burning jealousy as she came apart quietly on my hand. Something had shifted between them since he'd been shot, though, and I had no doubt he'd be back in her bed and between her thighs in no time.

It still didn't stop me from feeling smug as fuck now, while her arm wrapped around my waist and I kissed her hair as we crossed the private airstrip's tarmac.

Rhett, sullen asshole that he was, rubbed sleep from his eyes, then frowned at me. Then at Billie. Then grabbed her hand and tugged her swiftly out of my embrace and into his own. Slick fucker.

Billie's laugh filled the night, and I extended my middle finger to Rhett, who returned it with one of his own. Sharing her with anyone other than Jace would really take some getting used to, but it helped that Rhett and Grayson seemed to be decent enough dudes. They worshiped her, and that counted for a lot.

My phone buzzed while we waited for Hannah to sort out all our customs paperwork, and I sighed when I saw the caller ID. It was a call I'd been waiting on, but I still didn't really want to take it. The day I could cut my father out of my life for good couldn't come soon enough.

I quickly showed the screen to Jace before stepping away from the group to answer the call.

"Angelo!" The snap of my name was familiar. I'd

heard it every day of my life since I was old enough to remember life.

"Father," I replied formally.

"Why haven't you checked in?"

Good question. Maybe because I don't trust you, you old fuck. "It's been hectic. The tour, that is. Trying to keep up with new songs and learn how these tours work is taking all of my time and energy. But rest assured, Ricci assets are in safe hands. Everything is running smoothly."

There was an extended pause. "What are you referring to, *figlio?*"

"The shows of course," I replied with the same pause. "Were you referring to something else?"

The reason for this phone call was probably related to the missing Ricci men, the ones Grayson had dealt with in what had been, no doubt, a bloody and fitting end. Giovanni was checking in on his assets. The ones that mattered to him anyway. He didn't give a fuck about the success of the band and would, I was certain, try to destroy it when its usefulness had expired.

"Father?" I pressed. "Are there other jobs happening over here? I mean, I assumed so since you were fairly easy to convince that I should be part of the tour. I know you'll make money from this, but you always

371

have a concurrent plan. If you want me to keep an eye on it, you need to let me in on the job."

"No, no, no, son. I want you to live your dream for a short time before returning to take over your rightful place as head of this family." He said all of this in a rush, putting on the accent of his *cheerful Italian* persona. That was a dangerous tone from him, but I was too experienced with his shit to ever fall for the con. At his nicest, he destroyed you the worst.

It also told me that he was a hundred percent using this tour to run astronomically high levels of drugs through Bellerose, all the while setting them up to take the fall should anyone become aware of it. Or not aware. Knowing Giovanni, he probably planned to take them down this way no matter what.

"Was there another reason for this call, then?" I pressed, noting that Hannah had finished wrapping up the paperwork to get us into the country. I was running out of time.

"Ah, yes," he continued, still with all the Italian cheer. "Have you seen or heard from Valentina?"

There was not an ounce of fucking cheer in my reply. "No. Why is that?"

"Her father is most worried about her. She hasn't been seen for a few weeks, and we don't know if a rival family has her or if she's been killed. You're her husband. Why do you not know where she is?"

This fucker would pick up even the smallest detail if I let it slip, but again, I was too experienced with him to ever betray Vee like that. "You know we don't have a close relationship, Father. She does her thing and I do mine. We don't regularly check in except to fuck when she's fertile. For the Ricci-Altissimo heir."

"That should be soon then, correct?"

The fact that he knew her cycle should be terrifying, but I had zero doubt that Vee's father kept a close eye on that and kept mine informed. Old fucking perverts.

"Correct. But I'm not in America, which I assume she's aware of since I left her a voicemail before we took off. I'm sure she'll turn up eventually. When she needs money."

It pissed me right off that I had to act like Vee was just another brainless mafia wife, spending our money and gossiping with the other wives. Vee could have run the whole fucking family with half of her brain tied behind her back, but she couldn't show that. Neither of us could. Until we destroyed the leaders of the family, our only way to stay safe was to not break the traditions of the older generation, like strict gender roles.

"You will contact me the second you hear from her, Angelo."

"Yes, Father," I said dutifully. "Is there anything else you need me to take care of while I'm here?"

Billie, who I'd had one eye on since starting this conversation, released her hold on Rhett and wandered in my direction, no doubt to tell me that it was time to get into the row of black cars waiting for us.

"Just keep Bellerose in line. That fucking Adams kid thinks he's top shit, but I run his show now."

I barely heard his disdain for Jace; he'd always hated the effortlessly talented and charming personality of my oldest friend. Nope, I was too focused on Billie as she smiled mischievously, running her hand down the buttons of my shirt.

It felt as if I could still taste her on my tongue, and that just made me want more. I barely fucking stopped myself from groaning into the phone, and wouldn't that confuse my asshole of a father.

"Bellerose just plays their show and travels to the next," I bit out, voice gruff. "There's nothing else to worry about."

"What about all the fucking?" Billie breathed, just audible enough that I could hear, but I was fairly sure Giovanni wouldn't. "There has been a lot of fucking."

This time my groan was covered in a strangled laugh because there really hadn't been enough fucking. Not with us anyway.

"Angelo?"

"Got to go, Father. They're waiting on us."

I hung up the phone, knowing I'd pay for it later, but I had my girl's dirty mouth to deal with now. "All the fucking," I said softly, dropping the phone into my pocket so I had both hands free to reach out and wrap around her waist. "Is that right?"

She gasped softly when I yanked her into me, lifting her slowly until her face was even with mine. The flush on her cheeks reminded me of the girl I'd first fallen for and how she'd look after we fucked. "I think we're up to the third date now, right?" she breathed, pupils dilating as she licked her lips.

A possessive sort of rumble I hadn't expected shot through my chest, and when I pulled her into my body, she immediately wrapped her arms and legs around me, holding on like she'd been desperate for this sort of hug all morning.

"Third date done and dusted," I whispered against her hair. "Next time, I will have all of you, Bella. I'll settle for nothing less."

The jerk of my cock, buried between us, only reiterated that statement.

"Thank fucking fuck," she breathed. "I was actually concerned that you were practicing a new torture technique: sexual deprivation."

"If anyone was being tortured, little love, it was me."

"Hey, fuckhead, you need to bring our girl to the car now." Rhett was hanging halfway out the window of the first car as he bellowed. "We have a schedule to keep."

A burst of laughter from Billie followed, and she started to wiggle, indicating she wanted to be let down. But I just shifted my hold under her ass to keep her more secure and set off for the second car. Vee was in the first one too, but she'd be fine. I needed to show Rhett that he could demand all he fucking wanted, but that asshole didn't own Bella. He was going to have to learn to share better, and I was about to become a fantastic teacher.

A few of his curses reached us as I placed Bella in the middle seat, next to Jace, before sliding in on the other side of her. "Rhett is going to murder you in your sleep," Jace said with a laugh.

A derisive snort was my initial response to that. "Not fucking likely. The last time someone got the drop on me while I was asleep was when we were thirteen and you fart bombed me. I still owe you for that, by the way."

Jace tipped his head back and laughed, such a free, joyful sound. It reminded me of when we were kids; I was fairly sure he hadn't laughed like that in a long time—a fact confirmed by the way Billie shifted her head and watched him, her eyes shiny and filled with all the memories of the past that had just hit me.

"You got me back, bro," Jace finally said, clearly having no idea he'd just triggered Billie and me into a stroll through memory lane. At least those memories were the good ones. It was the years after that which had really fucked us up. "I could name at least twenty times I woke up in a bed full of frogs. What your fucking obsession with those slimy fucks was, I'll never know."

"Giovanni hated them," Billie said sounding sad. "Angel was aware, even then, that his father was an evil dictator."

She still knew me better than anyone else, and considering I'd never mentioned out loud the real reason I'd adored frogs for the first ten years of my life, it showed her keen observation skills.

"He feared them," I said with a nod. "And that man hates anything he fears. It was a tiny piece of revenge to leave frogs randomly around the house to jump at him. He still has no idea it was me. The memory of his screams got me through some really bad shit."

Jace just shook his head. "Your childhood is so fucked up; I think we need to get you into therapy too."

Billie laughed briefly before she managed to shut it down. Jace shot her a dirty look, and she choked on another laugh as she grinned back at him. "I just—" More laughter. "You probably need therapy more than any of us. Maybe we should inquire into a group discount."

Jace managed to hold onto his annoyance for a few seconds, before a resigned chuckle emerged. "Yeah, you're probably right. Guess that's why we all work so well together. We get the trauma."

We really fucking did.

The rest of the journey was quiet, Billie leaning over Jace and me as she took in the Berlin landscape. There were multiple Bellerose billboard signs up along the way, and it was still hard to believe I was here. On fucking tour.

When we arrived at the hotel, we were directed into a back parking lot, which had its own private elevator up to a set of suites that were all interconnected by a large central living room. Hannah translated everything, though the concierge spoke excellent English.

"Okay, rest up," the tour manager said, once the hotel staff had vacated the room. "If you want to venture out, you can find members of the security team outside and in the elevators to escort you, but otherwise we'll see you at the venue tomorrow for soundcheck."

"See you tomorrow," Jace said, all but ushering her to the door so he could close it behind her. Hannah didn't seem worried by it, shooting us a friendly smile before heading out.

When she was gone, everyone relaxed, dropping down into the couches. Vee slid in on one side of me, and I gave her a hug.

Rhett had Billie back in his arms on the next couch over, but I was okay with it. For now.

"Okay, now that we're alone," Jace said, striding back to drop down on the other side of me. "What's the plan moving forward? Angel, did you confirm that Giovanni is running the drugs?"

"Not in so many words," I replied. "But he was cagey, and there's only one reason for him to call right after Grayson fucked up his plan. He was clearly fishing to find out whether I knew what happened to his missing men and the cases of drugs."

"Where are the cases?" Vee asked, leaning forward.

"They're with the other band equipment," Grayson said shortly. "To save suspicion, I just changed out the locks on the back of that truck and told the crew that it was our personal items and to leave them unopened for this Berlin show. Gives us time to figure out what we're going to do with it all."

I had a few ideas, but before I could voice them, Grayson continued.

"I think we should arrange for the local gangs here to steal all the cases. There has to be a few million in cash and that amount again in drugs just in that one truck. It's well worth their while. I've got some contacts here I could reach out to—"

"I can do it," Vee cut in quickly. "Giana has cousins from Berlin, and I spent a few years with her here after I graduated from high school, while Angel was *allowing me* to experience some freedom."

How it had to look to our fathers, anyway.

"I know the local cartels quite well. Altissimo has done business with several of them in the past. You can leave it to me to organize."

Grayson regarded her closely for a beat, before he nodded once. "Okay, you reach out to your contacts. Discreetly, of course. None of this shit can come back on Bellerose."

Vee nodded, already jumping up. "You can rely on me. This is the shit I live for."

No fucking lie, she was known as the Mafia Princess for a reason. The life I'd been born into was a burden, but for Valentina Altissimo, it made her feel alive.

Her only sin was being born a female in a male-dominated world, but I fucking hoped that one day soon, that shit wouldn't matter.

The best person for the job was Vee, and I intended to make it happen.

thirty-five

BILLIE

This time, Vee and I went along for soundcheck. I didn't feel like hanging out in the hotel room until it was time to leave, and now that Grayson and I were moving toward some healing, it felt right to just be with the band as much as possible.

"Everything is set for tonight," Vee said, dropping down next to me in the stadium seats. Bellerose was working through their set list, and we had front row seats. I turned to find a broad smile on her face, her cheeks flushed as excitement filled her features. "It was actually nice to catch up with a cartel that allows women to be in powerful leadership positions."

"A woman runs the syndicate?" I asked, not even trying to hide my surprise.

Vee nodded. "Oh yeah. She's one bad ass bitch, and I hope that I'm as awesome as her when I grow up."

We were in our mid-twenties, but I got the sentiment. Some days it felt like I had a shit ton of growing up to do.

"What is the plan for tonight, then?" I asked, pitching my voice lower. We didn't have anyone nearby, except for a couple of security lingering in the aisles, but I wouldn't take any chances.

Vee turned back to the stage, relaxing into her chair as Bellerose launched into "Silent Trauma."

"After the show, we'll arrange for that truck to be left open in the back of the transport entrance to this venue. Juniper will show up with their trucks, remove the drugs and cash, and leave all the Bellerose equipment and gear there for it to head out to the next show."

"Is there any way to stop the drugs from circulating tonight?" I asked. "Or do you think the Ricci group will be laying low until they figure out what happened with the missing men and equipment truck?"

Before she answered, Vee sang along with Jace's chorus, and I had to smile. She knew every single lyric, and I had a feeling she might have been a Bellerose fan before she ever became part of their world. "They'll lay low for the next few shows," she confirmed. "And he'll send more of his most trusted across to ensure the rest of the tour goes as scheduled."

That was good. It meant that we had time to get this lot offloaded and figure out how to ensure there were no further Ricci drugs at the concerts.

The sooner Bellerose got out from under Big Noise, the better.

We chatted for a few more minutes before Hannah made her way along the row to us. "Ladies, could you head back to the side of stage?" she asked. "We need to get this area secure before the show."

"No worries," I said, getting to my feet.

As we made our way to the area where the roadies and crew were hanging out, Bellerose moved on to another of their hits, one that always came near the end of their set, which meant they were about to wrap up soundcheck.

Vee hurried over to the refreshment table and ate like a starving woman, and I enjoyed seeing her let loose. She wore a Bellerose band tee with the sleeves cut off, tight black jeans, and short black boots. Her hair was wild and curled down her back, her eye makeup dark and stormy.

She looked like a sexy rock goddess, and I was so happy she was on this tour with us.

"Hey there," a smooth voice said from my left. I turned away from Vee to find the lead singer of Lightstones, the opening act for Bellerose, standing there.

His name escaped me as I said, "Hey, can I help you?"

He wasn't classically handsome, not like Jace, but he had a nice smile, and he was shooting me the full wattage of it as he ran a hand through his short black hair. "I don't know, can you? I see you sitting here all by yourself, looking like every rock star's fantasy, and I figured I should come over and introduce myself."

It hit me then that this guy was flirting with me. It had been a long time since a random stranger had approached me like this, and I almost laughed at how uninterested I actually was. "I might be a rock star's fantasy, but that rock star isn't you," I said shortly. *Please just go the fuck away.*

He clearly had thicker skin than I expected, and of course, there was no greater incentive than rejection for a dude to dig in harder. "Aw, come on. Don't be like that. I promise that I have all the skills of Bellerose, in a much larger package."

Considering he was only a few inches taller than me, and his tight black jeans hid nothing, I doubted that very much. "I'm seriously not interested," I said as I crossed my arms over my chest. "And you need to walk away before you get yourself into trouble."

The jovial smile finally fell, and what looked like annoyance creased his forehead. "You think you're so good, the whore of Bellerose. Bitch, they have a different one of you in every—"

His words were cut off by a huge fucking hand around his throat. Grayson wore his neutral expression, the one I was starting to realize was the scariest of all, as he lifted the struggling singer up and whirled him around, all but throwing him into the nearby wall.

"Gray," I choked out, grabbing him before he could break the guy's neck or something. "It's okay. He was learning how to take no for an answer."

His reply was a rumble of pissed-off drummer, and the loser on the floor took the hint, scrambling to his feet with one hand pressed to his throat as he raced off.

"Will he be able to sing now?" I asked, some amusement creeping in at how terrified the guy was.

"Who the fuck cares. He sounds like shit anyway."

Grayson turned his full focus on me, running his gaze over my body, as if checking for injuries. "Did he hurt you? Touch you?"

I shook my head quickly. "No, no. He was just

flirting really badly, and when I rejected him, he got a little nasty."

Clearly the lead singer of Lightstones had seen the *Dirty Truth* articles about me or had witnessed me being passed around by my guys at one of the venues. The asshole had formed his own opinions from that, thinking I was just a band groupie to be used and abused.

No doubt that's what it looked like from the outside, but I knew the truth.

"Are you sure you're okay?" Grayson pulled me back to the present, and I couldn't help but step closer to him, wrapping my arms around his waist.

"I'm okay," I replied. "Thank you for having my back."

His chest rumbled again, and it sounded louder when I was pressed against him. "Always, Prickles. I will never fucking let you down again. I promise."

He'd never let me down in the first place.

The rest of the band was off stage now too, heading for the refreshments. Grayson had clearly seen what was happening with the Lightstone's front man and had bailed a few minutes before the others.

"Do you think we'll be able to figure out who actually initiated the hit on my mother?" I asked suddenly. It was a topic close to mind these days. "Angelo swears that he's been looking and nothing ever came through official Ricci channels. But he did confirm she worked for his dad, though."

"She worked for multiple criminal organizations," Grayson added. "I've managed to find out that much. Her reputation as an accountant was strong, and it was known that she kept her mouth shut and the money clean. Clearly, though, she pissed off the wrong person."

"How would she even get into accounting for gangs and cartels and the mafia in the first place?"

I mean, we were just middle-class suburban people, Mom an accountant and Dad a mechanic. None of it made sense.

"She caught the eye of the wrong person at the right time," Grayson said, still holding me close. We were able to have our whispered conversation like this, and everyone left us alone, no doubt happy to see our rift healing. "And once her rep got around, others would have approached her too. She never exclusively signed to any one criminal organization, and she probably had no idea how risky it was to work for multiple."

That was *probably* where all that money I'd inherited had come from. She'd either stolen it or earned it by doing really terrible shit. My instinct to never touch it had been a good one. No doubt I'd have found my throat slit too if I'd messed with that blood money. Messed with the wrong people.

Just like my poor dad.

He'd been an innocent caught up in mom's illegal bullshit. Just like Penelope.

These new revelations had me feeling like I was losing them all over again.

The wounds were still so raw and aching that not even my usual techniques from Dr. Candace could stop tears from spilling free. Only a couple, hidden against Grayson's shirt. He didn't say anything else, just held me tightly, and I felt like some of my broken pieces almost fit back together under his touch.

"It's going to be okay, baby girl," he told me, when we finally pulled apart. "We will get to the bottom of it, and I promise that everyone involved that hurt you and Penelope will pay with their lives."

He'd do it too; the truth of that was written across his face.

As I pushed up on my toes, he dropped his head so that our lips could touch. It had been too long since I'd kissed Grayson, and despite the very brief taste, it calmed a corner of my heart that had been aching for the last ten or so days. A piece of my soul righted once more.

"Come on, Gray, we need to get ready," Jace

shouted, shooting me a smile and a wink. He seemed happier than ever, and I wondered if that was because he'd felt the same pain in the rift as I had. This was Jace's band... his brothers, and he wouldn't like any of them being on the outs.

Gray kissed me one last time before Rhett swept in and twirled me around, kissing the hell out of me. Hannah shouted for them to get their asses moving, and once they were gone, I realized I was starving.

I joined a grinning Vee. "Girl, get your energy levels up," she said as I grabbed a plate and started filling it.

"You think I'm going to need it?"

She picked up a second plate. "Hell yes, you are. I'm filling one for you too."

Vee and I spent the next couple of hours, eating, laughing, and waiting for the concert to kick into gear. The stadium was absolutely packed, the noise near deafening as the crowd screamed for Bellerose to come out on stage. The opening act started, and I almost laughed at the rasp in the lead dickhead's voice. He made it through somehow, but he'd be paying for it tomorrow.

Not that I cared. He got what he deserved.

As Lightstones left the stage, Bellerose was announced, and the crowd lost its shit. Like, I'd thought it was noisy before, but this was next level. Vee clutched my arm, and I was a little sad that in this venue the boys were going to enter from beneath the stage, which meant I couldn't give out my customary kisses for luck. Oh well, I'd have to save all the kisses for afterward.

Vee squealed, and I almost did the same when the boys filed onto the stage, taking their places behind their instruments. Grayson's drums were closest to us —that was how he'd been able to see the scene earlier from the stage—and he shot me a slow smile as he twirled his sticks around his fingers.

Fingers that I already knew were talented in ways well beyond drumming.

Jace took his position in front of the thousands of screaming fans. "What's up, Berlin?" he yelled, and the crowd screamed back, only growing quiet when he spoke again. "We're so excited to be here tonight in your beautiful city. So let's get this fucking show on the road."

Rhett's guitar filled the stadium as he launched into the opening chords of the first song on their set list—a crowd favorite here in Berlin if the response was any indication.

It was also one of their few songs that wasn't about me or the heartbreak of the past, and I felt like they'd done that deliberately. Angel joined in with Rhett a moment later, and the drums added the beat beneath them as Jace started to sing.

It was electric, and already emotional from my healing with Grayson, I wasn't surprised when the burn of tears filled my eyes and throat. Vee, still holding my arm, pulled me even closer. She didn't say a word, but her comforting presence was strong and sure as I let the what-ifs of the past crowd in on me.

This was the life I should have always had, on tour with Jace and Angel, my first loves—made even better by the newer loves in my life: Rhett and Grayson. The four of them completed my heart in a way I hadn't understood until Grayson and I repaired the final quarter. That final crack that had been weeping for days, burning through my soul and happiness.

Now I was whole.

At least that part of me was, and in this moment, watching my boys—four of the most amazing, talented, hot-as-fuck musicians onstage this decade—I hoped that we would finally be able to put the past to rest. It wasn't going to be easy, but I had a damn list, and I was determined to cross out each item.

1. Find out who ordered the hit on my parents.
2. Cut ties with Big Noise and, in turn, Angelo's ties with Giovanni.

3. Free Vee from the cage of her family so she could love who she wanted.

Easy as fuck.

Well, if I could land four rock stars, I could do any fucking thing.

Right?

thirty-six

BILLIE

The first part of our plan worked flawlessly. The trucks were "hijacked" after they left the concert venue in Berlin in a highly dramatic highway robbery that resulted in a sickening amount of collateral damage—thankfully, only cars and property, no people. Okay, so maybe it wasn't *flawless* because the mess left along the Autobahn wasn't part of the plan... Maybe we should have specified hijacking on a road that actually *had* a speed limit.

Ether way, the drugs and money were *gone* and our hands were clean. For the next week of touring, we were inundated with news reports of the robbery and wild theories about what had been stolen. The popular fan theory was that someone stole Bellerose's instruments—their *babies*—and we leaned into that idea by having the guys use their backup equipment at the next shows.

Giovanni lost his *shit* over it. Of course he did. He even sent some of his guys over under the guise of security to snoop around and work out what had happened, but we remained confident that they'd never tie it to us —easy enough, when Giovanni genuinely didn't think we were capable of it. Angelo suffered a harsher inquiry, though, and Vee had to go into hiding as soon as we heard Ricci enforcers were joining the tour. She hadn't wanted to go, more than happy to just "deal with things" if her family found her, but we outvoted her. She meant too much to Angelo—and to me since we'd been getting closer every day. Vee was my best girl, and I wouldn't risk her getting shot by some mafia wannabee goon.

On the upside for Vee, the easiest place for her to hide was with Giana. So as sad as she'd been to leave us, I could see how badly she wanted to reunite with her love. I was disgustingly happy for her.

"Are you all looking forward to your break?" Hannah asked as we arrived in Monaco. We'd done all the travel since Berlin by road, since everything in Europe was so close, and Hannah had taken to travelling with us closer than ever. Which, on the one hand, pushed the guys into working on new music. On the other, it seriously tossed a dampener on our frenzied sex life.

So was I looking forward to spending a week in a luxury villa with just my four sexy rock stars and no interruptions? Hell yes. Hell *freaking* yes. I was so ready I was probably leaving a wet spot on my seat as I squirmed with excitement.

"Did the label make all the arrangements we asked for?" Jace asked in a bored voice, playing his celebrity role well.

Hannah nodded. "Yes, all confirmed. I'll check it myself once we arrive, too."

A ridiculous list of requirements was just expected of a famous music group while travelling, and vacationing, on tour. So we'd come up with a whole bunch of dumb shit like a freezer full of 42 Below Feijoa, a bowl of red peanut butter M&Ms, and—at Rhett's request—sixteen flavors of lube. Amongst those diva requests, though, we had included things like one-way glazing on all the windows to prevent paparazzi shit and video surveillance and perimeter alarms on all doors, windows, and garbage chutes. If Giovanni wanted to try any shit, we'd know.

My knee bounced with nervous energy, and I checked my new phone for the thousandth time. Vee had text me earlier with a picture of her with Giana, the gorgeous bronze-skinned woman kissing her on the cheek.

"She looks happy," Jace commented, looking over my shoulder.

I glanced up at him, meeting his eyes only a few inches away. "Yeah, she does. Is it weird that I miss her already? We haven't exactly been friends for years."

"Not really. Sometimes when you meet a person, you just connect on a different level. Like platonic soul-mates." He shifted into the seat beside me, his shoulder resting against mine as he glanced down the bus. Gray, Rhett, and Angelo were chatting to Hannah, and I could see what he meant. Jace's bandmates were his platonic soulmates. His heart friends.

"That's really beautiful, Jace," I said softly as he looked back to meet my gaze. "You should write song lyrics with that kind of prose. You could be really good at it."

He grinned and rolled his eyes. "Funny, Rose. Real funny. Actually... I wanted to ask you for a favor."

I narrowed my eyes with suspicion. "Uh... what

kind of favor?" Ever since that night in Edinburgh when he'd rejected my booty call, things between us had been... I don't even know. Weird. Not in a bad way, like I'd been prepared for. Just confusing.

Jace ran a hand over the back of his neck, which drew my attention to his ink-covered bicep, and then I started to think filthy things about that arm wrapped around my waist as he hoisted me up onto a counter and—

"Could you take a look at some lyrics for me? I was working on something back in the UK, and it was flowing really well, like, better than I'd ever vibed with a song, and then..." He trailed off with a small, frustrated groan.

"What killed the muse?" I smiled because Jace had always been like that. He'd be *pouring* music out of his soul, and then the slightest disruption would break his focus and it'd be gone.

He pouted in a stupidly attractive way. Boys pouting shouldn't be that sexy. "Grayson. Anyway, would you take a look?"

I shrugged. "Sure. I'll see what you've got."

Jace flashed me an appreciative, if embarrassed smile, then pulled his notebook out. The cover and pages were dog-eared and well-worn, but he flipped through quickly to find the song he wanted help on.

Spreading the pages, he passed it over to me with a small frown of worry on his face.

Intrigued, I raised a brow at him before starting to read the lyrics. He'd scribbled messy music notes below the lines of poetry, so it took up a dozen or so pages, and I quickly found myself immersed in the story his song wove. I could almost hear the melody in my mind, with Jace's honey voice singing the lyrics to me. Because at the heart of it, this song was from Jace *to me*.

When I reached the end, where his pen had scrawled across the page as Grayson interrupted him, I sniffed and wiped my damp cheeks.

"Jace," I whispered in a hoarse voice. "This is…"

"All true," he murmured, his eyes downcast to the notebook in my hand. "And should have been said a long time ago."

I swallowed hard, focusing on the page where his pen trailed off. Then I frowned. "Why is the paper crusty?"

Jace sucked in a sharp breath, his cheeks flaming red. "Oh, uh, I spilled something."

I wrinkled my nose, scratching at the crusty paper to try and save the ink beneath. "Were you eating yogurt or something? Fuck, Jace, you could have ruined the whole book."

"Yeah. Yogurt. It's a good, um, composing snack.

Anyway, that's beside the point. Can you help me finish it? I thought... maybe it's something we need to do together?" His eyes filled with hope and an apology, just like the song in my hands. The question wasn't whether I could help him write a song, it was whether I could forgive all the shitty things he'd said to me in the last few months. Whether I could forgive him for walking away from our love so easily all those years ago.

I drew a deep breath. "We used to write so well together," I murmured, running my thumb over the damaged page again, a tornado of conflicting emotions swirling through me.

"We still could," he replied in a soft voice, his hand finding mine and squeezing gently. "Couldn't we?"

I wasn't so sure. I *wanted* to say yes... but I also wasn't totally sure I was ready to forgive him. So many mean comments could be easily brushed off, but his anger and resentment about the loss of our baby was a tough one to swallow. Whether he apologized now, or not, I couldn't forget the things he'd said and the way he'd felt. Not yet. Not so easily, and goddamn, that hurt.

My lips parted, my eyes locked with his, but no words came out. A moment later, the bus slowed to a stop, and Hannah announced that we'd arrived at our vacation house.

"Rose..." Jace pleaded, but I peeled my hand out of his grip and handed the notebook back.

"I'm sorry," I whispered, sliding out of my seat. "I just don't..." I trailed off before I could really start crying. Unable to face the crushing disappointment in his gaze, I turned away and hurried off the bus.

"Everything okay?" Angelo asked, glancing back to the bus. "That seemed intense."

Gritting my teeth, I gave him a brittle smile. "Fine. We good to go in?" Our security had arrived a few minutes before us, by the look of things, and one of the guys at the door gave us a wave to indicate it was safe to enter.

Angelo looped his arm around my shoulders as we made our way inside, and I snuggled into his body. Fucking hell... what would I do about Jace?

"...five bedrooms, six bathrooms, steam room and sauna, home gym, infinity-edge pool," a smartly dressed woman I vaguely recognized as the property agent was saying, "and of course, a recording studio, in case the muse feels right and you want to extend your stay. The owner is a big fan and all too happy to accommodate whatever you request."

Hannah steered the agent away, talking to her about... I don't even know what. Angelo and I checked out all the rooms quietly, and I picked one with a little balcony and gorgeous natural light. It seemed like the right thing to have my own bedroom. That way I wasn't playing favorites... right?

"Can I sleep here with you tonight, Bella?" Angelo asked, his hands finding my waist as my back found the wall. I moaned as his lips found mine, and I melted into his kisses for far longer than I should have.

"Uh-huh," I replied in a breathy sigh when his lips moved to my neck and his hands slid under my shirt. "Definitely."

Whoops, so much for not playing favorites.

"Hey! Ricci! Hands off my girl," Rhett interrupted, giving Angelo a slightly rougher than playful shove and stealing me out from his embrace.

A flash of anger and frustration passed over Angel's face, but it eased when I laughed. "*My* girl," he growled, but with a lopsided grin to show he was joking. Sort of.

"Prickles!" Grayson bellowed from deeper into the house. "Come here! I'm making cocktails. You want Sex on the Beach?"

I grinned, letting Rhett lead me down the hallway to the kitchen. "I'm game," I told Gray when we reached him. "But I'm not sure if sand will get places it shouldn't be."

"Don't tempt me," he rumbled with a heated glance.

"It's too cold for the beach," Rhett complained. "I'm not against the hot tub though. What do you say, Thorn? Cocktails in the hot tub? No clothes allowed." He winked, and my belly fluttered with excitement.

"Angel, can I get your help on a song?" Jace asked, strolling through with a guitar in hand. He glanced my way with a pained expression, then disappeared in the direction of the recording studio.

Angelo gave me a long, conflicted and worried look, then followed Jace.

"Just the three of us, then," Rhett purred with a sly grin. "Definitely no clothes."

I arched a brow in question at Grayson, and he smiled back at me. "I'm game if you are, Prickles. Go warm up with Rhett; I'll bring drinks shortly."

Rhett didn't need to be told twice, giving a whoop of excitement as he tossed me over his shoulder.

Two hours later, my fingers and toes were all wrinkled from soaking in the tub too long, and my whole body was boneless jelly as Grayson carried me up to my bedroom. I'd lost count of all the orgasms, but the guys had definitely been trying to prove a point and take advantage of Jace and Angelo being distracted with songwriting.

"That…" I groaned as Grayson set me down on the end of my bed, "was fucking awesome."

He smirked. "*Fucking* is right. I don't think I've ever had such a short refractory period in my life."

I yawned, stretching the aching muscles of my back, then my stomach rumbled. "I'm starving. Do we have food in the fridge?"

"Fully stocked," Gray confirmed. "Get dressed; I'll go see what we can sort out for dinner."

I did as I was told, pulling some sweats out of my suitcase and dressing quickly. Then I headed out to the kitchen, where I found Gray chatting with Angelo… who was elbows deep in cooking us dinner. The rich aroma of tomato and herbs made me groan, and I almost came again. Or maybe that was just jizz-drip from the hot tub session.

"Hannah stopped by while you were *busy*," Angelo informed us. "Apparently the Madrid show got cancelled due to a plumbing issue at the venue. So we're cleared to stay here another week if we want."

My brows shot up, and happiness fizzed in my chest. "Yay!"

"Dinner is almost ready," Angelo said. "Gray, go call Jace and Rhett so it doesn't get cold."

"Can do," the big guy rumbled, slipping back out of the kitchen.

I circled around the counter to hug Angelo's waist, and he kissed my hair.

"Jace played his new song for me," he said quietly. "He's got a lot of regrets."

I swallowed the lump of emotion building in my throat. "I know. But he can't just—"

My words cut short as the power to the whole house switched off suddenly, plunging us into darkness. I stiffened, and Angelo's body tensed under my embrace. No alarms sounded for a perimeter breach, but would they work if the power was off? I had no clue.

"What...?" I whispered, but Angelo gave a me a squeeze that seemed to tell me to stay quiet.

A second later, a loud crash echoed through the house, followed by several more thumps and a hoarse male shout. The lights snapped back on, and Angelo shifted to push me behind him. Because we were no longer alone.

There in the kitchen, several heavyset men dressed in black held Jace, Rhett, and even Grayson, on their knees with hands bound at their backs. Guns were pressed to the backs of their heads and tape covered their mouths, but that didn't stop the intensity of their glares.

The men holding my guys wore black ski masks, but there was something weirdly familiar about one of them. Just the color of his eyes, the shape of his brow, they sparked an disturbing note of familiarity.

"Well... this is uncomfortable," Angelo said in a cool voice, still blocking me with his body. "I didn't cook enough for guests."

The leader, I assumed, gave a chuckle. "I'm on a diet anyway. Keto. No carbs, you know?" His voice was heavily accented... maybe German? "We'll let you get back to your dinner shortly, Ricci. We just came to get something from you."

Angelo kept his hand on my hip, holding me behind him. "If you're looking for the shipment of drugs, they're long gone. To *your* people, if I'm not mistaken... Nikolas. And there's nothing else."

The guy laughed again. "To my people? No, no, no. We hit the convoy as discussed, yes, but the drugs and money weren't there."

What?!

"We don't have them," Angelo snapped.

"I know," Nikolas said with a nod. "Your wife does, though. Or she did, before making a trade with the Albanians for a crate of weapons. She's got big plans, pretty little Valentina, doesn't she?"

My ass just about fell out of my body. *Valentina screwed us over.*

"So if you know she has them, why are you here?" Angelo's grip on my hip was so tight it hurt, but I wasn't complaining. Holy *fuck*. How could she do that to us? Had it all been a ruse from the beginning?

Nikolas shrugged. "Your wife is making bold moves to become a powerful player," he commented, tilting his head to smirk at me cowering behind Angelo. "So we thought, what better way to secure the favor of a new boss... than to offer her a welcome gift? Say... the head of the woman fucking her husband?"

Oh *shit*.

"Come on, then, we don't have all night. Hand over your whore, and we'll leave you to your dinner." He sniffed and hummed in approval. "Smells delicious, by the way."

Everything happened at once. Determination etched across Jace's face, fear and anger on Rhett's, but cold murder filled Grayson's eyes—all just a split second before they made a desperate move. And I suddenly, with a staggering jolt of clarity and disbelief, remembered why the masked man, the back-up goon who had a gun to Rhett's head, looked so familiar.

But that wasn't possible. My dad was dead.

Multiple shots fired, and my whole world stopped.

To be concluded in
BEAUTIFUL THORNS
April, 2023

Printed in Great Britain
by Amazon

20738810R00239